ABOUT THE AUTHOR

Maggie Anderson writes paranormal and contemporary romance, urban fantasy, supernatural crime thrillers and YA thrillers. She is currently working on the fourth book in her Dark Legacy series followed by the third book in the Moon Grove Paranormal Romance series. Maggie resides in Brisbane, Queensland. You can find out more about her books on her website: www.m-anderson.com.au

BOOK TWO

WOLF CURSE

A MOON GROVE PARANORMAL ROMANCE THRILLER

MAGGIE ANDERSON

Bella Luna Books
Australia

First Edition
Bella Luna Books, Australia

Front and back cover photos from
canstockphoto.com and pixabay.com
Cover design by Amy Elizabeth Photography, Australia
and Maggie Anderson

ISBN-13:9780992513979

Published by Bella Luna Books
AUSTRALIA

ONE

Paige wandered through the house in search of Eli but couldn't find him anywhere. It had been a wonderful day of turkey with all the trimmings, pecan pie and other scrumptious holiday morsels which Paige had prepared with Clarissa's instruction, wine and their favorite Christmas carols playing in the background. The older woman had taken a nap, tucked up on the sofa in front of the fire. Now all Paige had to do was find Eli. Where could he be?

She had noticed his Christmas spirit wane toward the end of dinner and wondered what he had on his mind. She could tell there was something.

Paige heard Clarissa's voice echo into the entry hall. "He's out on the front porch, dear. Said he needed some air. Bundle up it's chilly out there."

"Thanks, Clary. I will." Paige shrugged into her thick, woolen jacket, pulled her knit cap over her ears and opened the front door. "Won't be long."

"Take your time, dear. I'm fine."

Paige closed the door behind her and walked along the porch. Eli stood at the railing staring up at the clouded moon. "You disappeared right after dinner. Everything ok?"

His gaze moved to her. "Come here." He reached for her, pulled her into his arms and kissed her forehead.

Paige frowned up into his eyes, a feeling of foreboding washing over her. Something was definitely wrong. "What's going on?"

"I've been doing some thinking and I've come to a decision."

Paige's stomach flipped over under her jeans causing a wave of nausea. "What… kind of decision?"

He stared into her eyes for the longest time without answering. What was he searching for? A reason to change his mind?

"Eli?" she urged.

He gave a heavy sigh. "I can't…" He sighed again. "I don't want you to be my Alpha female, Paige."

She tugged free of his embrace. "You can't make that decision for me. It's my choice and I *want* to be with you."

"I'm sorry, sweetheart, but I have. I can't let you give up your life for me – for this." He motioned to the street, meaning Moon Grove.

"Eli, I love you. There is no choice."

"And I love you, too, but I don't want you to be a part of this."

"Don't you think it's a bit late for that? I am part of it." She reached for him. He stepped back.

"It's because I love you that I have to let you go, Paige." Tears burned the backs of his eyes and he blinked. "Pack up and move back to Washington where you belong and live a normal life. Find someone. Have kids. Grow old together."

"No!" She stepped up to him, a scowl on her face. "I'm not going anywhere and you have no right to ask me. I belong here… with you."

"You don't belong here. You never did." His heart ached as he said the words. It felt as though someone was ripping it from his chest.

Paige gasped and tears welled in her eyes. "Do you mean that?"

"With every breath." He wanted to hold her but wouldn't. He had to make a clean break.

"And you really want me to leave and never come back?"

Eli nodded without answering. He didn't trust himself around her anymore. He knew if she stayed they'd make love and it would be over. She'd become Lycan.

Tears spilled down Paige's face. "I thought…" She frowned at him, although he wasn't looking at her now, then without another word she turned on her heel and rushed inside.

After several minutes Eli entered the house.

Clarissa heard him come in and called him into the living room. "Don't do this, Eli. She loves you and you love her. And you know without her you'll lose your strength in time. She's a part of you. A very important part."

"I don't care, Gran. I can't allow her to give up her life for me and the pack. It wouldn't be fair to her."

"Even if you manage to persuade her to leave do you really think she'll stop loving you?"

"In time, yes. She has to." He paced.

"You're bound to each other, my boy. There's nothing either of you can do about that. It was both parents' decision all those years ago. Your mother wanted it for you. She wanted to know you'd have someone to share your life with long before she knew she was dying."

Eli sat down opposite his grandmother. "Why did the Lycan curse kill her?"

A sad look crossed Clarissa's face and her eyes brimmed with tears. "She wasn't strong enough." Her voice was a whisper. She blinked back the urge to cry and gave her grandson a thin, wistful smile. "It happens sometimes."

"What if Paige isn't strong enough?"

"Oh, but she is. She's proved that already."

Eli shook his head. "I don't know."

"Yes, you do. Go to her. Tell her you're sorry. Tell her you love her and want to be with her. You have no choice, neither of you do, so you may as well make the best of it. At least together you'll be able to keep each other safe."

Eli gave a heavy sigh. Could he ask her to give up her humanity?

Paige sobbed into the pillow, her heart breaking. How could Eli want her to leave after everything they'd been through? Everything they felt for each other? Her feelings for him had grown so quickly and now she understood why. They had been destined to be together their whole lives. She felt a pang of sadness and frustration because it was her choice to follow her fate and be with him. Not his. But she did understand the reasons behind his decision, even though she didn't agree with them. He wanted to keep her safe, to protect her, and that only made her love him even more. Tears continued to slide down her cheeks.

A knock on the door startled her, pulling her thoughts

back into the present. She sat up, sniffled, and wiped her tear streaked face. "Come in." Her heart beat just a little bit faster, thinking it was Eli. Hoping he'd changed his mind.

The door creaked open and Clarissa peered around the edge. "Are you all right, dear?"

Paige swung her legs over the side of the bed and sat up. "I don't know, Clary."

The older woman stepped into the room, walked over and sat down beside her, clasping Paige's hand in hers. "Eli headed home. I tried to reason with him…" She gave the young woman a thin smile. "He's only doing what he thinks is right. Give him some time. I'm sure it'll all work itself out in the end."

"Do you truly believe that?" Paige gave her a doubtful look. "Eli is strong-willed. I can't imagine him changing his mind. Not about this." He'd left without saying goodbye so she knew he wouldn't reconsider his decision. Their relationship was over even before it had begun.

Clarissa patted Paige's hand. "He loves you."

Paige gave her a sad smile. "I know he does and that's why I also know he'll keep to his word… to keep me safe."

Clarissa hoped the young woman was wrong because without their union Eli would lose his strength over time and his wolves would be vulnerable. The cohesive potency of the pack depended on their Alphas.

As Eli drove toward home his mind remained on Paige and the devastated look on her face when he told her it was over between them. His heart ached to be with her but there was nothing he could do about it now. He'd made the break and it had to stay that way, for her sake. He turned onto his driveway, eased his Jeep up beside the front porch and climbed out. Gazing up at the waxing gibbous moon he knew trouble was brewing. He could feel it in his gut and in the air. With the full moon less than twenty eight days away, he didn't know what kind of trouble, but something was coming and he had to keep vigilant. The town depended on him and his pack to keep it safe.

He climbed the steps, key in hand, and when he stepped onto the decking his hackles went up. Eli turned his head, his intense gaze moving to the right of him. The shadowed figure seated in the wicker chair at the end of the porch stood up. "It's been a while. Hasn't it, Eli?"

Trouble came in many forms and it appeared it was one step ahead of him once again.

"What can I do for you, Alistair?"

The figure moved out of the shadows. "I'm here as a courtesy because we were once friends." He stepped up to Eli, his pale immortal eyes iridescent in the moonlight. "You have something we want and I've come to give you the opportunity of delivering it to us without serious repercussion."

"We haven't been *friends* for a long time, Alistair." Eli eased his six foot four inch frame away from the vampire. Not out of fear. He hated it when someone invaded his personal space – creature or human. "And what is it the council thinks I have?"

A smug smirk spread across the immortal's diaphanous, handsome face. "Come now, Eli, don't play coy."

The sheriff's frowning gaze remained on him. "Well, unless you spell it out for me I have no idea what you're talking about. It's been a long night." He turned on his heel and headed for the front door.

The vampire whipped past him, blocking his path. "We want the moonstone ring. We believe you are in possession of it." Alistair's canines snapped into place and his eyes almost glowed in the dark as he attempted to intimidate the sheriff.

Eli knew he had to be careful. The venom of a vampire bite would put him out of action for quite some time and he couldn't afford to leave his pack or anyone else he loved unprotected. His grandmother had perfected an antidote but it would take days to travel through his bloodstream as his wolf heart rate was slower than a human's.

"*If* I had the ring why would I give it to you? It belongs to our pack."

"The council controls this town, Sheriff, don't forget that. It would be in your best interest to surrender the ring as soon as possible. The consequences far outweigh your need to play hero, wouldn't you agree?"

Eli folded his arms and stretched his spine, standing his full height. He didn't like being threatened. "What kind of consequences?"

"Let's just say defying the law has a…" he searched for the right word, "avalanche effect. You wouldn't want someone you love to be affected by your uncooperative decision, would you?"

Eli's honey colored eyes glowed with anger. "Don't threaten me, Alistair."

The vampire's features transformed to human. "As I said, I'm here as a courtesy. If the other members of the council have to act it will be most unfortunate."

"You can go back and tell them to stay the hell away from me and anyone I know. You rely on my pack to keep this town under control. What do you think would happen if I called my wolves off?"

Alistair's eyes widened. "You wouldn't do that. You have an obligation to this town."

"No, I don't. I'm just doing my job. But it could all change."

The vampire descended the front steps then turned around. "Some advice. Don't antagonize them, Eli. You're not indispensable." With that said, his dark form dissolved into the shadows.

TWO

With the case solved, and the coroner signing the release, it was time for Paige to make arrangements to lay her uncle to rest. The funeral home was in the next town and as she drove toward Bellehurst she remembered what Eli had told her about not viewing Jake's body. Because she hadn't seen him in such a long time she felt she owed it to him and herself to say goodbye. To have some kind of closure. Eli's words echoed in her head, *"Please, Paige, promise me you won't go over there. As next of kin you have the right to view his body but I'd appreciate it if you didn't. For your sake."* A shiver ran through her. What horror had her uncle endured that wouldn't allow her to be able to see his body? Should she heed Eli's warning or do what she felt in her heart was the right thing to do? It was something she'd have to decide once she arrived there.

The town was visually similar to Moon Grove although somewhat bigger, with a population of just over three and a half thousand residents. The main street stretched for a good few blocks with a variety of stores, other businesses, and a supermarket. Trees lined the neighboring streets and quaint, two-toned painted houses sat in rows with picket fences and well-maintained, front yards. Paige wondered if Bellehurst was anything like her old home town with its own dark secrets. Were there werewolves and other supernatural creatures residing here too?

She turned off the main road, drove along Petunia Lane, pulled into a parking space outside the funeral home and ran her eyes over the property. The split level, red brick building had burgundy awnings above arched windows with a matching marquee umbrellaing the main entrance. Its circular asphalt drive sat beneath tall, white oak trees and curved out to the street on either side through lush, green manicured lawns. The double-posted, white sign with elegant, black cursive script read: Mitchell's Funeral Home: Serving Families With Dignity and Compassion For Over A Hundred Years.

She pulled the key from the ignition, opened the door and stepped out of the car, gazing around at the stores and homes on the opposite side of the road. At least Jake would be laid to rest in the Moon Grove Cemetery where she could visit him whenever she wanted. Paige gave a heavy sigh and headed for the front door. When she opened it and entered the cozy, home-style foyer a woman in her mid-thirties, with short, brown hair and pleasant face dressed in a burgundy skirt suit with Mitchell's Funeral Home embroidered in gold on the breast pocket approached her, hand extended. "Hello, you must be Paige O'Connell. I'm Virginia Burch. I'm so sorry for your loss."

Paige shook the woman's hand. "Thank you, I appreciate your kindness."

"Won't you come this way? I have the information you requested and we can talk in our sunroom." She directed

Paige straight ahead and through an open, double set of white French doors into a bright, attractive sitting room. "Please, have a seat."

Paige sat down in an upholstered, pale mint green and wood armchair in front of a sophisticated, gray marble topped coffee table with a potted white orchid sitting in the center. Virginia sat on the cream, two seat sofa opposite.

"I have a question, if that's ok?" Paige crossed her legs at the ankles and placed her hands in her lap.

"Of course." The woman smiled, giving Paige her full attention. "What would you like to know?"

"Is my uncle here?"

"Yes, he is. Arrived yesterday."

"Can I see him?"

The cheerful smile vanished from the woman's face. "Well, uh, you could... but I wouldn't advise it." Her eyes moved to the pen in her hand.

"May I ask why?"

Virginia's gaze returned to Paige. "Did the sheriff tell you what happened to him, hon?"

"No. He just said it would be better if I didn't see him."

An empathetic half smile returned to the woman's face and she nodded. "He's right."

"So we can't have an open casket for his service?"

"It would be... difficult."

"Can you tell me what happened to him?"

The woman's eyes widened. "Oh, well, I –"

"If I can't say goodbye to him I'd like to know how he passed." Paige fidgeted with her hands. "He's... he was my only remaining relative."

Virginia reached across and rested a hand on Paige's knee. "I'm so sorry, hon. Maybe query Sheriff Blackwood again and see what he has to say. I'd hate to be the one to have to tell you."

Paige gave a heavy sigh. "Why?"

"Because it would be too distressing for you. I'm sure the sheriff can explain it better than I could."

By the time Paige left the funeral home it was late afternoon. All of the arrangements were in place. Had she made the right decision by not pressing to see her uncle one last time? It seemed she would never have any closure as far as his death was concerned. Eli wouldn't give her the information, even if he was talking to her. How awful could Jake's death have been? What terrible agony had he suffered that she would never know about? Had he been torn apart by the black wolf? It would be the only logical explanation as to why she couldn't view his body. So many questions and no one to provide the answers.

When she reached Moon Grove the sun had almost set and as she drove along the main street she noticed a light burning in the Tribune newspaper office. Was there a new editor in town that she hadn't heard about because she wasn't privy to grapevine gossip? Paige pulled into the curb on the opposite side of the road, climbed out and crossed the street. She peered through the glass door and couldn't see anyone, at first. Then she noticed him. He saw her at the same time and made his way over to the locked front door. The catch snapped back with a click as he opened it. "Hello. Do you need some help?"

Paige took a step backwards. "Oh, no thanks, I was just wondering why a light was on in the office at this time of night." She couldn't help staring. He was tall, dark and incredibly good-looking: chiseled jawline and clear skin, and he had the palest blue eyes she'd ever seen. Realizing her gaze had remained on him for longer than it should she averted her eyes.

"Do you go around Moon Grove checking on who's left the lights on at their businesses?" he asked, amusement in his voice.

"No, of course not." Her eyes moved back to his handsome face. His smile was just as gorgeous. "It's just since Wendy Ellis…" her voice trailed off.

"Yes, nasty business." He extended his hand. "I'm Archer Hamilton. I'm the new editor and chief of the Moon Grove Tribune."

Paige was reluctant to shake his hand but thought it would be rude not to. His hand was cool and slightly clammy and she felt her arm go rigid when their palms connected and tried to relax it. "I'm Paige – Paige O'Connell."

His handsome smile widened. "It's nice to meet you, Paige O'Connell. Did you want to come in?" He turned and motioned inside.

"Thanks, I should get home. It's been nice meeting you though." She took another step backwards and glanced over her shoulder at her car. Something about him drew her in and she wasn't sure she liked the feeling. Was he like the other supernatural creatures that inhabited Moon Grove? She turned to look at him. How could he be? He'd come from out of town.

"I'm sure we'll see each other again." His beautiful eyes met hers and she couldn't help but gaze into them. The pale blue irises were almost iridescent, and so mesmerizing.

"Uh, yes, I – I'm sure we will." She turned on her heel,

crossed the street and took one last quick glance over her shoulder before climbing into her car.

Archer watched her drive away before closing the door. She was someone he'd have to get to know. For many reasons.

THREE

Eli was aware of the new editor in town and would make a point of calling by to discuss the township's etiquette with him. New residents were monitored for the first few months after arriving to make sure they blended in without any complications, whether they were human or supernatural. Council law stipulated it, and as sheriff of Moon Grove it was his duty to maintain those laws. He'd requested information about Archer Oliver Hamilton and learned he'd been Wendy Ellis's assistant editor back in New York, and that was the reason for him being in the town now. He'd had no prior convictions, not even a minor misdemeanor or parking ticket. So it appeared he was squeaky clean, although the sheriff doubted it.

Leaning back in his office chair, Eli's mind wandered to Paige and he wondered how she was doing. He missed her, but knew he'd made the right decision. He couldn't bring himself to steal her humanity just for the sake of himself and his pack... nor for Moon Grove. It wouldn't be fair. The one thing he did know was he'd never be able to stop loving her, no matter how hard he tried. But there was nothing he could do about his feelings. It had to be this way for Paige's sake. He was a man of honor and would live up to the choice he'd made of setting her free.

Eli had heard that Jake's funeral was the following morning at eleven and would pay his respects at the cemetery, while keeping his distance. He would have liked to attend the service but knew it would be far too emotional with Paige being there. She would be distressed enough without him adding to her discomfort. He closed the file on Archer Hamilton, walked over to the cabinet in the corner and slid the manila folder into a sleeve in the top drawer. Tomorrow morning was soon enough to make an official visit to the Moon Grove Tribune.

Rosemarie popped her head around the open door. "It's late, Eli. Are you heading home soon?"

The sheriff closed the drawer and turned around. "In a bit, Rosy. You go on home."

"Are you sure? I can stay if you need me."

"No. It's fine. You head off."

She gave a small smile. "If you're sure?"

Eli nodded. "I'll close up."

"Ok. See you in the morning."

"I'll be coming in a bit later tomorrow, Rosy. I have some council business to take care of first."

Rosemarie's left eyebrow arched. "The new editor?"

"Yeah. Best to get it sorted early."

"Anything we should know about?"

"Not that I'm aware of yet. But if there is I'll call a meeting."

"Will we see you at Jake's funeral?" she asked.

He nodded again. "Yeah, I'll be there. Just not near the graveside."

"You know best. Goodnight." Rosemarie picked up her purse and headed for the front door.

"Goodnight, Rosy." Eli sat down at his desk again, Paige still on his mind.

Paige climbed into bed and pulled the covers up to her chin. Her childhood nightmares had completely disappeared and she assumed it was because they had figured out the reason why she'd been having them all those years. Her father's remains had been located although her mother's hadn't. So the mystery continued. What had happened to her? And where was her body? She gave a heavy sigh. Tomorrow. Tomorrow she'd lay her uncle to rest. Her heart gave a painful twinge and tears stung the back of her eyes. She had no family now. She was alone. She thought she could start a new family with Eli but it seemed fate had something else in store for her. Paige knew he would always live in her heart no matter what happened in her future. He was part of her and she him. Nothing could change that.

She gave another sigh, snuggled beneath the covers, turned on her side and gazed out the window. She missed their conversations, his handsome face and smile, his beautiful wolf eyes, missed him looking out for her, missed *him*. Was there anything she could do to change his mind? Paige knew the answer so there was no point in rehashing it over and over in her mind. She had to accept it and let it go. Could she?

After a while, her eyelids grew heavy and she drifted into a peaceful sleep.

When Eli arrived home his instincts told him something was wrong. He threw the Jeep's door open, flew around the car and up the front steps to the door. He used his wolf senses but could hear nothing, which didn't mean someone wasn't still inside. He shoved the key into the lock, pulled his pistol and jerked the door back. His home had been ransacked: furniture overturned, shelves emptied, the books strewn across the living room carpet, cushions slashed with the white stuffing spread across the sofa and floor beneath. Had the council decided to play dirty? He hoped it was the council and not some new, half-crazed monster in search of the ring or perhaps the new threat he'd felt. News traveled fast in supernatural circles and he would need to be on his guard at all times from now on.

The sheriff stepped into the room, eased the door closed, and ran his gaze around the kitchen before moving to the hallway. So far so good. He inhaled a deep, Lycan breath through his nostrils to pick up any scent. None – not human or supernatural. What kind of creature didn't leave some kind of distinct odor lingering on the air? Vampire? Could it have been Alistair or one of the other vampires on the council?

After doing a thorough check of his home, Eli began the lengthy task of putting his house back in order. It was going to be a long night. He made a mental note to tell his pack, just in case whoever had been through his house thought another member might be hiding the ring. If that's what they were looking for.

FOUR

The next morning, Eli arrived at the Moon Grove Tribune at around ten o'clock. He wanted to speak to Archer Hamilton and get the town protocol out of the way before heading over to Jake's funeral. He missed his friend and felt a certain sense of remorse for his father's actions. If only Jake hadn't taken the ring he'd still be here for Paige. She needed some family around her now. He hoped Brent would keep his word and come back to see her at some point, even though he understood why the young man and their mother were in hiding. The council was ruthless and would stop at nothing to keep its secrets. If anyone on the governing body discovered the location of Paige's brother and mother they would be dead, without a doubt. As far as Eli knew, they believed she was already dead and he would do his utmost to keep it that way for as long as he could.

He pushed open the door and stepped into the newspaper office. The editor was at his desk at the back of the room. When he saw the sheriff he pushed back his chair and stood up. "Good morning, Sheriff Blackwood. Is there something I can do for you?"

"This is an official visit." Eli walked the length of the long room and stopped at Archer's desk.

"Oh? Have I somehow broken the law?"

Eli ran his discerning gaze over the man standing before him. "Not yet. The town council welcomes new residents but likes to make them aware of the protocols of our community so something like that doesn't happen." His Lycan instincts were telling him something was different about this guy. His firm gaze remained on the editor.

"Well, I appreciate you coming by." He motioned to the chair in front of his desk. "Won't you have a seat?"

The sheriff's eyes moved from Archer Hamilton to the padded leather chair. "Thanks. I think I'll stand."

Archer's right eyebrow rose. "Suit yourself." He took his seat and clasped his hands on the desk blotter. "So what am I required to know, Sheriff?"

The funeral turned out to be a small gathering. Paige stood at the graveside, dressed in a black knee-length dress and jacket with Rosemarie by her side sniffling into a white, embroidered handkerchief, her eyes filled with tears. Paige felt numb as she stared at the dark wood casket with sheaths of colorful flowers lying on the heavy lid. The thought crossed her mind, *why does a coffin need such a heavy lid? It isn't as though the person inside is going to climb out.*

She ran her gaze around the group of attending mourners and wondered who knew Jake well enough to be here. Were they here because they genuinely cared about him or were they here to relay back to the grapevine what had taken place? Bobby and his wife stood opposite her on the other side of the coffin and when their eyes met the deputy gave Paige a hatted nod. She appreciated the support. Clarissa had wanted to be there but was still recovering from her ordeal at the hands of Eli's father. She had sent a beautiful spray of flowers, which was a lovely gesture.

As her eyes continued to move around the gathering, she noticed Myles Chesterfield among the intimate assembly. He gave her a thin smile and threaded his way around to her. "How are you, Paige. I'm sorry we're meeting again under such sad circumstances."

"I'm doing ok. Thank you for coming."

"I need to speak with you about an important matter. Can we talk after the ceremony?"

"Can't it wait until another time?"

"I think you'll want to hear what I have to tell you. But, yes, it can wait."

Paige's curiosity piqued. "All right. I'll meet you over by the…" She gazed across the lawn and spotted Eli standing under the white oak tree she was about to point out to the lawyer, hands pushed deep into the pockets of his police issue, dark blue jacket. Her heart leaped in her chest at the sight of him and she considered walking over and asking him to join her at the graveside, but just as the idea entered her mind Myles' voice interrupted her thoughts.

"Perhaps I could come by your house later today, if that would suit?"

Paige turned to look at him. "Yes, thank you."

"Say around two?"

"Two? Yes. I'll see you then."

The lawyer smiled and walked away.

Archer Hamilton stepped up to her. "My heartfelt condolences, Miss O'Connell." He extended his hand.

Once again, she hesitated before placing her hand in his. Eli would be watching. She glanced sideways in his direction. He was. She reached out her hand. "Thank you. I appreciate you coming." *Why is he here? Is he covering the funeral for the Tribune?*

Archer kept her hand in his for longer than was necessary, making Paige feel self-conscious despite the pull he seemed to have on her. She eased her hand out of his cool grasp and he took up position on the other side of her.

Rosemarie's frowning gaze peered around Paige at the editor. *What does he want with Paige? And why is he here?* There was something about him she already didn't like and she didn't even know him yet. Was she being judgmental?

After the service, Paige's teary eyes roamed the cemetery looking for Eli. He was gone. Her heart sank. She had hoped to speak to him and thank him for making the effort to come. Not having him in her life left a huge hole in her heart and she wondered if she would ever be able to fill it. They belonged to each other whether Eli cared to admit it or not. How could she walk away?

Rosemarie leaned in to kiss her cheek. "You take care now, Paige. And come see me some time."

Paige forced a smile. "Maybe we could have coffee together?"

The plump woman's face lit up. "I'd like that."

"I'll call you."

"I look forward to it." Rosemarie headed to her car.

Archer came over to Paige. "I hope you didn't mind me snapping some photos on my phone. I thought I'd run a piece on the funeral out of respect for your uncle."

Paige's eyes met his and she couldn't look away. "No, I didn't mind. I'm glad there'll be something for the town to remember him by."

"I'll make sure to deliver a copy to you as soon as it comes out."

"Oh, you don't have to do that. I can pick one up at the grocery store." She could feel the magnetic pull between them again and averted her eyes.

"It's the least I can do." He took her by the arm and walked her over to her car. The gesture was far too intimate and she hoped the people who attended wouldn't get the wrong impression, especially Bobby. Everyone had known about her and Eli and it had only been a few weeks since their break up. *And* she wasn't looking for a rebound relationship with anyone right now.

Archer eased the remote key out of Paige's hand, pressed the button and opened the door for her. A nice gesture. Once in the driver's seat, he handed the key back. "I'll get a copy of the article to you as soon as I have it."

"There's no need to…" Something about Archer Hamilton set alarm bells ringing. He seemed like a decent guy and yet something was warning her off and she knew she shouldn't ignore it.

"It would be my pleasure, Paige." He closed the door and she pressed the button in the armrest to lower the window. "Take care." His smile caused her heart to flutter.

"Thank you. You too."

"I always do." He turned and walked away.

Paige watched him as he crossed the lawn to his black Mercedes Benz. What was it about him that caused her body to react the way it did?

Eli had seen Archer Hamilton walk Paige to her car. What did the editor want with her? Was he interested in her romantically? The sheriff's gut tightened at the thought of someone else being with her, but it had been his decision to let her go so he had to resign himself to the fact that she would meet someone new. But if he had his way it would not be the editor.

FIVE

Paige climbed the front steps, crossed the porch and stepped onto the welcome mat. As she slid the key into the lock a shiver ran through her. She frowned and turned around, her nervous gaze scanning the street. No one. It wasn't as though she'd experienced that disconcerting tingle between her shoulder blades, nonetheless, she felt as though someone's eyes were on her. She turned the key and when she tried to open the door something blocked her path. Paige pressed her shoulder against the wooden doorframe and shoved, causing it to jerk back leaving just enough space for her to squeeze inside. *Not again!*

Her house looked as though a tornado had ripped through it. Someone had been searching for the moonstone ring. Why? Didn't those in the know realize Eli had it?

She pulled her cell phone from the pocket of her black jacket and hit speed dial. She hadn't taken Eli's number out of her phone and was glad it was still in her address book. The phone rang for a long time and Paige wondered if he would answer her call. As she was about to press end she heard Eli's voice.

"Hello, Paige, everything all right?"

"Someone's ransacked my house again," she told him, breathless, her eyes roaming the chaos.

Eli sprang from his office chair his instincts to protect her hitting him like an adrenaline rush. "I'll be right there."

Paige knew the police routine and, after shifting the obstruction from behind the front door, she stepped out onto the porch and sat down on the swing seat to wait. At least Eli would have to speak to her now. Her heart did a little leap in her chest and tears stung the backs of her eyes. It had been a while since they'd spoken.

Ten minutes later, Eli's Jeep screeched into her driveway and Paul's van pulled up at the curb.

The sheriff climbed the steps, his colleague in tow. "Wait here while we do a preliminary crime scene sweep."

Paige nodded and gave Eli a thin smile, her heartbeat thumping against her ribs at the sight of him. He was here, so close to her and yet so far away. She couldn't run into his arms for comfort and it hurt. Those stinging tears threatened to spill and she turned her head and glanced out at the tree-lined street.

The men entered the house.

After what seemed like ages, Paul came to the door. "We'll be done in a few minutes. How are you holding up?"

Paige gave him a wry smile. "It was a shock, but I'm ok. Thanks for asking."

"Good to know." He smiled and disappeared back inside.

Had Eli asked him to check on her? Had he wanted to know if she was all right?

It was up to Eli to talk Paige through what they'd discovered and he was having a difficult time getting his head around the fact that he'd have to speak to her face to face. It had been a few weeks since he'd broken off their relationship and they hadn't seen each other until the funeral today. He heaved a sigh, stepped onto the front porch, and walked along to where she was sitting. "How're you doing?"

The question sounded perfunctory to Paige. She hoped he was asking because he still cared.

She nodded. "I'm ok."

"Well," he turned and glanced back at the open doorway, hands on hips, "we didn't find any new fingerprints in the house. Yours are everywhere, of course. And some of Jake's, mine and Stephanie's too. The only explanation for this break in is someone's still looking for the ring. The same thing happened at my place." He'd known the situation with the ring wasn't over but he hadn't expected things to escalate so soon.

Paige gasped. "When?"

"Last night."

"Do you have any idea who did it?"

"I'm sure it wasn't Lycan." The official conversation between them felt uncomfortable, strained, and the distress on Paige's face made him want to take her in his arms and hold her. Feel the warmth of her body against his. But he couldn't. Not now.

"Then who?"

He shook his head. "Maybe the council. I had a visit from one of them recently. And there was no wolf scent at my house, which is why I believe it could have been other members of the governing body."

"Aren't there Lycan on the council too?"

"Not anymore. There are other supernatural creatures…"

"What kind of creatures?"

"You don't have to worry about that anymore."

Her eyes moved to the open doorway. "Maybe I do." She returned her gaze to him. "Are you going to give them what they want? Perhaps it will end all of this and our lives can get back to normal." She doubted their lives would ever be normal. How could they with everything that went on in Moon Grove?

"No, I'm not. I'll destroy it before I'll hand it over to the council." He folded his arms and frowned into her eyes. "Can you imagine the power they'd have if they got their hands on it?"

She sighed. "I really don't care, Eli. I just want my life back and all of this to be over. I don't want to come home and wonder what I'll find behind my front door every time I climb those steps." Her eyes moved to the front steps then back to him.

Eli gave her a serious stare, his gaze remaining on her longer than it should have, then turned on his heel and strutted back into the house. There wasn't any point in prolonging the discussion. And he knew if he stayed around her any longer his resolve would begin to dissolve and he couldn't allow that to happen.

Paige stood up, walked over, leaned against the railing and folded her arms. She knew Eli was only trying to keep the town and its residents safe, but at what cost? Was the ring worth more lives? She sighed and gazed along the street. Who would ever think the picturesque township was controlled by supernatural forces? Moon Grove looked like the perfect place to live; only it was far from it.

Paul and Eli stepped out onto the porch and Eli said, "We'll be in touch."

So that's it? She frowned into his eyes and he averted his gaze.

He wasn't staying to help her clean up this time.

Of course not.

They're relationship was over and he didn't want to be in close proximity to her any longer than he had to be.

A single tear slipped down her cheek as she watched the cars drive away.

Why had everything gone so horribly wrong?

She walked along the porch to the front door, ran her eyes over the mess and sighed. She'd better get to it if she wanted the house in any kind of order by the end of the night.

Archer picked up the newspaper page and ran his eyes over the article on Paige's uncle's funeral. While he worked with Wendy they'd been researching all the unusual incidents that had happened in Moon Grove over the years and he knew he was compelled to come here. He'd volunteered to come. He had delved deeper into the supernatural aspect of the unassuming, country town and had discovered things he hadn't shared with his editor. Although, after sifting through the dossier she'd compiled on some of its residents he'd found hidden in the bottom of a filing cabinet, she wasn't as ignorant about the place as he'd first believed. What she knew about the town had to be the reason why she'd been murdered.

So, the sheriff was Lycan. Archer had caught a whiff of his scent the moment he'd stepped through the office door. How many were there in the town? There would have to be at least five or six. Usually a pack had eight wolves but Eli Blackwood's didn't. And what of the elusive council that no one in the town ever laid eyes on? What kind of creatures controlled Moon Grove?

He asked Harold Norris, the printing press operator, to deliver a copy of the paper to his desk as soon as it ran. He would take it to Paige himself. There were things he wanted to know about her. And now that she was no longer dating the town sheriff he might have the opportunity to find out. Archer headed back to his desk and just as he was about to sit down a well-dressed man entered the office. He thought he'd locked the front door. "Sorry, we're closed today."

"Yes, I know. I saw the sign in the window and thought it was a good time to stop by."

"And you are?"

"Mayor of this fine town." He approached the editor's desk, hand extended. "Ross Redmond."

Archer Hamilton didn't shake it. Instead, he folded his arms across his black sweater. "To what do I owe the pleasure, Mr. Mayor?"

"I felt it was my official duty to welcome you to Moon Grove… and to also tell you that if you do anything to upset the balance of our community there will be serious consequences." He gave the editor a thin, smug smile, intimidation his forte.

"Sheriff Blackwood has already paid me an official visit, so I don't understand why you're here, Mr. Redmond. Perhaps you could make it clear for me."

"A reliable source tells me you're here for unscrupulous reasons." He took a seat at the desk. "And I have a rather large file sitting on my desk about your... shall we say... eccentricities."

Archer's dark gaze rested on the Mayor. "I do believe you're bluffing, Mr. Redmond. The sheriff said nothing about a file with my name on it."

"Believe what you will, Mr. Hamilton." Redmond stood up and stepped around the chair. "I have other methods of finding out what I need to know. I'm privy to certain information that doesn't extend to the law enforcement of this town. If you understand my meaning." He gave the editor another self-satisfied smirk as he turned and headed for the door. "Good to meet you. I'll be watching you."

A knock startled Paige and she dropped the cushion in her hand, her eyes moving to the curtained, white wood and glass paneled door. Her mind had been elsewhere, due to the break in and clean up, and she'd forgotten to give the lawyer a call to cancel their meeting. She picked up the shredded cushion, stuffed it into the black plastic rubbish bag, crossed the entry hall and opened the door, brushing several stray strands of hair off her face. "I'm sorry, Myles, I meant to call you. Can we make it another time?"

The lawyer could see she was frazzled. Her face was flushed and she looked tired. "What's happened?"

Paige stepped aside to reveal the mess inside her home.

Myles frowned, his eyes moving back to the young woman. "Who did this?"

"I wish I knew. It's the fourth time I've been broken into since I moved here. What does that say about Moon Grove?"

"I can assure you, Paige, nothing like this happens here on a regular basis, if at all."

"Well it's happened to me too many times." She brushed more hair from her face and sighed.

"I'm so sorry."

Paige gave him a thin smile. "It's not your fault you don't have to apologize."

"I feel I must under the circumstances. Moon Grove is a relatively peaceful, law-abiding town."

Either he didn't know what lay beneath the rural township or he wasn't aware she knew.

"What did you want to talk to me about?" She plucked her jacket off the coat rack, stepped onto the porch, and headed to the swing seat.

Myles followed. "It's about your childhood home."

Paige's head swung around. "What about it?"

"You, once again, are the sole beneficiary of the house and surrounding land." He sat beside Paige on the swing, opened his briefcase, and retrieved a business envelope. "You're the rightful owner."

"I don't want it."

"Do with it what you will, Paige, it's yours." He handed her the deed and other documentation inside the A4 sized, yellow packet.

"I plan to have the house torn down. Nothing good can come from it remaining there."

"What you do with it is up to you, my dear. I've done what I came here to do." He glanced over his shoulder at the open doorway. "And, again, I truly am sorry this has happened to you. *Again*." He stood up and headed for the front steps.

"Mr. Chesterfield. Myles."

The lawyer turned around. "Yes?"

"Thank you." She smiled.

"You're welcome." He crossed the lawn, climbed into his Lincoln Continental and drove away.

Paige stared at the large envelope in her hand and sighed. "What else can happen?" The last thing she wanted was anything more to do with that death house.

SIX

Clarissa was in her kitchen making a cup of chamomile tea when the feeling of darkness washed over her. She turned and glanced over her shoulder through the doorway into the entry hall. A rash of goosebumps spread up her arms and she shivered. It was a sensation she knew only too well but didn't welcome because she knew it meant trouble was on its way. She stepped back from the kitchen counter and wandered into the hallway, her witch senses piqued. The vibration was strong, which meant there was a new supernatural creature or creatures in town. She would need to tell Eli, unless he already sensed it himself.

She went back into the kitchen, picked up her tea, took it into the living room and sat down on the sofa. The tarot cards in front of her on the coffee table beckoned her to read them, the ancestral voices calling to her. She picked up the pack and shuffled it. The cards had been in her family for over a hundred years and were always accurate in their interpretation. She laid out the Celtic cross spread and hesitated before turning over the first card, her hand hovering above it, the energy beneath it strong. All of a sudden, she had an unsettling feeling about Paige. After everything the poor girl had been through what more could happen to her?

Clarissa turned the first card – three of wands – setting things in motion. *What things?* She studied the card with a frown before turning the next one – five of cups – sorrow, loss, disappointment. The old woman's heart stuttered in her chest. She continued to turn over the rest of the spread with tentative fingers. Seven of wands – standing your ground, fighting off others. She knew something terrible was on its way and that Paige and Eli were involved. A vampire had come to the town. For what purpose? Was he part of this new danger? She had to find out who it was.

She set about casting a location spell. This spell was different to finding humans or lost things, this spell located supernatural creatures. She lit a candle, placed the town map in the center of the table, turned out the living room light and began. Nothing. She huffed out a frustrated breath and repeated the chant: "By the darkness in his soul I call light to guide and protect me so that the vampire is found this night." She lit a red candle and let the flaring, yellow flame linger a moment then recede before continuing. "By the scent of his dark soul I call the sense of smell to guide me so that the vampire is found this night." She lit another candle. "By the heart of his dark soul I call upon instinct to guide me so that the vampire is found this night." Still nothing. Their power was much stronger than hers. What could she do to find them? She had to locate the vampire, she had no choice.

As Paige climbed into bed, exhaustion settling over her from the long day of cleaning up after the break in, she gave a heavy sigh and closed her eyes, willing a peaceful slumber. But, instead, Eli's handsome face stared back at her. Her eyelids snapped open and she turned over with a huff, plumped her pillow, and tried to dislodge his picture from her mind.

She closed her eyes again and as she drifted off Archer's face appeared to her but he looked different somehow. Frightening. She gasped and sprang up in bed. What had she witnessed in the realm of dreams? Paige sighed, threw back the covers, and decided to go downstairs to make some warm milk with honey.

When she reached the bottom of the staircase a knock on her front door echoed into the entry hall causing her to stop short midway. Paige glanced at her cell phone, 10.45 PM, and wondered who would be on her front porch at such a late hour. "Paige, it's me," the familiar voice said through the door.

Paige raced down the remaining stairs and unlocked the door. "Clarissa, what are you doing here at this time of night?"

The grave expression on the old woman's face sent a shiver through her. Paige had felt something in the air but had hoped she'd been mistaken.

"I have to talk to you. It can't wait." She crossed the threshold and Paige followed her into the living room.

"What is it, Clary?"

The older woman perched herself in the center of the sofa, immediately popping up again and pacing. "Something's coming. Something dark and sinister. A new supernatural creature has arrived in Moon Grove but I haven't been able to locate him yet." She gave Paige a distraught stare. "I've tried and tried. They must be hiding from me. They must know I can feel their presence."

Paige crossed the room to the old woman, took her by the hand and sat down with her on the sofa. "Are you sure?"

"Very sure, dear." She wrung her hands together. "We must find out who it is and what they want, otherwise things here will get far more dangerous than before. Haven't you felt it?"

"I thought I was imagining it." A heavy weight dropped into Paige's solar plexus and she swallowed hard. What more could happen to them? "Both Eli and I had our homes broken into again. Does this new danger have something to do with the moonstone ring?"

"Of course, dear. There are many who are willing to do anything to get their hands on it. Look at what happened with Eli's father."

Paige didn't want to remember. It had all been so horrible. At one point, she thought she'd lost Eli in a fight to the death. Who was the new creature in town? And how could they find them before things got out of control – once again?

"But that's not all." Clary's anxious face was pale with fear. "Something bigger is on its way. A war is coming."

Eli tossed and turned but couldn't get to sleep. The dark vibration in the air meant the trouble he'd been expecting was already in Moon Grove. Why was he holding onto the ring? Why hadn't he destroyed it? He knew why. The power it contained would protect him and his pack, if he chose to wear it. Should he? He didn't want to believe that once he put it on his finger the person he was would change into someone else. Eli ran the thought around his mind for some time before sliding the top drawer of his nightstand open and retrieving the small, black velvet pouch. He opened it and dropped the moonstone ring into his palm. He could feel the pull its power had on him. Perhaps it was time to wear it, especially with what he could feel was on its way.

The milky, iridescent stone gleamed in the moonlight, drawing him in. Without hesitation, he picked it up and slipped it onto the ring finger of his left hand – worn close to the wearer's heart for protection. Would he be the same man when he woke up in the morning? He tried to slide the ring off his finger. It was stuck tight.

What would it do to him? He hoped nothing except give him the strength to defeat whatever was coming to Moon Grove.

SEVEN

After everything that had happened, and not being able to find a receptionist, Paige had postponed opening her practice. She knew she would have to sooner rather than later but without help it would be difficult to give her clients the best possible support. She decided to place another want ad in the Moon Grove Tribune and hoped to get a response this time.

The next morning, as she drove along the main street heading for the corner office, she noticed how quiet the town was. She guessed everyone could feel the unsettling vibration permeating the atmosphere and chose to keep out of sight. Paige pulled into the curb outside the Tribune, took the keys from the ignition and climbed out, gazing along the almost deserted street. A chill ran through her and she shivered. Whatever was on its way had the residents who knew spooked.

She stepped onto the sidewalk and hesitated for a moment before walking into the Tribune office. The editor had a magnetism she couldn't deny and every time they were together it pulled her in even more. Her gaze moved through the pane of glass to him and she pushed the door open, her stomach doing nervous flip flops as she entered.

Archer stood up when he saw her come in. "Hello, Paige. What an unexpected pleasure. Is there something I can do for you?" He came around the desk and extended his hand with a dazzling smile.

Paige swallowed the tangle of nerves lodged in her throat wishing she didn't have to shake his hand but reached out and took it anyway. "Thank you. I'm here to place a want ad."

The editor's left eyebrow arched. "Oh? What kind of want ad?"

"I need a front desk receptionist for my practice."

"You do?" He motioned for Paige to take a seat. "I can certainly help you with that."

"Thanks. I appreciate it."

He circled his desk and sat down.

"I placed an ad with Wendy. Can you just run the same one again?"

"Let me have a look…" He typed into the computer. "Ah, yes, here it is. How long did you want to run it?"

"Uh, I guess a couple of weeks or until someone answers it. Can I let you know?" She gave him an uncertain smile.

"Of course you can." He keyed in some information and hit enter. "All done. It should be in the classified section tomorrow." His grin widened.

Paige's heart stuttered. His smile and his eyes were gorgeous and for some reason she couldn't look away. "Thank you. How – how much do I owe you?"

"Consider it a gift." His eyes remained on her beautiful face. He liked what he saw and wanted to get to know her further.

Paige's mind felt fuzzy. She blinked and averted her gaze. "Oh, no, I couldn't let you do that."

"It's my pleasure, Paige. Oh, by the way, here's the article on your uncle's funeral. I've been so busy I didn't have a chance to drop it off to you." He passed the paper across the desk.

"Thank you. I appreciate you doing this for him." Her gaze perused the article and her uncle's photo.

"Again, my pleasure. Jake was a good man, so I'm told. He deserved some kind of recognition." Archer leaned back in his plush, office chair and clasped his hands across his abdomen. "I was wondering."

Paige's eyes moved from the newspaper in her hand to his handsome face. "Wondering what?"

"I'm new in town and don't know anyone… would you like to have dinner with me?"

"Oh, I – it's not that I don't want to it's just – I've recently come out of a relationship and…"

"It's only dinner, but of course, it's up to you."

Paige felt a pang of guilt squeeze her heart. He was a new resident and, as he'd said, he didn't know anyone. Eli popped into her thoughts and her conflicted emotions burned in her chest. They weren't together anymore, by his choice, so what harm could it do? Although, there was that nagging little voice in the back of her head warning her to be careful. "All right, yes, I'll have a welcome dinner with you as your first new friend."

"Awesome. Can I come by and pick you up tomorrow night?"

Paige remembered the disastrous first dinner date she and Eli had gone on. "Why don't you text me the details and I can meet you there?" She picked up a pen and pad from off his desk and jotted down her cell phone number.

"If you'd prefer, of course I can." His magnetic smile widened even more and his beautiful, pale blue eyes remained on hers.

A shiver ran through Paige as the vision of Archer she'd had when she'd been falling asleep the previous evening popped into her head and a sudden feeling of panic washed over her. Was he the new supernatural threat Clarissa had been so anxious about? Perhaps dinner was a good idea, after all. She could find out more about him and see if he offered something that could indicate what he was, if anything.

Paige stood up, smiled, and moved around the chair. "Then I look forward to it."

"Me too." The editor watched her leave. At least it was a starting point.

As Paige crossed the sidewalk to her car she spotted Eli's Jeep on the other side of the street. Was he following her? She pushed her hands into her jacket pockets and walked over to the four wheel drive. He wasn't inside. She gazed up and down the road but there was no sign of him. Paige gave a disgruntled huff, walked back to her sedan and climbed in. At least if he had been sitting in his car watching her she'd know he still cared.

On the drive home, Paige thought about Archer. He was tall, dark, and attractive which to her mind meant he had to be some kind of immortal being. All the men in Moon Grove who were supernatural had a certain aura about them, were very good-looking, and had amazing eyes. She looked forward to having dinner with the editor. It would be nice to have a man to talk to again. A thought slipped through her mind: even though her heart still belonged to Eli she needed to feel loved and cherished by someone. Could Archer be her new relationship?

The thought vanished when Paige checked her rear view mirror and noticed a sleek, black sedan with tinted windows behind her. She didn't know all the cars in Moon Grove, but she was sure she hadn't seen it before. Had she become too suspicious or was it following her? She pushed the accelerator down and continued along the road. The other vehicle hung back. By the time she turned into her driveway the sedan had disappeared. Still, she'd had the distinct feeling it had been tailing her. An unnerving, cold shiver poured over her as she pulled the keys from the ignition and stepped out of her car. If someone had been pursuing her... who was it?

EIGHT

Eli crossed the street and entered the Tribune. What had Paige been doing there and why was she talking to the editor for any longer than business required? He felt like a stalker, but despite the fact they were no longer a couple he would always do his best to keep her safe, at least from a distance.

Archer glanced up and stood as soon as he saw the sheriff. "What do you want this time, Sheriff Blackwood? I'm pretty certain I haven't broken any council laws." He smirked.

"What was Paige O'Connell doing here?" He had no time to mince words. He'd discovered certain disturbing facts about the editor and felt it his duty to warn him off. For Paige's sake.

"Miss O'Connell came in to place a want ad. Is there some kind of law against it?" He folded his arms and stared into the sheriff's honey colored, wolf eyes.

"No. No law against placing an ad. What concerns me is her relationship with you." Eli stepped up to the chair and gripped the backrest.

Archer gave an unamused chuckle. "Relationship?

What relationship? We don't have one... yet." His left eyebrow arched.

"And you won't." Eli could feel his Lycan hackles rising. He had to stay in control. Was it the moonstone ring causing him to react this way?

"You're not her boyfriend any longer, Sheriff. I think the decision is up to her, don't you?" His dark gaze remained on Eli. He didn't like being told what to do, not in any area of his life.

"I know what you are and I'm telling you to back off." He raised his right hand and poked the air with his index finger.

"And what do you believe I am, Sheriff Blackwood?"

"A vampire."

"What does that have to do with anything? My inclinations are none of your concern unless I break the rules around here, which I don't intend to do."

"Paige is different. She's..."

"Not all human? Yes, I'm aware. Lycan blood flows through her veins."

"Then what do you want with her?"

"Isn't it obvious? She's an attractive woman and I'm interested. Nothing more."

Eli's wolf eyes narrowed. "Why don't I believe you?"

The editor shrugged. "I can't answer that."

Frustration and mounting fury curled its way through Eli. He attempted to shrug off the unsettling feeling. "I've been doing some digging and have learned a lot about you and your past." He stared into Archer's immortal eyes, seeing for the first time his dark depth, knowing he was in Moon Grove for a reason. "You'd do well to heed my warning."

"I don't like being threatened, Sheriff. What I do in my *private* life is none of your concern. If Paige wants to have dinner with me it's her decision, not yours."

"Dinner?" Eli said, his voice sounding throaty even to him. He could feel his Lycan rising to the surface. Under any other circumstance he could handle his wolf, although for some reason it wasn't working this time. It had to be the ring.

"Yes. She wanted to welcome me to Moon Grove."

"*Tell* her you can't make it." Eli's heart pounded against his ribs. He could feel himself losing the battle to keep his Lycan sensitivities in check.

"No. You cannot tell people who they can and can't see. I will have dinner with Paige and nothing you can say will change my mind." The editor stood his ground, knowing the sheriff was losing a hold on his humanity.

Eli sucked in a deep breath, his eyes glowing amber. "This isn't over, Hamilton." He turned on his heel and stalked out of the office before he did something he couldn't take back.

Eli pulled the Jeep into his grandmother's driveway and turned off the engine. What was happening to him? If he hadn't left the Moon Grove Tribune when he did he knew what would have ensued. He and Archer Hamilton would have gotten into a supernatural brawl with him coming out the worse for wear, if the vampire bit him. Why was he acting this way?

The front door opened before he climbed the front steps. "Come in, come in, my boy."

"Hi, Clary." He leaned down to kiss his grandmother's cheek.

The older woman frowned up at him. "Are you all right, Eli?"

He shook his head. "I don't think so. I was just at the Tribune talking to the new editor and I wanted to rip his head off."

Clarissa raised a finger to her lips. "Oh, dear, that can't be good. Why on earth would you want to do that?"

He raised his left hand. "I think it's the ring's influence."

"Oh!" His grandmother closed the front door and motioned for him to follow her into the kitchen. "Sit." She pointed to a chair at the table.

Eli did as he was told. "I tried to get it off but it won't budge."

"Of course not, darling. Once an Alpha places the moonstone ring on their finger it becomes part of them. If anyone tried to take it from you they'd have to kill you and chop off your finger."

It wasn't the news he wanted to hear. His eyes moved to the iridescent stone set in silver and he wished he hadn't put the ring on after all. He didn't want to be affected by the power it held, but it was happening whether he liked it or not.

Clarissa moved around the kitchen pulling containers and bottles from different overhead cupboards. "I can make something to take the edge off. It should all settle down in a few days." She glanced over her shoulder. "When did you put it on?"

"Last night." He watched her bring the ingredients she needed over to the table.

"Once I make this elixir, you must be sure to take it every day until you feel calmer. It should only take a week for the ring to become attuned to you... and you to it. After that you should be fine." She mixed different colored liquids together and sprinkled an assortment of powders and granules into the potion.

After adding everything on the table, she poured the mixture into a small, brown glass bottle with an eye dropper lid, gave it a good shake then passed it to her grandson. "Two drops onto your tongue twice a day for five days."

Eli raised the bottle to eye level and stared at the concoction. "And you're sure it will lessen these unsettling feelings?"

She gave an emphatic, single nod of her head. "Yes."

"Can I take some now?"

"You need to start right away."

Eli opened the bottle, inhaled the astringent aroma, and wrinkled his nose.

"Don't sniff it, Eli, drip some onto your tongue so it can take effect."

"How will I know it's working?" Just as he asked the question a feeling of calm washed over him and his shoulders relaxed.

A smile spread across Clarissa's face. "Feel better?"

He frowned at the bottle in his hand. "Yeah, I do."

"It circulates your body quicker than a human's because of your Lycan temperature."

Eli replaced the dropper cap and pushed the bottle into the pocket of his jacket. "Thanks, Gran." He gave her a cheeky grin knowing how much she disliked the formality.

The older woman play slapped him. "Now we've sorted out your problem want to stay for some tea?"

"Thanks. I'd love some tea."

The same afternoon, Paige was at the computer on the reception desk setting up empty client accounts in anticipation of acquiring new patients when a knock echoed into the moderately furnished office. When her eyes moved to the door she noticed a woman standing outside. She stood up, crossed the room and opened it. "I'm sorry, I'm not open for business just yet."

The woman smiled and extended her hand. "I'm Linda McCarthy. I'm here about the want ad."

Paige's eyebrows rose. "Oh? Please, come in." She motioned for the woman to enter the office.

"Thanks." Linda stepped through the door and ran her gaze around the room. "Nice. Very welcoming... and calming."

"Thank you." Paige offered her a seat on the sofa. "I didn't want the place to feel clinical. I want my clients to feel comfortable and relaxed."

"Well I think you've accomplished what you set out to do."

"I appreciate your honest appraisal, thanks."

"You're welcome." Linda passed Paige the black business folder in her hand. "My CV."

Paige took it, pulled up a chair, and sat opposite Linda. Her eyes perused the documents inside. "So you're working for Ross Redmond at the moment?"

"Uh, yes I am, but please don't hold it against me." She gave a brief smile.

Paige smiled back. "I won't." She continued to go through the pages one at a time. After several minutes her gaze moved back to the woman in front of her. "Well, you're the first person to answer the ad so give me a few days and I'll get back to you."

Linda stood up. "Thank you for your time. I'll look forward to hearing from you."

"And you will whether or not you're the person I choose." She walked the woman out. "Thanks for coming by. I'll be in touch." Paige locked the door, walked back to the reception desk and sat down. Linda's credentials were impeccable; even so she wasn't all together comfortable with the fact that the woman worked for the mayor, especially after everything that had happened and the possibility of him being involved. Would more people apply for the position? She'd have to wait and see.

Linda got into her car, closed the door, and reached for the cell phone in her purse. She keyed in the number and waited. "I did what you asked."

"How did it go?"

"She said she wanted to wait and see if there were other applicants before making a decision. She'll get back to me in a few days."

"Let's hope no one else applies."

"It's unlikely considering no one did the last time."

"I guess we wait and see then."

"I'll let you know when I hear something." Linda rang off, started the car, and drove towards the council building. Ross Redmond would be waiting with a long list of things for her to do. If he ever discovered she was Wendy Ellis's informant she would end up like the editor and the others who had disappeared from Moon Grove. It was time for her to move on.

NINE

Zachary Ridgeway dumped his bulging, Louis Vuitton travel bag onto the bed and plonked himself down beside it. He was back in his old hometown. He wondered what kind of reception he'd get from Eli Blackwood once the sheriff knew he'd returned to Moon Grove. They had never been friends during high school; in fact, you could say they'd been frenemies. Not quite friends or enemies, although close enough. Zach had established a successful freelance photography career in Philadelphia, once out of college, and thought it was time to take a well-earned break. Besides that, there were other motives for his return to the picturesque township rife with sinister secrets.

He walked over to the window, brushed back the lace curtain with his hand, and gazed out at the main street below. The Moon Grove Inn hadn't changed in all the years he'd been away and it felt welcoming somehow. Just as he had remembered it before he'd left. Zach knew Rebecca worked at the Inn and would do his best to keep his distance. He didn't want her to find out he was back in town and warn Eli before he had a chance to make an appearance at the police station. Stepping into wolf territory was dangerous, he knew, but he wanted the sheriff to know he wasn't in Moon Grove for a vacation. He was back for a reason.

A knock on the door pulled his thoughts into the present and he crossed the room and opened it.

Rebecca's eyes widened, the towels in her hands dropping to the floor. "What are you doing here?"

"Hello, Rebecca, it's good to see you." He gave her a thin smile and wished he'd ignored the knock.

"How long have you been in Moon Grove?"

"I arrived half an hour ago."

"Does Eli know?"

"Not yet, and I'd like to keep it that way." He swung the door back. "Why don't you bring those in." His gaze moved to the dark blue bundle of towels lying at her feet.

Rebecca scooped them up, stepped into the room, and regretted it the minute the door closed behind her. A knot of nerves tingled in her stomach and her Lycan instincts kicked into play, her wolf hackles rising.

Zach gestured to a chair at the small table by the window. "Please, take a seat." He eased the towels out of her grasp, tossed them onto the bed and followed her over. "I decided to come home. There's no crime in that, is there?"

"It depends on why you're here. Didn't you agree never to come back?" Her eyes remained locked on his handsome face. He was even more attractive as an adult than he had been as a teenager. And those eyes. Her heart stuttered against her breastbone.

"It was a long time ago. I'd like to tell Eli myself. Can you at least allow me that?" He perched himself on the bottom corner of the bed close to her. He had hoped to avoid this situation. He'd been looking forward to surprising the sheriff.

"Then you need to go speak to him *today*. Because if you don't I will." She stood up. "If he found out I knew and didn't tell him he'd be angry with me, and he'd have every reason to be."

Zach's inclination was to attempt to mesmerize her but he suspected the effect wouldn't last long enough for him to make his appearance at the station. She'd tell Eli at the first opportunity, once it wore off. The only course of action was to appeal to her feminine instincts. Try to coerce her.

"We were close once, Bec. What happened to our connection?"

Rebecca folded her arms, her back rigid. "You're a vampire, that's what happened. And don't call me Bec. You lost that privilege when you left without a word of goodbye."

"I'm sorry, I know, I should have. But in my defense, I did have to leave in a hurry." He stepped up to her and stared into her eyes. "It never bothered you before that I was... different. Why now?"

"I had no idea what you were, Zach. You didn't tell me and back then I was too young to realize it myself. You being able to walk in the daylight never indicated to my raw Lycan instincts what you were." She'd been attracted to him in high school and they'd gone to the movies a couple of times, but it had never gone any further and she was still angry with herself for not figuring out he was a blood drinker. Rebecca didn't want to relive those days. They were in the past. "Just go see Eli before he finds out

57

and comes looking for you." She marched across the room.

"I will, I give you my word." He followed her over and opened the door for her.

"You have today." She stepped into the hallway and continued to the stairs without looking back.

Zach smiled. It would be worth seeing the look on Eli Blackwood's face when he walked into the police station later in the day.

When the door to the police station opened Rosemarie's eyes widened along with her mouth. She blinked twice expecting the vision before her to vanish. It didn't. Her heart rate ticked up a notch or two and she glanced over her left shoulder into Eli's office. The sheriff wasn't there. Perhaps he was in the kitchen getting coffee. She hoped so. "Well, Zachary Ridgeway, as I live and breathe, what are you doing here? Do you want to get yourself...?" Just as she was about to finish the sentence she heard Eli's voice behind her.

"What the hell are you doing in Moon Grove?" The sheriff plonked his coffee mug down on Rosemarie's desk and rounded the counter.

The astonished look on Eli Blackwood's face was priceless.

Zach raised defensive hands. "Now, wait a minute, I come in peace."

Eli stepped up to him, hands on hips. "I doubt it. You were told never to come back here. What part of *never* didn't you understand?"

"It was a long time ago, Eli. I thought..."

"Well you thought wrong. There's no place for your kind here."

"This is my home. I have a right to be here just like any of you. And isn't Moon Grove the perfect place for creatures like us?"

"Why are you here, Zachary? What could possibly bring you back to a town that wanted you dead?"

"I was banished for something I don't believe I had any part in and that needs to be resolved."

"All the evidence pointed to you and the others in your gang, at least what I've read in the police report did. Can you prove otherwise?"

"I'd like to try, with your help."

Eli folded his arms. "The kids you hung around with killed an innocent girl. You were there and did nothing to stop it. Why would I help you?"

"Because you're an honorable man and I know you wouldn't want anyone blamed for something they had nothing to do with. Even me." He pressed a pale hand to his chest.

Eli's scrutinizing gaze remained on the vampire for some time, trying to ascertain whether or not he believed him. "I'll look into it."

"Thank you. That's all I'm asking."

"Don't thank me yet. See what turns up."

Zach nodded and turned to walk out the door.

Eli called after him. "And, Zach, watch your back. There are certain people in this town who head hunt. And I'm sure yours would make a sought after trophy."

"Thanks for the warning, Sheriff. But I can take care of myself."

Eli crossed the station and stepped up to Zach. "Be

59

warned. There's another vamp in town. Stay away from him."

Zach's right eyebrow arched. "Oh. Only one?" He smirked.

"I'm serious. Keep your distance. I don't want another incident happening again like the last one."

"I don't plan on getting involved with any other vampires. Whatever they do is on them, not me." He opened the glass paneled door and a blast of cool air rushed inside. Before leaving he turned around. "Did the council go through with their plan to murder my friends?"

Eli's stern gaze met his. "Have you ever known them not to?"

Zach stepped onto the front porch, gave Eli one last look, and headed to his car. The real reason he'd returned to Moon Grove would become apparent, eventually.

TEN

The following evening, as Paige stood at the mirror in her bathroom applying a coat of passion pink lip gloss a shiver ran the length of her five feet, seven inch frame causing goosebumps to spread up her arms. Her eyes met her reflected gaze and the overwhelming feeling of dread poured over her. Could having dinner with Archer be a mistake? Could he be the dark force they had all felt? He seemed nice enough, although there was something about him she couldn't quite figure out. Something behind those beautiful eyes. Why didn't her Lycan sensitivities act as a radar when it came to supernatural creatures the way Eli's did? Perhaps it would in time. She hoped so because she needed all the help she could get now that the sheriff was no longer a part of her life.

The ship's bell clanged downstairs and Paige knew Archer was at her door. She screwed the cap onto her lipstick, dropped it into her purse, grabbed the jade colored shawl from off her bed and headed downstairs. When she opened the door she was surprised to see Clarissa on her welcome mat. "Hi Clary, is everything ok?"

The older woman stared up at her and held out her hand. "I'd like you to wear this." A beautiful, silver pendant with a glistening, clear crystal in its center sat in her palm.

"It's lovely, but…"

"It's for protection, dear. *Never* take it off."

"Oh?" Paige reached out and took the necklace from Clarissa's hand. "Thank you."

"You're having dinner with…" She stopped herself from saying 'the vampire' and gave Paige a sheepish glance.

"I'm having dinner with?" Paige coaxed.

"The editor tonight, aren't you?"

Paige frowned into the older woman's eyes. "You weren't going to say that, were you? Tell me what's on your mind, Clary."

Clarissa shook her head. "It's better you don't know."

"Is it? You've implied there's something about Archer I'm not aware of so why don't you tell me what it is?" Paige held up the sparkling jewelry. "Is he the reason for this?"

The older woman nodded and let out a soft sigh. "He's… a vampire, dear."

Paige's eyes widened. Werewolves were one thing, but vampires? "Vampire?"

"Yes. He's not terribly old, as immortals go, only a few hundred years, still he is powerful."

"A few *hundred* years! Should I even be going out with him tonight… or any night?"

"You can always call and say you're not feeling well."

Just as the suggestion left her lips, Archer pulled into the driveway. Clarissa turned to Paige. "Too late now."

Pointing to the necklace she whispered, "Put it on."

Paige undid the clasp and set the silver and crystal pendant in place around her slim throat. "Thank you."

"You're welcome. I'll leave you to it then." Clarissa hurried down the path and across the street under Archer's scrutinizing gaze. He could see the magic aura around the old woman and knew right away she was a white witch.

He closed the door of his Mercedes and crossed the lawn, glancing over his shoulder at the woman as she disappeared into her house. When he reached the front steps he said, "Hi. Who's that?"

"Oh, just a neighbor." Paige closed the front door and came down the steps to him. "Ready to go? I'm starved." She smiled, the tangle of nerves in her stomach making her feel queasy, and hoped he couldn't sense her unease.

His eyes roamed her body and he noticed the necklace. "Clear quartz crystal. A protection stone."

Paige frowned and lifted the pendant. "You know about things like this?"

"I know a little about a lot of things. Comes with the territory." He gave her a thin smile. "Shall we?"

When Archer drove straight through Moon Grove's main street, heading for the highway, Paige's nausea increased tenfold. Where was he taking her? "Um, where are we going?"

"I thought we might have dinner at my place." He flashed her a smooth smile. "Why? Is there a problem?" He could sense her discomfort, hear the rhythm of her pulse quicken.

"No, no problem. I just thought you might've mentioned it, that's all." Paige now wished she hadn't agreed to let him pick her up and had stuck to the original plan of meeting him at whichever venue he'd chosen.

"I can assure you I have no ulterior motive other than to have your undivided attention for a few hours."

"How far is it?" Paige felt her throat constrict, her nerves getting the better of her.

"We'll be there before you know it."

As they drove along the tree-lined drive, Archer's house came into view. It was a large, yellow wood, two story cabin set among the trees with floor to ceiling windows that accentuated the beautiful, natural surroundings. To the left stood a white wood pergola with table and chairs and a BBQ and to the right a kidney–shaped swimming pool which was covered with a blue vinyl mat to keep falling leaves out of the water.

When she stepped through the front door, Paige felt the rush of warmth wrap itself around her and as she gazed into the living room could see a roaring fire in the large stone fireplace set in the middle of the side wall. The comforting heat made her feel at ease until the door closed behind her and Archer helped her with her shawl. She was alone with him. Alone with a vampire.

ELEVEN

Bobby knocked on Eli's office door, opened it and poked his head in. "Anything else you need before I go?" He'd been working back because they were one man down and he hoped to get home to see his kids before they went to bed. It had been a long day. He stepped into the office, crossed the room and dropped into the chair in front of his boss's desk. "Are you heading home soon? You look beat."

"I'm just finishing up this report then I'm on my way. Go home and see your kids, and say Hi to Barb for me."

"Thanks, Eli. I sure will." Bobby pulled himself out of the chair and walked over to the open doorway. "Oh, by the way, Barb was wondering if you wanted to come over for dinner Saturday night." He'd ask now and square it with his wife later. Eli needed a break and, as his best friend, it was up to Bobby to make sure his pal was doing ok, especially after the break up with Paige.

Eli's gaze moved from the laptop in front of him to his deputy and he smiled. "Sure. Thanks. Sounds great. Better than eating alone. And it'll be nice to spend some time with those kids of yours. Tell Barb thanks."

"Terrific. I'll let her know." Bobby crossed reception to the coat rack, plucked his police issue jacket from its hook and shrugged into it then put on his Stetson and headed out the door.

Eli pulled up Zachary Ridgeway's file which included reports and statements about the incident involving the death of Charlene Brooks back when they were teenagers. Was Zach as innocent as he claimed?

Sifting through the information on the screen, Eli stopped at a set of photos: Zachary, Joshua, Caleb and Riley. All had been before the council for their renegade behavior on many occasions and finally in front of a judge for the death of one of their classmates. Although the group had been reprimanded for the brutal attack, they were unable to be charged with murder because they were minors, so the council decided to take matters into its own hands and execute the vampire teens, all except Zachary. His parents had organized for him to be transported out of Moon Grove in the back of a delivery truck in the early hours of the morning, and from there, on to live with relatives in Philadelphia. Far away from the council's deadly reach. Only one council member knew and he had warned Zachary never to return, for obvious reasons.

Zach had always maintained his innocence, but no one believed him because he was a member of the gang. Had he been telling the truth all those years ago? And if so, how could Eli prove it? The one person he could have asked, Wil Wallace, was dead so who else could help him? Just as the thought entered his head, Alistair stepped into the office.

"What do you want?" Eli's serious gaze met the vampire's.

"Have you given any more thought to my suggestion?" Alistair crossed the room, hands deep in the pockets of his calf-length, black overcoat, and took a seat.

"Well, now that you've made yourself comfortable, perhaps *you* can help *me* with something."

Alistair's left eyebrow arched. "Why would I when you haven't obliged the council's wishes?"

Eli held up his left hand. "There it is. Now what do you plan to do about it?"

"Why did you wear it? I've been trying to protect you. Now there is no way to prevent what they will do to you."

"Haven't you felt the vibration in the air? Something's coming and I need all the help I can get. This ring will give me the power I need to defend our town, unless, of course, the council wants Moon Grove destroyed."

"They are aware of what is on its way to the town."

Eli's eyebrows rose. "Oh? Why? Did Remus arrange it?" He folded his arms. "Who is it?"

"The answer is something you will have to discover for yourself."

"I need some answers, Alistair. Zachary Ridgeway is in town. Is it…"

"Yes, I know."

"Can you tell me if he was involved in the death of Charlene Brooks?"

"Ah, so young and hungry during their coming of age, the craving for virgin blood makes neophyte vampires crazy. To be fair, those boys had no idea what they were doing and I still feel a sense of remorse over their deaths. But the decision had to be made otherwise more teenaged girls would have lost their lives at their hands."

Eli leaned forward. "What about Zach? Was he

involved or was he in the wrong place at the wrong time?"

"He was there. Whether he partook..." He licked his lips at the thought of virgin blood. "...I cannot say."

"Someone must know something." The sheriff sat back in his seat.

Alistair shrugged. "If someone does I do not know who. Will Wallace worked the case as I recall."

"Yeah, I know. But he's dead." Eli let out a frustrated sigh. "Come on, Alistair, what aren't you telling me?"

"I have no knowledge of whether or not Zachary Ridgeway drank from the young woman." He clasped his hands in his lap. "Now, about the ring."

Paige sat in front of the cozy, open fire and discretely sniffed the wine in her hand hoping her Lycan senses would pick up anything unusual about it – they didn't. She gave a soft sigh and brought the glass to her lips. The Cabernet tasted normal, as far as she could tell, and she hoped she was right. If there was something in her drink perhaps her werewolf genes would somehow counteract the potency of whatever it was and prevent a reaction to it. Why had Archer brought her all the way out here? There had to be a reason, didn't there?

He returned to the living room with a cheese and fruit platter and set it down on the coffee table behind Paige. "Help yourself. Dinner will be ready in thirty minutes, so my cook tells me."

The heavy weight on Paige's shoulders lightened and she felt a sense of relief. Someone else was in the house. She scooted around on the ottoman and perused the selection on the platter. "Thank you. It all looks delicious." She reached across and plucked a piece of apple off the plate and a cube of hard cheese.

"If you think this looks delicious wait until we sit down to dinner. Bronson has whipped up a feast fit for a queen."

Paige inhaled a deep breath through her nostrils. The aroma coming from the kitchen smelled amazing and her stomach growled. Thank goodness the queasy feeling had subsided. She didn't want to appear rude by not eating anything.

"It smells wonderful."

Archer's gaze moved to the kitchen doorway. "Yes, it does. And I know you're going to love it." He came around the table and sat down on the floor beside her. "I'm glad you're here, Paige. I'd love to know more about you."

Paige's stomach did a nervous flip flop. Was this the beginning of a new romance… with a very appealing, if not sexy, vampire? Her heart gave a little tug at the thought of Eli but she couldn't think about him now. He'd made his choice and she needed to try and move on.

TWELVE

The confrontation with Alistair had proven fruitless. Either he knew something he wasn't sharing or, as he had stated, he knew nothing. Eli wasn't sure he believed him. As a member of the council, and a vampire, it was more than likely he was lying to save his own undead skin. And without any proof as to whether or not Zach had been involved in the blood ritual what could he do? Something in his gut told him there was more to it, so how could he find out the truth? And why had Zach returned after all these years, considering he'd been warned to stay away? What was the real reason behind it?

His thoughts were interrupted by his cell phone vibrating on his desk. He snatched it up and checked the caller ID. "Yeah, Bobby, what's up?"

"Someone's broken into the church…"

"I'm on my way." Eli was on his feet and heading for the front door of the police station as he spoke.

So, it had begun.

When Eli drove the Jeep into the parking lot behind the church Bobby was beside his patrol car waiting, arms folded, and a grim expression on his face. His eyes shone in the headlights, exposing his inner wolf. He rounded the four wheel drive and Eli pressed the button on the armrest. "Is it bad?"

Bobby nodded. "Yeah, someone's done a real number on the place. Statues smashed, seats overturned, office ransacked."

The sheriff gave a heavy sigh. "Hell." He stepped out of his car. "Where're the others?"

"I haven't called them yet. Do you want me to?"

"Let's take a look around before we do anything else." Eli marched along the concrete path parallel to the outer wall of the towering, white washed church, Bobby behind him. Even the front doors had been torn from their hinges. Eli ran his eyes over the splintered decimation. "Looks like more than one creature was involved in this."

"I was thinking the same thing." The pair stepped inside.

When Eli saw the chaos his inner Lycan reared its angry head and he knew he'd lose it if he didn't take some of the drops his grandmother had concocted for him. He reached into his jacket pocket, retrieved the brown glass vial, opened it, dripped two drops onto his tongue, screwed up his nose and coughed as the bitter tincture slid down his throat.

His deputy gave him a curious stare. "What's that for?"

Eli held up his left hand. "It's to take the edge off until the ring and I become attuned to each other."

Bobby's eyes widened. "Man! You're wearing the moonstone ring." He frowned. "How does it feel?"

"Like I've been hit by a bus to be honest, but I couldn't let it fall into the wrong hands so I made the decision."

"It could be a good thing and a bad thing."

"Yeah, I know."

The two continued through the mess to the back office. Filing cabinet drawers lay open, the contents strewn across the floor, desk, and tops of the metal lockers. "Wow, it looks like a tornado swept through here." Eli wandered around the room.

"Told ya." Bobby stood with hands on hips and ran his gaze around the office. "Wonder what they were looking for?"

"Maybe the ring."

"Nah, whoever it was would've known it wouldn't be here. It's too valuable."

Eli crossed the room to the safe. The door stood ajar. "They managed to get into the safe and take the Book of Laws."

"Why would anyone want to take it? It's not going to do them any good."

"It has information in it about ways to defeat us, remember? Whoever took it wants the knowledge it contains to use against the pack."

A cold sweat washed over Bobby. "I thought we were looking at a couple of vampires, but this looks like more than a couple, if it is vampires who did this."

"The darkness we've all felt is somewhere in Moon Grove and we need to find out where before we're picked off one at a time." Eli stalked back into the church hall, his deputy right behind him. "Can you organize a cleanup?"

He nodded. "Already on it. They should be here within the hour."

"I need to see Alistair and find out what he knows about this."

Bobby frowned. "You think the council's involved?"

"Anything's possible at this point. And I wouldn't put anything past Remus."

Paige felt light-headed as she sat in the passenger seat of Archer's black, Mercedes Benz soft top on the way back to her house. She didn't think she'd had a lot to drink and thought she'd eaten enough to counteract the effects of the alcohol in her system; nonetheless, she was drowsy and ready for sleep. As the editor pulled into the driveway behind her car, she gave a relieved sigh. She'd spent a pleasant evening with him, but definitely needed some personal space right now.

Archer turned off the engine and glanced across at her. "Well, it's been a wonderful evening. I hope you enjoyed yourself."

Paige's unsteady gaze moved to his attractive face. His smile caused butterflies in the pit of her stomach. "Yes, I've had a great time. Thank you." She couldn't figure out why she felt so woozy. It had to have been the wine.

The editor stepped out of the car and came around to her door. "Let me help you." He extended his hand. Paige was about to reach for it when she remembered how it felt each time she'd placed her hand in his. She groaned inwardly and allowed him to pull her up out of her seat. He closed the door and led her to the front porch. "I hope we can do this again some time."

Paige climbed the steps, Archer right behind her, and fumbled in her purse for her keys. She shoved the key into the lock and turned it. "Yes, of course." She was about to step through the door when the editor leaned in and kissed her goodnight. The groggy feeling she'd experienced on the way home vanished and she stepped backwards.

"I'm sorry. I shouldn't have done that on a first date."

"Archer, this wasn't a date. We were having dinner as friends."

"You're right." He gave her a sad little boy face. "Forgive me?"

"Yes, of course I do."

"Good. All's well?"

She nodded.

"Then I'll leave to your dreams." He walked down the steps and crossed the lawn.

Paige stood and watched him leave before going inside and bolting the door. His kiss had caught her by surprise, although she hadn't disliked it, but it was too soon to begin a new relationship with anyone. Still, Archer was someone she could develop feelings for, despite him being a vampire.

THIRTEEN

The next morning, Paige woke up with a splitting headache and thought it had to have been the wine she'd consumed at dinner the night before. *How many glasses did I have? Two? Maybe three?* The events of the evening seemed fuzzy. Why? She shook it off, climbed out of bed, and went to take a quick shower before heading downstairs for a cup of coffee, which was all she could stomach right now as it appeared she had a hangover. As she reached the bathroom door she raised her hands to her throat and was about to take off the necklace Clarissa had given her when she realized she wasn't wearing it.

She glanced over her shoulder at her dresser. It wasn't there either. She walked back across the room and checked her nightstand before getting down on her knees and peering under the bed. Where could it be? Paige was angry with herself for misplacing the gift Clary had given her. What could she do? It was gone. She'd check with Archer some time in the week to see if, perhaps, it had fallen off in his car. She hoped that's what had happened and headed for the bathroom.

Coming down the stairs, towel drying her hair, Paige thought she heard a noise on the front porch. She twisted the towel around her head, poked the corner into the edge at the nape of her neck, and took the last few steps on tip toe, glancing around the doorframe at the window. A shadowed, hooded figure stood outside, face pressed against the glass, peering through the sheer curtains of the dining room. Paige eased herself off the last carpeted step, sidled across the entry hall, snatched the heavy, wooden doorstop from off the floor and threw open the front door. "Hey, you!" she shouted, her rapid heartbeat pumping against her ribs.

The figure swung around, cleared the railing in one fluid leap and took off across the lawn.

Paige raced down the path to the street but by the time she made it to the sidewalk whoever it had been was gone. She frowned and ran her gaze along both sides of the road. No one. *How could they have gotten away so fast?* Was it someone planning another break in? Her stomach twisted into a tight, nervous knot and the urge to rush back into the house, pick up her cell phone and speed dial Eli pulsed through her. But she couldn't. Although it was a police issue, she didn't want to involve him in her woes anymore. Somehow, she'd handle it herself.

Paige turned with conviction, marched back up the path and into the house. She would not be intimidated in her own home any longer. It was time to take matters into her own hands. She was going into town to buy a gun. She cringed at the thought of having a weapon in the house, but what else could she do? She needed to be able to defend herself against the creatures that continued to invade her home and her life. No one else would come into her personal space and frighten her – no one! Lycan blood ran through her veins, dammit, and she needed to toughen up.

Paige was amazed at how easy it was to purchase a gun. The guy behind the counter had completed a security check on her in less than three minutes and she was walking out of the store with a small, SIG SAUER P232 revolver sitting in her purse along with a box of ammunition. Did she feel safer? She wasn't sure. At least if someone did try to get into her home again she'd be able to shoot first and ask questions later – shoot to injure, not to kill, of course.

She drove from the pawn shop to her office. There had still been no further applications for the receptionist position, apart from Linda's, and Paige decided she had no choice but to hire the woman. She'd give her a call once she was safe inside the building and set up another meeting with her to go over the processes and procedures before she opened her door for business, which she hoped would be in the next week or two.

As she pulled into a parking space in front of her office she spotted Eli crossing the street. Her heart sank and she let out a heavy sigh. He was on his way over to her car. Why? It was difficult enough seeing him at a distance without having to engage in conversation with him. She put on a brave face and gave him a smile. "Hi, Eli," she said, stepping out of her sedan and pressing the remote. "What can I do for you?"

"I heard you had a visitor this morning." He stood with

hands on hips, his gaze remaining aloof. He couldn't bring himself to look into her eyes for fear of seeing the hurt behind them. Pain he had caused.

"How did you...?" She realized Clarissa would have seen what happened and contacted her grandson. "Never mind."

"Do you want me to have Bobby look into it?"

So, he wasn't interested himself, he just wanted to do his police duty and nothing more.

"No, thanks, everything's under control." Paige found it hard to maintain her pleasant demeanor. It seemed they were on official speaking terms these days and it brought the frustration she felt about their breakup to the fore.

Eli folded his arms. "What does that mean?"

She reached into her purse and pulled out the revolver with the pearl pink grip. "I have protection now."

The sheriff's eyes widened. "Are you crazy?" He huffed out an exasperated breath. "Do you want to get yourself killed?"

Paige scowled. "Excuse me?" She dropped the weapon back into her bag and mirrored his movements. "No, I'm not crazy, thank you very much. I'm doing the best I can to stay alive in this... this Godforsaken town of yours."

"A gun isn't the answer, Paige."

"Why don't you let me decide what's best for me?" She rounded her car and crossed the sidewalk.

"Wait." He followed her over to her office door. "I'm sorry. It's just... a gun isn't going to protect you. You know that, right? It's dangerous."

"What I know is I'm not going to cower inside my house and be afraid anymore." She unlocked the glass door. "If you don't want to help me then I'll help myself."

She stepped inside and closed the door in his face. Even though she was angry, it was too difficult being so close to him. Her heart still ached, the kind of ache she knew would never go away.

Eli stood outside the office and shook his head. Paige was in danger and only making things worse for herself. He glanced at the closed door then turned on his heel and crossed the street to his four wheel drive. He'd send Bobby and the new deputy around to speak to Paige later in the day. Someone had to talk some sense into her before she got herself killed.

Bobby knocked on Paige's front door, his Adam's apple bobbing above the collar of his denim shirt. He felt a sense of discomfort being outside her home after everything that had happened between her and Eli. To his mind, his best friend had made a serious mistake by breaking up with her. She was meant to become the female Alpha of their pack and without her they were vulnerable. He hoped, in time, Eli would come to realize that.

The door opened and the scowl on Paige's face did not go unnoticed. "Hello, Bobby, what can I do for you?" She knew Eli had sent him over to give her a pep talk about the dangers of having a gun in the house. Something she was already acutely aware of.

"Hi, Paige. Mind if we come in for a few minutes?"

Paige eyed the uniformed young man beside Bobby. The deputy noticed.

"Oh, sorry." He pointed to the guy. "This is Cooper our new deputy. He's not... he knows the situation here."

Paige's right eyebrow arched. "So he isn't...?"

"Nope. One hundred percent human."

Cooper extended his hand. "Nice to meet you, Miss O'Connell."

She shook it. "Nice to meet you, too, Cooper. Please, call me Paige. Everyone else does." She gave a thin smile.

He nodded and smiled back. "Thanks, I'll do that."

Bobby motioned to the doorway. "May we?"

Paige stepped aside making room for the two men to enter her home, pointed to the living room, and closed the front door. She followed the pair in. "I suppose Eli sent you over to talk some sense into me." She took a seat in one of the armchairs opposite the sofa.

Bobby and his deputy remained on their feet. "I'm here to check the papers for your weapon."

Paige huffed out a sigh, stood up and walked into the entry hall to retrieve her purse. She reached inside, pulled out the paperwork she'd been given, and handed it to him. "Satisfied?"

Bobby ran his gaze over the documents. It looked like everything was in order. He glanced up at Paige and handed the papers back to her. "Seems like it's all legal."

"Do you think I'd do it any other way?" She sat her purse in the armchair and folded her arms.

"We just needed to be sure. Guns are a dangerous accessory, Paige. Please be careful with it."

She ran her eyes over both deputies. "Anything else?"

Bobby gave his partner a sideward glance then returned his gaze to her. "Just be careful with the pistol. Ok? I wouldn't want to see you get hurt because of it."

The tension in Paige's shoulders relaxed and she smiled. Bobby was looking out for her and she should be grateful. "I will. I promise I won't do anything stupid."

"I guess that's all we can ask." He gave her a thin smile and headed to the door, Cooper in tow.

"Thanks for coming by. I appreciate your concern." Paige opened the door for them and both men stepped out onto the porch. "Tell the sheriff he has nothing to worry about. I'll be careful."

"I'll tell him." Before heading to the cruiser, Bobby turned around. "If you need anything just call, okay?"

Paige nodded and waited for the pair to wander down the path and climb into the patrol. Once they drove off, she closed the door and locked each lock – a shiver running through her. She had the distinct feeling someone's eyes were on her. Her gaze moved to her purse sitting in the armchair. At least she had protection now, and she wasn't afraid to use it. She would not be a victim any longer.

FOURTEEN

When Bobby and Cooper entered the police station Rosemarie glanced up from her computer. "How is Paige doing?" she asked, watching the pair remove their jackets and hats. She and Paige hadn't had a chance to get together for that coffee and the receptionist hoped the young woman was okay.

"She's fine, Rose." Bobby crossed the office and sat down at his desk. Cooper walked over and took a seat at the desk Craig had previously occupied.

Rosemarie's left eyebrow arched. "Is she? I heard she bought a gun today."

"Well, now, yes she did. But it doesn't mean anything. She just wanted some kind of protection is all." Bobby clicked the mouse to boot up his computer.

"And I heard someone was skulking around her house this morning."

"Geez, Rose, news travels fast around this town. Who else knows?" Bobby folded his arms.

"Why are you asking me?" The receptionist gave him a sheepish glance and sighed. "A few people, I guess."

"Did you tell 'em?"

Rosemarie's cheeks reddened. "I may have mentioned *something*."

Bobby's forehead creased into a deep frown. "Rose! You cannot go around telling people police business."

"I only mentioned it to a couple people. People who are concerned for Paige's well-being."

The deputy gave her an incredulous stare. "And who would they be exactly? The people of this town haven't given her the time of day as yet and probably never will."

"I'm sorry."

"Just don't let Eli find out."

At that moment, Eli came through the door from the kitchen with a mug of coffee in his hand. "Don't let Eli find out about what?"

"It's nothin', boss." Bobby's anxious gaze moved to the sheriff.

"Doesn't sound like nothing to me. What's going on?"

Rosemarie raised her hand. "It was me, darlin'. I'm the one who told Emmett and Clara about someone being at Paige's house this morning." Tears stung the backs of her eyes. Why couldn't she keep her big mouth shut?

"Don't worry about it, Rosy. Everyone in town has already heard. The grapevine in Moon Grove knows things before we do most times."

The receptionist let out a long, relieved sigh. "I promise I won't do it again, Eli. I swear." She crossed her heart.

"I believe you." He gave her wink and a smile, sipped his coffee, and headed for his office door. "Oh, Bobby, can I see you for a minute?"

"Sure, boss." He swiveled out of his chair, pushed open the swinging wooden gate on the partition, and followed Eli into his office, closing the door behind them.

"How did it go at Paige's?" Eli rounded his desk and sat down.

Bobby crossed the room and dropped into the chair opposite. "The paperwork's all legit."

"Did you try talking some sense into her?"

"I asked her to be careful. What more could I say? She's a grown woman, Eli."

"I don't like her having a weapon in the house. It's a recipe for disaster. Someone could use it on her."

Bobby wondered if he should broach the topic of their relationship while Eli was in a concerned state over Paige's well-being. What did he have to lose? Only his job. "Eli, can I say something?"

Eli's frowning stare met Bobby's sincere gaze. He had a fair idea of what was coming. "What?"

"You know you should be with Paige. We both do. She's part of our pack. Or she would be if you'd let her. Did you know she's seeing the bloodsucking editor? What's his name?"

"Archer Hamilton." Eli sat his mug of coffee on the desk and folded his arms. "Yes, I'm aware."

Bobby's eyebrows rose. "And you don't want to do anything about it?"

"I already spoke to him. He's not budging. He said he likes Paige."

"Surely you don't believe him?"

"Look, Bob, I appreciate your concern for Paige and me, and I know it's coming from a good place, but I have no say in what she does anymore."

"Then you should mend your relationship before it's too late. You still love her, don't you?"

"Of course I do but it's not that simple."

"Hell, sure it is. Go talk to her. Tell her you're sorry."

"I can't."

Bobby frowned. "Can't or won't?"

"Can't."

"Why not?"

Eli raised a defensive hand. "Bobby, just leave it alone. I can't and that's all I'm prepared to say."

"If you don't right the situation, Eli, we're all doomed. Something's here, something dark and dangerous, and we need to be a whole pack. That includes Paige."

"I'm not prepared to..." He shook his head. "I'm not prepared to discuss it any further." He stood up. "Thanks for the update."

Bobby pulled himself out of the chair, crossed the office and opened the door. "You have an obligation to your wolves, Eli. You might want to consider the consequences."

Eli watched his friend stalk back to his desk through the glass window. He knew Bobby was right, but he couldn't bring himself to take Paige's humanity in the heat of Lycan lust – no matter what the cost.

Paige sat in front of the fire staring at a picture of her uncle Jake and her when she was around ten years old. She missed him and wished she'd had a chance to see him again before... She sat the photo on the coffee table, picked up her glass and sipped the Merlot. Had moving to Moon Grove been a terrible mistake? Her life had changed forever and there was nothing she could do about it. Her cell phone jingled in the silence and she jumped.

Reaching across, she picked it up off the table and glanced at the screen. She didn't recognize the number. She declined the call, noticing the time, 9:00 PM, and set her phone down again. The meeting with Linda had gone well. The woman knew her job and Paige was grateful to have her on board. The doors to her new office would open the following Monday – one week from today. She gave a satisfied sigh. She needed the distraction otherwise her life might spiral out of control, and as a psychologist she couldn't allow that to happen.

Not having Eli in her life made it all the more difficult. She couldn't pretend she didn't care because she did. It seemed he was doing an expert job of hiding his feelings, if he still felt the same about her. Even though she liked Archer Hamilton he wasn't Eli. He was a vampire. Another creature in her life. How many more were there out there? Paige sighed and swallowed the last of her wine. She felt lonely all of a sudden. Her cell phone rang again and this time she answered it.

"Hello?"

"Hi, Paige, it's Archer. How are you?" He had a seductive quality to his voice that drew her in the moment he spoke.

"I'm good. How are you?"

"Always good. I was wondering…"

"Yes?" Paige felt a warm rush pulse through her body she couldn't ignore.

"Could we get together some time? Maybe for dinner again?"

"When did you have in mind?" Her heart rate ticked up a notch and she realized she wanted to see him.

"Oh, say Friday evening?"

The end of the week was a long way off. "Oh, Friday?"

"Do you have other plans?" He paced in front of the floor to ceiling window in his living room gazing out at the dark trees surrounding his property.

"No, no, I don't have plans for Friday. I was hoping it might be sooner."

Archer smiled. "Sooner? How about Wednesday?"

"Wednesday sounds wonderful." Whenever she heard his voice something came over her and all thoughts of Eli disappeared. "I'll look forward to it."

"Would you like me to pick you up? Say around seven?"

"Yes, I would. Where are we going this time?"

"Do you mind if we eat at my place again? It's quiet and…"

"Not at all. Sounds perfect."

"Great. I'll see you Wednesday at seven."

A smile spread across Paige's face. "See you then."

Once Archer was off the phone Paige started to doubt whether or not she should see him again. Her heart belonged to Eli. Why was it that when she was with the editor or spoke to him on the phone all thoughts of the man she was truly in love with vanished? Was it a vampire thing? She made a mental note to be more aware of herself and her feelings around Archer. Maybe he used some kind of mind control. Was it something vampires could do? She couldn't ask Eli because, officially, they weren't speaking to each other. How could she find out?

Paige dragged her laptop along the coffee table, opened it, and typed in vampires in the search bar. She'd need to do some research to safeguard herself. She had Lycan blood coursing through her veins and had to be careful of otherworldly creatures. Even Archer. Did he actually like her or was there something he wanted from her? Did he have some kind of agenda? The question sent a shiver through her.

FIFTEEN

The figure dressed in black ran his gaze around the neighboring houses in the tree-lined street, all was quiet and everyone appeared to be asleep. Good. He stalked along the sidewalk until he reached the gray and white, wood clad, two story house and stopped at the adjoining fence line. Was Paige asleep? He crossed the lawn and stepped onto the front porch, the rubber soles of his sneakers making no sound. There didn't appear to be any lights on downstairs. He crossed the decking and peered into the right hand window. No light, no movement. He checked the other window before stepping off the porch and heading to the sideway.

He leaped up and over the green metal gate and landed on all fours on the stone path on the other side. He stood up, continued around to the back yard and gazed up at Paige's bedroom window. No light on there either. *She must be asleep.* He moved across to the covered back porch and tried the outer screen door. Locked. It wouldn't have been difficult to dislodge the wooden door from its frame, but the noise would wake Paige and alert her to his presence. Something he didn't want. Not now.

After wandering around the yard for a few minutes, he climbed back over the gate and disappeared into the night. He'd be back.

Paige wandered through Archer's elegant home looking for him. Where had he gone? She pushed open the kitchen door and peered into the bright workspace. No one. Where was Bronson? Wasn't he supposed to be preparing dinner for them? An unsettling feeling crawled over her skin as she backed out of the doorway and let the door swing shut. She turned and crossed the expansive living room to the staircase. Had Archer gone upstairs?

As she stepped up to the banister an icy shiver traveled the length of her body and she stopped short. Maybe she shouldn't go up there. But why? A feeling of foreboding washed over her and rather than climb the wooden staircase she called up the stairs. "Archer, are you up there?"

No answer.

Paige swallowed the anxious lump pulsing in her throat and hesitated before stepping onto the bottom tread. She moved up onto the next step then the next and the next until she was on the upstair landing. "Archer?" A wave of nausea rolled in her stomach and she gripped the railing. "Please answer me." She could hear the high pitched tension in her voice. She swallowed hard and continued along the cream carpeted hallway.

Where could he have gone? He has to be in the house somewhere. Doesn't he?

Moving toward the closed double doors at the end of

the hall, a prickling feeling crept over her skin and she stopped again. Maybe she should wait downstairs. Maybe she shouldn't invade Archer's personal space. She turned around and was about to head back to the stairs when someone grabbed her wrist. "Where do you think you're going?"

Glancing over her shoulder, Paige let out a shrill scream when she saw Archer in vampire form – his eyes blood red, canines extended, and looking as though she were his next meal.

Paige sucked in a strangled breath, her throat tight. Her nervous gaze flickered around the darkness – no one was there. She threw the covers from her trembling body and leaped off the bed. Why had she dreamed about Archer as a vampire? Did he look as terrifying in person as he did in her nightmare? She hoped she'd never find out.

Slipping into her robe and slippers, Paige opened her bedroom door and strained her ears to listen before stepping out into the hallway. Not a sound in the house except the humming of the refrigerator. She turned on the light at the top of the stairs, came down the staircase and crossed the entry hall to the kitchen to make some warm milk. Her previous dream, the one she'd had since she was a child, had been a warning. Could this new nightmare be the same? Were her instincts about Archer using some kind of mind control over her accurate? Could the editor be the danger they had all felt?

The microwave oven dinged and Paige almost jumped out of her skin. She picked up the mug, wandered into the living room and switched on the lamp. She crossed the room and sat down on the sofa, sipping the warm, creamy liquid. It soothed her jangled nerves and gave her a sense of comfort. Seeing Archer as a vampire in her dream set alarm bells ringing in her head. It appeared the law of nature wasn't content for her to begin a new relationship with someone like him when she was of Lycan blood. Paige gave a heavy sigh and sipped more of her milk. Was she meant to live the rest of her days alone? There was no way to make Eli see reason so what more could she do except do what he'd suggested and move on?

SIXTEEN

The following morning, Eli parked his Jeep outside the Moon Grove Inn, climbed out and gazed up at the second story windows. He needed to speak to Zachary Ridgeway about finding out the truth of what had happened the night the young vampires had killed Charlene Brooks. The only thing Eli could think of was to take him to see Doc Taylor. Perhaps the psychiatrist could unlock the events of that night in Zach's mind and shed some light on what had actually taken place.

The sheriff walked up the path and onto the front porch, pushed open the glass paneled door and stepped inside. The warmth of the roaring fire in the dining room wrapped itself around him as he closed the door and crossed the entry hall to the reception desk. Rebecca was behind it. "Morning, Bec. Zach about?"

Her eyes moved to the room keys. Zach's wasn't there which meant he should still be in his room. "I guess so. His key isn't here. Room 8." She pointed up the staircase.

"Thanks." Eli gave her a smile, walked over and climbed the stairs. Wandering along the hallway, the sheriff wondered what else had brought Zach back to

Moon Grove. It was something else he'd need to find out before things got out of control. The threat to the town was palpable, he and his wolves had felt it, even Clarissa and Paige had too, so Eli needed to be sure Zach wasn't part of the looming danger.

He stopped at room eight and raised his hand to knock. The door swung open before his knuckles connected with the wood. "Is there something you want, Eli?"

"We need to talk. Can I come in?" The sheriff's serious gaze rested on the vampire.

Zach moved aside and motioned for Eli to enter his room. "What did you want to speak to me about?" He closed the door, crossed the room and sat down on the side of the bed.

Eli remained standing. "I think it would be a good idea to see Doc Taylor. He could put you under hypnosis and try to find out what happened that night."

"Hypnosis? It won't work on me. We do the mind control thing not the other way around."

"How do you know it won't? Have you tried before?" Eli folded his arms.

"No, I haven't tried it before. But I know it won't work."

"You could be wrong, you know."

Zach ran the idea around his mind. Did he really want to undergo mind manipulation? Was he prepared to incriminate himself now? "I don't know…"

"What have you got to lose? You asked for my help and I'm offering."

The young man's gaze moved to the sheriff. Was Eli feigning to help him or trying to find a way to involve him? One less vampire in Moon Grove would serve the

Alpha's purpose even though there were vampires on the council. "All right. I'll come with you to see Doc Taylor but I don't think it'll work. When did you want to go?"

"I already booked a session for ten this morning. Grab your jacket." Eli walked over and opened the door. He wasn't giving the vampire an option. If he left Zach to think about it he might decide to disappear again and the truth would remain hidden forever.

The drive to the psychiatrist's house was quiet and Eli could see Zach was rethinking his decision. They were only a few minutes away and he stepped on the gas. He needed to find out the truth as much as Zachary Ridgeway did and he couldn't have him change his mind at the last second.

He pulled the Jeep into the doctor's driveway, climbed out and rounded the wagon. Zach made no attempt to step out of the vehicle and Eli opened the door. "Come on, Zach. Let's do this so you can get the answers you're looking for."

The young man glanced at him sideways. "What if I find out things I don't want to know?"

The sheriff's right eyebrow arched. "Could you have been involved?"

Zach shrugged. "I don't remember. The blood lust had taken control and I wasn't thinking straight. I felt like I was on drugs or something. Everything about what happened is a blur."

"Then it's imperative you see Doc Taylor. He was able to unlock things in my mind and help me find out the meaning to a dream I'd been having for years. Don't discount what he can do. Let's see how it goes. Ok?"

Zach climbed out of the four wheel drive and Eli closed

the door and motioned for him to walk ahead of him.

John Taylor was behind the reception desk when the sheriff and his companion came into the converted garage office. "Hello, Eli. Good to see you."

"You too, Doc." He turned and pointed to the man standing beside him. "This is Zachary Ridgeway."

"Hello, Zach. It's good to meet you."

Zach gave the psychiatrist an uncertain frown. "Hi. Thanks."

"Why don't you come on through?" The doctor opened the door to his consultation room and Eli and Zach stepped in ahead of him. Once inside, he closed the door, crossed the room to his desk, picked up a pair of spectacles and placed them on his nose. "Have a seat, Zach." He glanced at Eli. "Why don't you wait outside while we get acquainted?"

"I'd prefer to stay. This is part of a new investigation into the death of Charlene Brooks so it's official police business."

John peered over the top of his glasses. "Very well." He motioned to an armchair against the wall by the door. "Have a seat over there."

Eli removed his Stetson and sat down. He knew the routine and would remain silent during the session.

The doctor stood up, came around his desk and sat down in a chair beside the sofa. "Why don't you make yourself comfortable?"

Zach's gaze moved to Eli then back to Doc Taylor. "Do I have to lie down?"

"It's important for you to be in a safe and comfortable position while undergoing hypnosis, so yes, please lie down."

Zach stretched out on the leather sofa, staring up at the white ceiling, hands clasped across his abdomen.

"Ok." John picked up the metronome and set it in motion. Tick, tick, tick, tick... "I want you to close your eyes and listen to the sound of my voice." The doctor knew vampires didn't breathe so there was no point in asking him to take some deep, calming breaths. "Are you comfortable?"

Zach nodded.

"Right. Let's begin."

The session didn't offer anything of value and Doc Taylor convinced Zach to make another time to attempt a deeper method of hypnosis. There had been a minor break through but nothing substantial enough to ascertain whether or not Zach had been part of the blood ritual. He'd remembered Charlene being with them and everyone in the group drinking beer, including her, but nothing more. The information was in his head somewhere and the psychiatrist was certain that if he had a longer session with Zach he could reach further into his mind and extract the truth.

When the three men stepped out into reception, John asked Eli if he could speak to him alone for a moment assuring Zach it was not related to their session. Eli handed his keys to Zach and asked him to wait in the Jeep. Once he was gone, John gave the sheriff a serious stare.

"I have to tell you something." The doctor removed his spectacles, folded them and sat them on the reception desk.

"Ok. What is it?" Eli folded his arms, his gaze remaining on Doc Taylor.

John sighed. "When we started your sessions I..." he

stopped for a moment, contemplating whether or not to continue.

"You what?"

"I was ordered to communicate certain information about what you remembered back to the council."

"What?!"

John raised defensive hands. "Look, I'm sorry, I had no choice. They gave me no choice."

"Everyone has a choice, Doc."

"They threatened my family, Eli. What would you have had me do?"

"You should've come and told me. I would've done something about it. The council doesn't frighten me."

"You're a werewolf. I'm human, an easy target."

Eli gave a heavy sigh. "I thought I could trust you."

"You can."

"How do you figure that after what you've done?" Eli moved to the door and opened it.

"I'll help you. I'll tell you what I know."

"I never thought you would betray my trust. Isn't there some law about doctor patient privilege?"

John swallowed hard. Would Eli lodge a complaint and have his license revoked? "Yes, there is but…"

"Maybe you should've considered the consequences before going against medical ethics." Eli pushed the door open and stalked along the driveway to his four wheel drive. As luck would have it, Zach was in the passenger seat.

SEVENTEEN

Linda and Paige were in the office making last minute preparations for the opening of her practice the following Monday. As they worked, the receptionist wondered if she should tell her new employer what she'd done while working for the mayor. She had been Wendy Ellis's informant, unbeknown to Ross Redmond. She had once been part of Eli's pack, too, but decided she wanted to lead a normal life, not roam the woods in search of danger. Eli had understood her reasons and allowed her to leave.

The reason she was with Paige now was as a favor to him. He wanted to be sure the psychologist was protected at all times and Linda being a wolf would ensure her safety, even though she rarely used her Lycan abilities anymore. She knew she would also be safe because, although she had left the pack a couple of years ago, Eli was still her Alpha.

Paige came into the office from the kitchen with two mugs of coffee and set one down in front of Linda. It was good to have someone to work with and talk to again. She missed her best friend, although there was nothing she could do about it. Stephanie had ended their friendship after almost dying at the hands of Elijah, Eli's demented father, and Paige had to take some responsibility for what had happened because she had been his target.

"Thanks," Linda said, turning from the computer keyboard and picking up the mug. "Your digital filing system is awesome. I can't wait to use it."

"It is pretty awesome. It's the same one I used in my practice in Washington. It makes record keeping a breeze." Paige pulled up a chair and sat down beside the reception desk.

"Can I ask you something?"

Paige set her mug down. "Sure. What is it?"

"Are you worried no one will want to come here?"

"The thought has been in the back of my mind the whole time I've been setting the business up." She gave a soft sigh. "But I'm hoping there'll be some people in Moon Grove who'll give me a chance. Maybe women who'd prefer to talk to a woman rather than a man."

Linda knew the insular town only too well. People here were rigid in their thinking. She felt a pang of sympathy for the woman sitting next to her because she didn't think anyone would give her the opportunity to prove herself. "Me too." The receptionist pointed to the glass paneled door and Paige glanced over her shoulder. "At least someone is curious."

"Yes. Let's hope it's a good sign."

"I need to tell you something." Linda's smile disappeared, a serious expression replacing it.

"Ok" Paige frowned.

"Two things, actually. First of all, I was Wendy's informant…"

Paige's eyes widened. "You were?"

Linda nodded. "Yes. I couldn't sit by and know about the things going on and not try to do something about it."

"What's the second thing?"

"You have to promise it stays between us."

"Absolutely."

"Eli asked me to apply for this job. He wants to make sure you're safe."

A small smile crept across Paige's face. "He did?"

"Yes."

"How are you supposed to keep me safe? I know there's safety in numbers but what can two women do against who knows what?"

Linda's eyes glowed.

Paige gasped and raised a hand to her mouth. "You're a wolf?"

"I used to be part of Eli's pack. Being the man he is he understood my reasons for wanting to leave and let me go." She gave Paige an empathetic look. "I haven't freaked you out, have I?"

"No, not at all. Now I know who you are I feel safer already." She smiled. "Not only do I have a top receptionist but a bodyguard as well."

Linda chuckled. "Thank you."

"You're welcome." Paige picked up the mug sitting in front of her. "You are aware I have Lycan blood too, right?"

"Yes, Eli told me." Another person appeared at the door. "Well, speak of the devil." Linda crossed the room and opened the door. "Hello, Eli."

"Hi. Can I speak to Paige alone for a moment?"

"Sure." Linda took her mug and headed to the kitchen.

Paige stood up and folded her arms. "What brings you here, Eli?"

The sheriff removed his hat and ran his hand through his tousled hair. "I need your help."

"Oh? What kind of help?"

"I took Zachary Ridgeway to see Doc Taylor and while we were there he told me he'd been relaying information from our sessions back to the council."

"What? You could get his license suspended for breaking patient confidentiality, among other things."

"I know. Right now I don't know how I feel about what he did. He said he could help and I'm thinking I might take him up on the offer."

"Can you trust him?"

"After what he's done I'd be hesitant to say I could. But who knows. Time will tell, I guess."

"So how can I help?"

"Zach had a session with him. Nothing significant came out of it though. Would you work with him? We need to find out what he remembers about the night Charlene Brooks was killed."

"You want me to hypnotize a vampire?"

"Yeah."

Paige sighed. "When did you want to bring him in?"

"I'd like to keep the momentum going while he's cooperative. Is tomorrow too soon?"

"Tomorrow? I'm not officially open yet." She thought for a moment then nodded. "Sure."

"Consider him your first client." Eli smiled and was about to reach out and touch her arm out of force of habit, but pulled back. "Thanks. I appreciate it."

"How does ten o'clock sound?"

"Great. We'll be here."

"Is there anything I need to know about him? He's not dangerous, is he?"

"Not as far as I'm aware, although you can never trust a vampire." He hoped his words might prompt her to be more careful around Archer Hamilton.

Paige gave him a curious frown. "Is there anything else?"

"I've been wondering why he came back to Moon Grove after all this time. Perhaps you could dig a little deeper during your session with him tomorrow and see what you can find out."

"Is it relevant?"

"It could be, especially if he's part of the danger we've all felt. We have two new vampires in town and it can't be a coincidence."

A cold weight plummeted into Paige's stomach and she shivered. "I'll see what I can do."

"Good. Thanks." Eli walked over to the door. "See you at ten.

Paige crossed the office and locked the door behind him. Was she prepared to delve into the psyche of a vampire? What secrets lived in a mind hundreds of years old? Another shiver caused goosebumps to spread up her arms and she was about to turn around and head to the kitchen when Archer Hamilton appeared at the door.

She snapped the lock back and swung it open, a broad grin spreading across her face. "Hi. I didn't think I'd see you until tomorrow night. To what do I owe the pleasure?"

Archer gave her a pained look. "I'm going to have to cancel our dinner plans. I have to go to New York and I'm leaving first thing in the morning."

"Oh? Ok." Her heart felt heavy in her chest and she couldn't hide her disappointment.

"Hey. Let me make it up to you when I get back. I'll take you to the Jade Dragon. I hear the food's good there."

"Yes, it is." She gave him a forced smile. "Sounds great. Have a safe trip."

"I will." He leaned in and planted a soft kiss on her left cheek. "See you in a few days."

Paige watched him cross the street and enter the Tribune office before locking the door and heading out the back to the kitchen.

Linda noticed her glum expression. "Everything ok?"

"Sure. Why do you ask?"

"You just look a little... blue. Is it Eli? Did he upset you?" The receptionist got up from the table and rinsed her mug at the sink.

"No, it wasn't Eli."

"Oh, did someone else come in?" Linda dried her cup and placed it in the overhead cupboard.

"Yes. Archer Hamilton, the editor of the Moon Grove Tribune."

"I see."

"We were meant to have dinner together tomorrow night but he had to cancel. He's going out of town for a few days."

"Did he say why?"

Paige frowned. "No, he didn't and I didn't ask. Why?"

"No reason."

"Is there something I should know?" Paige folded her arms.

"I'm not sure. Ross Redmond is keeping close tabs on him and so is Eli."

"Do you know why?" Paige pulled out a chair and sat down at the table.

"He's a new vampire in town. Maybe it's reason enough."

Paige allowed Linda's words to circle her mind for a moment. Was he a threat? Could it be the reason why the mayor and Eli were watching him? Should she distance herself before things got serious between them?

Later that evening, Paige had just finished the washing up when a knock on her front door echoed into the entry hall, startling her. She dried her hands on the tea towel, dropped it onto the kitchen counter, and headed to the entry hall. As she reached the door her hackles went up… the hairs on the back of her neck static, the cold feeling of dread crawling over her skin. "Who's there?" she called through the closed door, not wanting to open it until she knew who was outside. No answer. Paige's stomach flipped over causing a nauseous wave to roll beneath the belt on her jeans.

Another forceful knock.

She gasped, her body jerking backwards. "Who's out there?" Reaching for her purse on the small, dark wood stand by the coat rack, she snatched the revolver from it, moved across to the lock and snapped it back. When she threw the door open and pointed the weapon no one was there.

Paige eased her slim frame into the open doorway, leaned out and peered around the jamb in both directions. Who had been on her porch and where were they now? An icy chill poured over her skin, the fine hairs standing erect, and she darted back into the house, slammed the door shut and bolted it. A voice from behind her startled her and she dropped the pistol onto the hall mat as she swung around.

EIGHTEEN

Archer Hamilton wasn't happy about traveling to New York on such short notice but he'd been summoned by the vampire hierarchy of the city and had no choice. He'd needed to see Paige alone again and now he'd have to wait until he returned. He pushed his black leather toiletries case into the on board bag and zipped it shut. Perhaps he could pay the lovely psychiatrist a visit before he left. Walking across to his dresser, he picked up his cell and thumbed her number into the keypad. The phone rang for quite some time before voicemail kicked in. He frowned at the screen and pressed the red button to disconnect. It wasn't like Paige not to answer. Archer was certain she'd have his number in her address book by now and would pick up as soon as she saw his name appear on the screen. Why hadn't she?

Maybe he should pay her an impromptu visit to make sure she was all right and do what he needed to before heading to the Big Apple.

Paige took a step backwards. Could she get out the door before the creature standing in front of her grabbed her? Her heart throbbed against her ribs, her eyes remaining fixed on the darkly clad figure in her entry hall. She took another step back.

"I am not here to harm you, Miss O'Connell, only to talk. There is no need for you to fear me." He stepped toward her, his pale eyes piercing her soul. Her distress quickened him, even though he wasn't about to attack her.

Paige could feel her throat closing up and sucked in a sharp, strangled breath. She took another step back, her spine pressing into the curtained door behind her. "If what you say is true… why break into my home?"

He steepled his fingers in front of him. "I did not break in as you claim. Your kitchen door was unlocked."

Both doors had been locked. She'd checked them as she did every night before heading upstairs.

The word vampire jumped into her head. Couldn't they only come in if invited?

"Who are you?" Paige's nervous gaze darted to the gun lying on the floor a short distance away. There was no point in trying to grab it. Bullets didn't kill vampires. Not ordinary ones, anyhow.

"My name is Julius. I am an ancient immortal. I sit on the Moon Grove council." He extended his pale hand. Paige didn't accept it. "I need your help, Miss O'Connell." He gave a lopsided half grin and lowered his hand.

"Why would the council need my help?"

"You are close to Eli Blackwood. Are you not?" His eyes remained fixed on hers and she felt light-headed.

"Not anymore. We broke up several weeks ago."

Julius' right eyebrow arched. "We were not aware."

"So whatever it is you want… I can't help you."

"How unfortunate."

"You have your answer, now would you please leave?" Paige's stomach did another uneasy flip flop and she felt dizzy.

"Not just yet. I am still of the belief you can offer assistance…"

The ship's bell clanged outside, its mellow, metallic tone echoing into the entry hall. "Paige, it's Archer."

Paige's gaze shifted for the briefest moment and when she looked back to where the vampire had been standing he was gone. She breathed a huge, relieved sigh and unlocked the door. "I am so glad to see you."

Archer's charismatic smile lit up his handsome face. "The feeling is always mutual."

She ran her gaze around the entry hall, living room, and dining room once more. Her visitor was definitely gone. "Come in."

Archer could hear Paige's accelerated heartbeat. "Everything all right?"

"It is now." She closed the door.

The editor leaned down and picked up the pink handled revolver and studied it. "What's this doing on the floor? And why do you have a gun in your house?" He frowned at her.

Paige eased the pistol out of his hand and dropped it into her purse. "It's for protection."

"What's it loaded with?"

"Regular bullets." She led him into the living room.

"Then it's useless." Archer huffed out a humorless chuckle and sat down on the sofa. "What did you mean by 'It is now'?"

"I had a visit from the council. Well, one of its members." She remained on her feet and folded her arms. "He said he wanted my help."

"With what?"

"We didn't get into the specifics because you arrived, thank goodness. The frightening thing is he came into my house uninvited and came up behind me. I thought he was going to…"

Archer dashed across the room and wrapped his arms around her. "Thank God I decided to come over. Who knows what would've happened if I hadn't?"

Paige stepped out of his embrace and frowned up into his beautiful, pale blue eyes. "Why *are* you here?" Two vampires in one night couldn't be a coincidence.

"When you didn't answer your phone I thought I should come by and see if you were ok."

"Is that the only reason?" Her eyes moved to the patterned carpet beneath her feet.

Archer raised her face up to meet his gaze. "Not really. I wanted to see you again before I left."

Time seemed to stand still for the briefest moment before he pressed his lips to hers and she fell into the moment, wrapping her arms around his waist and stepping closer so their bodies touched. The heated kiss lasted a long time before Paige eased out of his embrace. "Archer, I'm sorry, I can't."

"I know you like me and you must know I like you so why is there a problem?"

"It's too soon. I'm not ready. Can we please take things slow?"

The editor stepped closer, brushing stray strands of red hair off her face. "Of course we can. I'm not about to do anything that would ruin what we could have together."

"Thank you." She reached up and touched his hand. "I need to ask you something. It didn't cross my mind when you came into the office today."

The editor gave her a curious frown. "What is it?"

"You didn't happen to find my necklace in your car, did you? I seem to have misplaced it."

"Oh? That's a shame."

"Yes. It was a gift."

"Perhaps I can find you a new one while I'm in New York."

"Sweet of you to offer but don't worry about it, I'm sure it will turn up somewhere." At least she hoped it would.

When Paige woke up the next morning she felt woozy and hungover again. Her thoughts were a jumble about the previous evening. She'd seen Archer, hadn't she? He'd come over. The memory of the dark figure in her entry hall jumped into her head and she gasped. Julius, wasn't it? What had he wanted? Oh, yes, her help. But with what? He'd mentioned Eli, hadn't he? She rested her head in her hands and tried to dislodge the wall of fog blocking her thoughts. What had occurred the previous evening? Did she and Archer have something to drink? Paige threw back the covers, climbed out of bed, and wandered downstairs to the living room. No glasses or wine bottle on the coffee table. She headed into the kitchen. An empty Chardonnay bottle and two glasses sat on the sink. She frowned at the trio of glass. She couldn't recall drinking any wine last night. A shiver ran through her. Why couldn't she remember?

NINETEEN

Gregor Petrov was of ancient, Russian vampire blood. He stood six feet five inches in height, was of solid build, had cropped dark hair and the palest green eyes. He also had a penchant for ridding the world of Lycanthropes, the fewer werewolves around the better. Standing at the end of the main road, he ran his perceptive gaze over the rural setting. Moon Grove was a charming little town with tree-lined streets and shingled roofs. It seemed a shame he had been sent to decimate it and the people who lived within its borders. At least, the supernatural creatures taking refuge in the picturesque township.

The first item on his agenda was to acquaint himself with Paige O'Connell, new resident and town psychologist. She had Lycan blood pulsing through her veins of which he planned to partake. Not yet a fully-fledged wolf, Paige's blood would enhance his ability to defeat the pack and forge a new alliance for the town. It had been unwise of the Alpha not to have consummated their relationship and turn her while he had the chance, but it would give Gregor the advantage now. He smiled.

Drinking from her would make him a hybrid creature and would offer him power beyond any other vampire or wolf.

He hadn't come to the town alone. Some of his team was already concealed within a property on the outskirts of the town, awaiting his instruction. More would come. They had retrieved the Lycan volume from the church – a necessary accoutrement to the plan of ridding Moon Grove of the wolves. It contained all he needed to destroy the pack, including its Alpha, Eli Blackwood, and secure the moonstone ring. Not for himself, of course, but for those who had paid him handsomely for his services.

He pushed his hands deep into the pockets of his jacket and strolled past the quaint shops, movie house, and businesses on the main street, heading to his car. Another visitor to the small township, taking in the sights. No one would suspect anything different. Although the town was remote to the rest of the US, tourists still traveled through it on their way to other destinations and to the people who saw him on the street he would be just another vacationer. He had been sanctioned by the governing body of the town and had traveled a long way to fulfil the mission he'd been assigned, and he was looking forward to the time when he would come face to face with Eli Blackwood in a fight to the death. It would be a pleasure to take his life.

Eli spotted the stranger wandering past the café and wondered who he was. His Lycan radar shot up. Vampire would be his guess. Why had another blood drinker come to Moon Grove? If he didn't know better he'd think there was some kind of upcoming immortal convention. The darkness they had felt grew more palpable by the day and he wanted to keep a close eye on new visitors to the town, especially the supernatural kind.

He crossed the street, stepped onto the sidewalk, and walked up to the man he'd had his eye on. "Hello, I'm Sheriff Blackwood. May I ask if you're visiting or passing through?"

The guy gave him an intense stare for the briefest moment then smiled and said, "Just passing through." It was a lie, of course, but Gregor wasn't about to tell him he was in the town to eradicate Blackwood's pack. He hadn't expected to run into the Alpha quite so soon.

"Good to know. Thanks. Uh, can I grab your name?"

"Is it necessary?"

"Just a need to know."

"Greg Petrov."

"Russian?" Eli frowned.

"Yes."

"You're a long way from home."

"I am on vacation. I have always wanted to visit America."

"Welcome. I'm sure you'll enjoy your stay in our fine country." Eli knew the vampire was lying but he couldn't interrogate him on the street in front of residents who were unaware of the supernatural element in the town. He'd have Bobby do a check once he returned to the station.

"Thank you." He glanced around. "I noticed your town does not have a lot of tourist traffic. Is that why you asked?" Gregor returned his gaze to the sheriff.

"We like to know who's visiting. Keeps the town and its residents safe." He gave a thin smile.

"Oh, of course. Good policy. If there is nothing further I'll be on my way."

"No. You have a nice day." Eli had the distinct feeling this visitor wasn't leaving soon. Was he part of the danger and darkness they had felt? And, if so, where was he staying?

Eli and Zach stepped into Paige's office at 10:10 AM. They were late and he knew their tardiness wouldn't sit well with her. Linda smiled up at them as they approached the reception desk and placed a clipboard with some documents for Zach to fill out on the counter. "If you could complete those I'll let Dr. O'Connell know you're here." She stood up and headed for the door to the private offices.

"Sorry we're late," Eli called after her.

Linda turned around and smiled. "Might want to give your apologies to Paige, she's the one who's been waiting."

Eli gave a heavy sigh and wandered over to where Zach had sat down and took a seat beside him.

Paige came through the door a short time later with a professional smile on her face. "How are you today?"

Zach glanced up, pen in hand. "Good. Thanks."

Eli's gaze moved to her and he smiled. "Sorry we're late. I had an encounter this morning I couldn't ignore."

"It's ok. It's not as though I have clients beating down my door."

"How are you?"

"I'm fine." She gave him a brief smile.

Zach finished filling out the paperwork and handed the clipboard to her. She ran her gaze briefly over his information then looked at him. "Why don't you come with me?"

Both men stood up.

"Uh, Eli, could you wait out here? I need to spend some time with my client alone."

"Sorry, can't." He stood with hands on hips. "We've reopened the case and as the investigating officer I need to be in there. Whatever he says under hypnosis has to be documented."

"It's ok, Dr. O'Connell, I don't mind," Zach told her.

"Very well. Come on through." She led the way down the short hall to the second door on the right and motioned for the pair to go in ahead of her.

Eli took a seat in the corner by the window, removed his Stetson and sat it on his lap. Today's session was an integral part of the new investigation to clear Zach's name and he hoped Paige could extract the information they needed and also find out the other reason why he was in town.

Paige set the metronome on her desk in motion, asked Zach to close his eyes, and told him to listen to her voice. She counted back from ten to one and stopped the device from ticking. Her patient was out.

TWENTY

Gregor drove the winding road out to the property where four members of his team were awaiting his arrival. The other five would travel to Moon Grove sporadically over the next couple of weeks so as not to raise suspicion. He turned left onto the dirt road, followed it to the end and pulled up outside a padlocked, black metal field gate. The cabin was another few hundred feet beyond the legion of tall, pines.

He stepped out of the car, gazed around at the hazy surroundings, then tugged the keys from his jacket pocket and unfastened the lock. After pushing the gate back, he drove through and stopped to secure it again before continuing on. The area was remote and well out of Lycan range. Gregor pulled the rental up outside the closed in porch, got out and climbed the steps. The door flew open before he could push the key into the lock and a young woman smiled up at him. "It's about time." She jumped into his arms, wrapped her legs around his waist, and planted a firm kiss on his lips.

Gregor lowered her to the floor. "Yana, remember what I said. We must be professional while we are here."

She scowled. "I do not know why. The others know we are together."

"Yes, I know, my sweet, but this is an important mission and we cannot be distracted with other pursuits. We must keep our heads in the game." He reached out and lifted her chin up so their eyes met. "We will have time later. I promise."

Yana gave him a seductive grin. "I will hold you to your promise, my love. By then my need for you will be *insatiable*."

He kissed her forehead and they both stepped inside.

Gregor greeted his team. "It is good to see you all here. We have a huge task on our hands and we must be prepared."

"We are ready!" Nicolai told him, pounding his fist into his chest as a sign of respect and loyalty.

The others in the group gave a loud, united 'Da.'

"I am privileged to be working with you. Spasibo (Thank you)."

Yana brought in a tray of vodka shots and they drank to a successful mission, each member downing the alcohol and slamming the small glasses onto the tray on the coffee table.

"Let me see the book," Gregor asked, holding out his hand.

Nicolai crossed the room to the bureau in the corner, picked up a thick, worn, leather bound tome, walked over to his leader and placed it in the palm of his hand. A smile spread across the vampire's face as his eyes met the Latin title. They now had everything they needed to end the pack and commence a new law enforcement in the town, one regulated by vampires.

Bobby snatched the digital handset off its base and answered the call. "Moon Grove County Sheriff's Office, Deputy McBride speaking." He waited for a response on the other end of the line but no one replied. He frowned, pulled the receiver from his ear, and stared at the display as though it would give him the answer as to who the caller might be. He pressed it back to his ear. "Hello? Is anyone there?" After a few more seconds, he poked the end button, plonked the handset back into its base, and glanced across the office at Rosemarie. "Well wasn't that the darndest thing."

"It's not like someone to call in and not answer," Rosemarie said, a concerned frown on her face.

"I know, right?" Bobby ran his hand over the stubble on his chin, his other hand on his hip. "I had the feeling someone was there."

She let out an amused snort. "There had to be, hon, unless a ghost called."

"Yeah, yeah, I know, Rose, but…"

"Something weird is going on in our town and I, for one, am not feeling good about it." The receptionist stood up. "Want some coffee?"

Bobby's gaze moved from the silent phone to her. "Sure, thanks, Rose."

"Cooper?"

"Huh?" The deputy looked up from his computer.

"Coffee?" She held up her empty, pink mug with Boss Lady on the front. A gift from Eli.

"Uh, no thanks. I'm good." He got up and crossed the

office to Bobby's desk. "So what do you think that call was about?"

The deputy shook his head. "Beats me. A lot of strange stuff is going on around here lately and…"

"Like what?" Cooper folded his arms.

"The church for one. Whoever broke in meant business. And now the pack is vulnerable because they have our Lycan tome."

"Maybe you should contact the sheriff and let him know about the strange call."

"Can't. He's not contactable right now."

"If I was him I'd want a heads up. If the kind of danger you're talking about is here then you should tell him. Just saying." Cooper turned and walked back to his desk.

Bobby knew he was right.

Eli's phone vibrated in his shirt pocket and his eyes darted to Paige, who frowned at him. "Sorry," he whispered as he stood and left the room to answer the call. "What's up, Bobby, I'm in the middle of something?"

"I had an unusual call a few minutes ago…"

"What kind of unusual call?"

"Whoever was on the other end of the line didn't answer when I picked up."

"Could've been a wrong number and they decided not to say anything."

"Yeah, it could've been, except they hung on the line for a while before I ended the call. I had the distinct feeling it was someone like us."

Eli's right eyebrow arched. "You're sure?"

"I can't say one hundred percent, but I think so."

The sheriff let out a long sigh. "A lot of strange things are starting to happen here, things making no sense at all." He paced the outer office. "See if they call back. Maybe they got scared or something. I have to go."

"How's it going with Zach?"

"Hard to say right now. Look, I'll be in later and we can talk more then. Can you round up the others? I'll text you when I know what time. I have to go."

"Sure. See you when you get here." Bobby rang off.

Eli frowned at the screen. It had to be the beginning of whatever had arrived in Moon Grove and they needed to be prepared. He'd organize a meeting at the station for later tonight once he finished with Zach. He'd talk to Paige, too, before he left. Just to make sure she was aware. Having Linda with her during the day was some comfort, at least.

The receptionist stood up and came over to him. "Everything all right?"

"Bobby's spooked by a call he got. No one answered but he could tell they were on the other end of the line."

"Could've been a wrong number and they felt embarrassed."

"I thought the same thing, but I know Bobby too well, so do you, and I'm sure he wouldn't be alarmed unless there was good reason."

"Then it has to be part of what's starting." Linda folded her arms.

"Yeah. And we're in a vulnerable position right now with that book being in the wrong hands. Once whoever took it knows our weaknesses we're destined for disaster if we can't stop them."

A shiver ran through the receptionist. "It's a frightening thought, isn't it?"

"You bet. But I'm going find out who has it and get it back." He held up his left hand, displaying the moonstone ring.

Linda gasped. "You decided to wear it." Her eyes ran over the milky stone set in silver. "How do you feel?"

"I'm ok. Clary made me this." He pulled the small brown vial from his jacket pocket. "Takes the edge off while we're getting *acquainted*." He gave her a thin smile.

"I feel so much better knowing you're wearing it. It will give you the strength you need to fight whatever's here."

"I hope you're right, Lin. So far all it's done is provoke an irrational, furious response to everything in my path, which I hope settles down soon."

"Maybe you need to be furious. The anger will boost your strength."

"Like it did the last Alpha who wore it?" He stared into her eyes, his gut twisting into a tight ball of apprehension.

TWENTY ONE

Paige climbed the front steps and was about to push the key into the lock when she caught sudden movement out of the corner of her left eye behind the swing seat along the porch. She swung her startled gaze across the veranda and saw the hooded, male figure standing with hands in pockets. She gasped, fumbled for the revolver in her purse, tugged it out and aimed. "You... you were here the other day. Who are you and what do you want?"

The figure moved toward her.

"Stop!" she shouted, "Don't take another step... or, or I swear... I'll shoot you." Her clammy, trembling hands gripped the pistol tightly as she pointed it at her intruder. Could she pull the trigger?

The figure pushed back his hood to reveal his face. "I'm not here to hurt you, Paige."

"Then why are you here? Who sent you?" She could hear the nervous tremor in her voice and swallowed the lump in her throat threatening to choke her. The guy was a few years younger than her and looked familiar somehow. Had she seen him in town? No, she would have remembered if she had. "Do I know you?" She frowned, her eyes never leaving him for a second. There was something about his face Paige felt she recognized.

He raised his hands. "No one sent me. Would you mind not pointing the gun at me? I'm here to talk to you, nothing more."

Paige kept the revolver raised. "Not until I know who you are and what you want with me."

"You're thinking I look familiar, aren't you?"

Her eyes widened. "How did you know…?"

"I have an… ability, you could say."

So he was another *creature*.

"Are you saying you can read minds?"

He nodded. "Yeah, among other things."

She was in no position not to believe him after everything she'd seen and learned during her time in Moon Grove. There was still so much she didn't know. "Ok. But you haven't answered my question."

He let out a sigh. "My name's Brent. Brent O'Connell."

"How do I know you're telling me the truth?"

He removed something from his right-hand pocket and held it out to her. "You need to look at this."

Paige stepped closer and snatched the object from his hand, still pointing the gun at him. Glancing down at the photo she gasped. It was a picture of her mother, but there was something different about her. Her tear-filled eyes moved back to him. "Where did you get this?"

"It was given to me by… your mom."

"My mom?" She shook her head. "Not possible. She died when I was five." Paige lowered the revolver, a tear sliding down her cheek, and passed the photo back. "So you're a relative? A cousin on my father's side perhaps?"

He took another step toward her. "I'm more than just a relative, Paige."

"What do you mean? She frowned.

"I – I'm your brother."

Paige gave an emphatic shake of her head. "You can't be. As I already said, my mother died a long time ago."

He took another tentative step. "Paige, she *isn't* dead."

More tears slipped down her cheeks. "Then where has she been all these years? Why didn't she come and get me?"

"It's complicated."

"Yes, it usually is." She dropped the weapon into her purse, pushed the key into the lock and swung the door open. "I think you should leave now."

"But there are things you need to know. Important things. Things that can keep you safe."

"Safe?" She folded her arms. "I've been attacked by a ferocious black wolf that turned out to be Eli Blackwood's father, who wanted me dead. Had my home broken into four times already by creatures looking for an ancient moonstone ring. My best friend was stabbed and almost died and now she won't speak to me. I was knocked unconscious at my office and ended up in the medical center over in the next town. How can what you have to tell me keep me safe from any of it? Did you know they found my father's remains in the woods? He'd been lying out there for twenty three years. They have what's left of him at the coroner's office over in Bellehurst. I can't even bury him because the investigation is ongoing as Eli still isn't sure who killed him." She was unaware that Brent had given the sheriff information about Elijah being the killer. She took a breath, about to continue her tirade, but stopped as the realization of what she'd seen a moment earlier hit her. The photo of her mom – she looked older.

Eli sat at his desk in the den of his home and contemplated the session with Zach. It seemed the vampire's subconscious was going to be harder to crack than he'd first anticipated. Paige had managed to unearth some minor details about the night Charlene Brooks was killed, but again, nothing substantial enough to prove Zach hadn't been a part of the blood ritual. How could they get inside his vampire psyche to acquire the information Eli needed?

He thought about the meeting at the station earlier. Filling in his pack on what was going on and about the vampire he'd encountered, which he wasn't able to find any information on, brought his pack up to speed. They all needed to be on alert now as the density of the danger had become more acute, leading Eli to believe Greg Petrov was involved and the reason he was in Moon Grove.

His cell vibrated on his desk, interrupting his thoughts. He snatched it up and frowned at the screen. Paige? Pushing the button, he answered, "Hi, Paige, what's up?"

"I had a visit from the hooded man again and I thought you should know."

Eli sprang out of his seat. "Are you all right? Is he still there?"

"Yes, he's still here."

"Do you want me to come over?"

"I'd appreciate it. Thank you."

"Ok. I'm on my way."

As Eli shrugged into his jacket and pushed his Stetson onto his head he wondered why Paige had seemed so calm. Had she been threatened? Was the intruder holding a gun to her head or a knife to her throat as she spoke to him over the phone? He climbed into his four wheel drive, spun the wheels, did a U-turn and hurtled down the drive to the road. He'd switch on the siren so he could fly along the highway to get to her home as fast as he could.

It took fifteen minutes to reach Paige's house, record time, considering he lived almost thirty minutes out of Moon Grove, and when he screeched into the driveway and stopped behind her sedan he was surprised to see her standing on the front porch with her brother. Eli threw open the door, rounded the vehicle and strutted across the lawn. "I thought you were in danger."

Paige folded her arms. "And I thought you were an honest man. Why didn't you tell me about Brent?"

Eli stopped at the steps. "He asked me not to." He gave the young man beside her an annoyed frown. "Didn't you bother to mention that?"

"So you knew about him before Christmas?"

"He was the guy I was talking to when you were looking for me in parking lot at the hospital the day we were bringing Clary home. Remember?"

"Yes, I remember. And you said he'd asked you for a cigarette. Which was a lie."

"Because he said you'd be in danger if you knew about him and your mom. They'd been hiding from the council all this time."

"I know. Brent told me."

"Then why are you angry with me?"

"Because you should've been the one to tell me. I trusted you."

"Didn't I just explain what he said? Your life would be in danger if you knew." Eli folded his arms. He'd come to make sure she wasn't in danger and now he was getting the third degree. He turned to leave then turned back. "Look, I'm glad you're ok and I'm glad you have your brother here now. I guess I'll see you around." He crossed the lawn and was about to get into his Jeep when Paige called after him.

"Don't you want to continue the sessions with Zachary Ridgeway?" Even though she was angry with Eli she still wanted to spend time with him when she could. She missed being with him, and if the only way to be near him was in a professional capacity, she'd make the most of it while it lasted.

Eli knew it was imperative to get to the bottom of Charlene's death, despite the friction between him and Paige. What choice did he have? He couldn't go back to John Taylor after what he'd discovered, and still wasn't sure what he planned to do about his confession. "I'll get back to you once I know when Zach wants to give it another try." He climbed into his car, backed out of the drive and sped off.

TWENTY TWO

Gregor stood across the street from Paige's house, hands pushed deep into the pockets of his knee length, black leather jacket. Not that he felt the cold, he didn't. He was a vampire, after all, a cold blooded, undead creature. The O'Connell woman had a Lycan visitor; he could smell the scent from his hiding place. And, as it turned out, the bloodline was the same as hers. A thin smile spread across the vampire's rugged, handsome face. He was eager to make her acquaintance because unbeknown to her she would assist him in destroying her ex-lover and his pack. It was time for fresh blood in Moon Grove. Vampire blood.

The hooded young man left the house around 10 PM. Gregor wondered if he should inform the council of the wolf's presence. Was he someone they could gain information from? The thought dissipated when he saw the living room light go out. Paige was on her way upstairs to bed. His smile widened. She was alone – and vulnerable. Now would be the perfect time to acquire what he needed from her, but he had other plans. He liked to toy with humans just a bit and it would amuse him to play with her for a while.

As Paige climbed the stairs her cell chimed, causing her to jump. She plucked the phone from the pocket of her robe and frowned at the screen. It was after eleven, who would be calling at this time of night? A smile spread across her face when she saw the name. "Hello, I didn't expect you to call."

"Well I thought I should because I've been delayed," Archer told her.

Her smile faded. "Oh. So how long will you be in New York?"

"Another few days. But when I get back we'll have that dinner I promised you."

Paige reached the landing and walked along the hallway to her room. "Then I'll look forward to it."

"I have to go."

"Take care."

"You too. I'll see you soon." He rang off.

Paige sighed and opened her bedroom door. Maybe she should have adhered to her initial plan of *not* getting romantically involved with anyone. It would've made life a whole lot easier, especially now that she was working with Eli on the Charlene Brooks case. She was still in love with him, even though she'd tried not to be, and she hoped the new relationship with Archer would help lessen those lingering, painful feelings. She knew she could never love him the way she loved Eli, but at least he was someone she could learn to love, in time.

She closed the door to her room, slipped out of her robe, dropped it over the back of the armchair, and climbed under the covers, giving a heavy sigh. Why had her life become so complicated?

Gregor remained hidden among the trees contemplating whether he should set his plan in motion now or wait a while longer. He wanted to ease himself into Paige O'Connell's life, get her to believe him, trust him, then implement his scheme. But was there enough time? The sheriff and his pack were aware of the vampire presence in the town, but not who as yet, so how much time did he have?

Dressed in black to blend into the night, he crossed the street like a shadow, whipped across Paige's front lawn and dropped down on the other side of the gate onto the path without a sound, his sensitive vampire hearing listening for any movement inside the house. She was asleep. He could hear the deep, rhythmic flow of her breathing and the slow, gentle beat of her pulse. He followed the path to the back yard, ascended the wood clad wall on hands and knees, like an oversized fly, and peered through her bedroom window.

Using mind manipulation, Gregor stared at the latch on the window, watching it twist open by unseen fingers, then slid the lower sash up and crept inside. He stood in the shadows beside the bed, his nocturnal eyes roaming the covers and Paige's sleeping form beneath. It would be so easy to drink from her while she slept. The thought caused a wash of saliva to pool beneath his tongue and his razor sharp canines snapped into place. He lowered his tall frame onto his knees, eased her hand out from under the bed clothes, brought her wrist up to his face and drew her scent deep into his nostrils. Exquisite. The bloodlust implored him to taste her, a jagged twist of pain squeezing his insides, the urge overwhelming, but he wouldn't give in to its demand. Not yet. He would orchestrate his plan and visit her place of business, follow through with his ruse of becoming a client. Before he did something he knew he would regret, he slipped out of the window, eased it shut and descended the wall.

Yana gave Gregor a dissatisfied stare from across the room. She knew where he had been. Knew he was infatuated with the Lycan bitch*. Did he plan to sleep with her? Was that the reason he had decided they should keep their distance while in Moon Grove? Had his feelings for her changed? She would need to be sure of her suspicions before acting on them. If she thought for one moment he had any kind of feelings for the woman she would end her, despite what she knew would happen if she did. Gregor belonged to her. Only her. They had been together for hundreds of years and *no one* would take her place beside him.

She crossed the living room and stood next to him with arms folded as he talked to his men, she being the only female vampire on his team. He planned to go into town the following morning and make an appointment for a consultation with the psychiatrist. Once he infiltrated her professional life he would make every effort to become part of her personal one too. Time was of the essence and he would have to move quickly.

Anger welled inside Yana as she listened to his scheme and her unbeating heart ached, but she knew if she did anything to disrupt Gregor's plan she would be disciplined harshly for it – regardless of their personal relationship. When it came to loyalty, her lover was stringent. You break his rules he breaks you! Even so, Yana wasn't sure she could hold the frustration inside for much longer.

*Dictionary definition: Bitch – a female dog, wolf, fox or otter. *Author note*

TWENTY THREE

Monday morning arrived quicker than expected, and when Paige walked through the door of her new office and saw Linda already working behind the reception desk she hoped she'd made the right decision to go ahead with the opening. After being in the town for a few months, the residents were no more welcoming than they had been when she'd first moved into her uncle's house and she wondered if their attitude toward her would ever change. She closed the door, crossed the office, and set a take away container of coffee down in front of her receptionist. "Any calls?" she asked, taking a cautious sip of her caramel latté.

"Not yet. But I wouldn't have expected it. It's only just after nine." Linda gave Paige an empathetic smile.

"Ok. I'll be in my office if anyone comes in." Paige sighed and headed down the hallway.

Linda walked over and gazed out of the front window through the vertical drapes, arms folded. Would anyone give Paige a chance to prove herself or was she wasting her time on the narrow minded, superstitious town? The phone rang and the receptionist rushed back to her desk to answer it. "Welcome to Peaceful Mind Psychiatry. You're speaking with Linda, how can I help you?"

"Hey, Lin, it's me," Eli said. "I want to make another appointment for Zach while he's still keen."

"Ok. When did you have in mind?" Linda opened up the appointment book on the computer screen. "Did you want it for tomorrow?"

"Tomorrow's fine. Say around ten again?"

"I'll pop Zach's name in for ten tomorrow."

"How are things? Any clients yet?"

"Not yet."

"Maybe all it needs is some time."

"Let's hope so, Eli, but you know how people are in this town."

He sighed. "Yeah, unfortunately."

"I'll text you a reminder in the morning."

"Thanks. But I won't forget. I want to get to bottom of this whole thing ASAP."

"Ok. Zach's all booked in for tomorrow."

"See you then." He rang off.

Paige came to the doorway. "A new client?"

Linda shook her head. "Eli. He made another appointment for Zachary Ridgeway for tomorrow at ten."

"Oh? Well at least I have one client." She gave a thin smile, turned and headed back to her consultation room.

Around midday, Linda stepped out to pick up their lunch from the Moon Grove Inn. While she was gone Paige sat at the reception desk in case someone ventured in. While skimming through Google pages to pass the time, the door opened and a tall, good-looking man entered. Paige popped up out of her seat, feeling flustered, her cheeks growing warm. "Good… good afternoon. Can I help you?"

He crossed the waiting area to the counter. "Yes, I think so. I'd like to make an appointment to see the doctor, please." Gregor had to play the game. He knew who she was, of course.

Paige pulled up the appointment book on the computer screen. "What day and time would suit you?"

"What about right now?" He smiled.

"We're on a lunch break at the moment. Perhaps we could make it later in the day, if you feel you need to start right away?"

"Of course. Would two o'clock be all right?"

"Yes, I can book you in for two." She poised her fingers over the keyboard. "What name shall I put?"

"Greg Petrov."

She glanced up at him. "Contact phone number?"

He gave her his cell number and Paige added it to the spreadsheet then swiveled around, wrote the time on an appointment card and slid it across the counter. "We look forward to seeing you later today."

Gregor picked up the business card, ran his gaze over the neat handwriting, and slipped it into the inside pocket of his jacket. "Thank you. I will be back at two o'clock."

Just as he opened the door, Linda arrived with a cloche covered plate in each hand. Gregor held the door for her then stepped outside and disappeared along the sidewalk.

Linda crossed the room and set the warm plates down on the counter before walking back to lock the door. "Who is that?" she asked, peering through the glass.

Paige's face lit up. "Our first client. Well, technically our second, but who cares. Someone came in!" She jumped to her feet, raised her arms in the air and danced around in a circle. "Woot, woot!"

"He was pretty cute, in a rugged sort of way, huh?" Linda came back to the counter.

"And Russian, I think. He had an accent of some kind."

"*Nice.* Tall, dark, hunky and European... a sexy combination."

Both women smiled at each other, picked up their plates and headed to the kitchen. The day had taken a definite turn for the better and Paige could tell it was just the beginning.

Linda eyed their client sitting on the sofa as discreetly as possible, her heart thrumming against her breastbone. He was undeniable eye candy. When he'd spoken to her earlier, the rich tone of his Russian accent had wandered her skin like a lover's hands and sent a distinct tingle to her feminine core. Charismatic was a word she'd use to describe him. Something about the man drew her in and held her fascination. And those pale green eyes. Oh my! He was the complete sexy package and the thought crossed her mind, *I wonder if he's single?*

Paige came through the doorway, picked up the iPad sitting on the desk, turned toward her client and said, "Greg, would you like to come through?"

Gregor closed the magazine he'd been feigning to read, dropped it onto the coffee table and stood up. As he passed the reception desk a hint of his musky cologne drifted into each woman's nostrils. He smelt wonderful and dressed well, too.

"Follow me, please." Paige turned and walked ahead of him down the short hallway to the second door on the right, motioned for him to step inside, followed him in and closed the door. "Please, have a seat."

"Thank you." He unbuttoned his black leather jacket and eased his tall frame onto the center of the charcoal gray sofa he assumed he would be lying on later in the session.

Paige brought up his file on the tablet in her hand and sat down behind her desk. "So, how can I help you? What do you need?"

He smirked inwardly, his pale eyes remaining on her concerned, pretty face. *If only she knew what I craved, what I need from her. Ah, well, she will find out soon enough.*

The session with Greg had gone well and Paige was confident she could help him. He had experienced some personal trauma which required guidance and reassurance, and once he successfully worked through it, with her assistance, she knew he would make a complete emotional recovery. At the conclusion of the session he'd been keen to make another appointment for the end of the week. It wasn't uncommon for a patient (client) to have two sessions within a few days of each other.

No further calls or walk ins had ensued throughout the course of the afternoon and by six o'clock Paige was ready to send Linda home, finish up, and head home herself. Tomorrow was another day, and she hoped someone else would be curious enough to want to make an appointment and see what she had to offer. She unlocked the front door, said goodnight to Linda, relocked it and wandered back to her desk. By the time she finished her notes on the session with Greg it was almost eight o'clock and she realized she was starving. After gathering her belongings she headed to her car.

When Paige pressed the remote and her sedan flashed to life, the hair on the back of her neck stood up and an icy chill poured over her skin. She could feel someone's eyes on her. Her nervous gaze scanned the dimly lit, deserted street. No one. She wrenched open the car door, climbed in, and snapped the lock closed, breathing a relieved sigh. Shoving the key into the ignition, Paige started the car and pulled away from the curb, checking her rear view mirror as she headed along the main street. Was she being paranoid?

As she drove toward home a set of bright headlights came up short on her trunk, the haloed glare hitting her in the eyes through the rear view mirror, almost blinding her and causing her to squint. Was it a local or the same car that had been behind her a few days before? It was difficult to tell in the dark. Paige's rapid heartbeat pulsed in her throat, the thick, clothy feeling blocking her airway, making her gasp. She pressed the accelerator to the floor, hoping to gain some distance between them.

The stark white lights remained close on her tail.

TWENTY FOUR

Rather than Paige hypnotizing him, which she assumed she had, Gregor had mesmerized her and planted certain seeds of information into her mind and a specific trigger so when the time came he could drink from her freely without resistance. A satisfied smile spread across his handsome face, his scheme to insert himself into her life had gone better than expected. He eased on the brakes of the black sedan, waited for her to pull her car into the driveway, then did a U-turn and headed back in the direction he had come from. His plan to unravel her was also working. He could sense the apprehension inside her as he followed her home.

Paige sat in her car, an anxious chill roaming her trembling body. Who had been following her again and why? Was she the target of a new supernatural predator? Could it be whoever ransacked her home? She checked the rear view mirror, snatched the keys from the ignition, opened the door and peered around the trunk of her car before stepping out. The street appeared empty. She wandered down the drive to the sidewalk and gazed along the street in the direction she had driven home from. No headlights. She knew she hadn't imagined it.

Regardless of her reservations, she decided to call the station. She keyed in the number as she climbed the front steps and unlocked the door. "Hello, Bobby, it's Paige. Can you come over to my house tonight?"

The deputy frowned. "Is something wrong?"

"I need to report an incident and I'd prefer not to have to come into the station." She closed the door behind her and shuffled the phone from ear to ear as she shrugged out of her jacket and hung it up. "I'd appreciate it if you didn't mention it to Eli. This needs to be done without his involvement for now."

"Sure, if that's what you want." He glanced at his watch. "I can be there in ten. Sound ok?"

"Thanks, Bobby. I appreciate it."

"I'll see you in a bit." He rang off.

Paige turned on the living room light, wandered to the kitchen door and flipped on the light in there as well. For some reason she was spooked, the hairs on the back of her neck static. Glancing over her shoulder, she turned around, rushed back to her purse and shoved her hand into it, breathing a sigh of relief when she felt the cold steel of the pistol lying at the bottom.

She headed back into the kitchen to make a cup of tea. It always soothed her nerves and gave her a sense of comfort the way warm milk did. She flicked the switch on the kettle, took a mug from the overhead cupboard and dropped a teabag into it. As she was about to pour boiling water into her cup a knock echoed into the entry hall. *Bobby's here already. That was fast.* Paige left the cup on the counter, along with the container of milk, made her

141

way to the front door and swung it open. "You were quick."

It wasn't him.

Bobby headed to the coat rack by the door. "I have to go out for a while, Cooper. Think you can handle things here without me?" He shrugged into his police issue anorak, pushed his Stetson onto his head and opened the glass door, catching a blast of the cool, spring breeze.

"How long you gonna be gone?" The apprentice deputy wasn't sure he *would* be ok alone.

"Don't know. Why? You're a big boy you'll be fine on your own. Got to do it some time."

"Yeah, I know, but…"

"I've got my shoulder mic so if you need me just holler."

"What if it's something serious?"

"Call Eli, then the pack, then me."

Cooper's eyes widened. "The pack?"

"Yeah. You can do that, can't ya?"

The young deputy nodded vigorously and hoped it wouldn't come to that.

"I'll be back as soon as I can. Ok?"

"Ok." Cooper gave a heavy sigh as he watched the door close behind his partner.

When Bobby pulled in behind Paige's car his hackles went up. He unclipped the holster on his hip, pulled his weapon and stepped out of the black and white cruiser, his eyes roaming the scene. The front door to Paige's house stood wide open and as he raced onto the porch and stopped at the threshold he shouted, "Paige, are you in there?" No answer.

This was bad. This was really bad!

He raised his pistol, stepped into the entry hall and scanned both rooms with eyes and weapon. No sign of her. He eased his tall frame along the wall of the hallway and peered into the kitchen. No one. A cup of tea sat on the counter along with a carton of skim milk. He walked over and pressed his fingers to the mug. Still warm, but not hot. His eyes roamed the room before heading back to the stairs. He climbed the carpeted treads two at a time and checked each upstair room. Empty.

Where is she?

Bobby came down the stairs like a man possessed reaching for his mic as he closed the front door and raced across the lawn. "Cooper, do you copy?"

Nothing. Static.

"Goddammit, Cooper, pick up."

The deputy came through the door zipping his fly and rushed over to the radio. "I'm here, Bobby, what's up?"

"Paige is missing. Get onto the others. I'm on my way back." The words oozed out of his mouth, tight and anxious.

"What?!"

"You heard me. I'm calling Eli now."

"Ok, ok, I'm on it."

Bobby rounded the police cruiser, jumped in and started the engine. *This is worse than bad!*

Paige came to in a pitch black space, her hands bound behind her, her ankles tied, and a sour-tasting cloth wedged between her teeth. She blinked back the haze and her eyes darted around her unseen surroundings, her heartbeat thumping against her ribs. *Where am I?* It took her foggy senses a second or two to catch up and then it dawned on her. She'd been taken. By whom? Someone was at her front door and she'd thought it was Bobby. Who was it? She gave her head a shake to rattle her brain into submission but nothing came to mind. The tangle of nerves in her stomach shrank into a tight ball of fear when she realized no one knew where she was. How much time did she have? Was whoever took her going to kill her?

Without the use of her tied hands, she struggled to ease her contorted body up the brick wall into a sitting position and attempted to recall what had happened and how she came to be here. It was all a blur. How long had she been unconscious? She noticed something warm trickling down her neck and her head started to pound. *Is that blood?* Then a horrible realization crossed her mind, causing her stomach to clench even more. Could she have been bitten by her assailant? Tears stung the backs of her eyes and she blinked them away. No time to fall apart now she had to stay alive.

A noise echoed into the room from outside and the dull amber glow of light pushed its way under the gap below the door not more than a few feet away. Her heartbeat revved up several more notches and her head spun.

Breathe, Paige. Breathe. You cannot *pass out, you have to stay awake!*

The door creaked open and an elongated, dark shadow stretched across the dirty concrete floor haloed by the bright rectangle of light.

Paige's eyes widened and she inhaled a sharp, shocked breath through her nostrils, her spine rigid against the bricks, her heart ready to claw its way out of her chest.

TWENTY FIVE

Eli threw open the police station door and strutted across the empty reception. Everyone was in his office waiting for him to arrive. He rushed through the door, a strained look of worry causing him to appear pale, and ran his gaze around the tense faces in the room. How could this have happened? He knew how. Because of his decision not to be with Paige. She'd been left alone and vulnerable despite his efforts to keep her safe. "Give me a brief of what you found when you got there, Bob."

"Let me start by telling you about Paige's call earlier." He gave Eli a sheepish look, knowing he should've told him regardless of what Paige had asked him to do.

Eli frowned at him. "What call? And why am I only hearing about it now?"

Bobby cleared his throat. "Well, uh, she called and asked me to go over there, which is why I was at her house tonight."

The sheriff folded his arms, his stern gaze growing even more severe. "Why?"

"She said she needed to talk to me about something and she didn't want you involved."

"And you thought it was a good idea not to tell me even though her life could've been in danger?"

"I would've told you once I knew what she wanted to talk to me about." His answer sounded lame, even to him. But it was the truth.

"So what did she tell you?" Eli rounded his desk and sat down.

"Not much." The deputy shrugged. "She didn't want to discuss it till I got there."

"Did she sound worried?"

Bobby's brow wrinkled into a deep frown and he thought about the question for a moment. "Well, yeah, she kinda did."

"Dammit, Bobby, why didn't you tell me?"

His deputy raised his hands and shrugged again. "I'm sorry, I should have."

Eli let out a heavy sigh. "Let's just get out there and see if we can locate her."

Just as he was about to mete out instructions, Linda appeared in the doorway. "Is it true? Has Paige been kidnapped?"

"Yes, it would appear so." Eli was surprised to see his former pack member at the station.

"Then I want to help." Linda stepped into the office and stood beside Bobby.

"Thank you, Lin. We could use all the help we can get right now." Eli's gaze moved to Rebecca. "Bec, take Lin and go over to Paige's and see if you can pick up a scent? We need to have some idea of who or what we're dealing with. Once you finish there, take a run through the woods. Maybe whoever has Paige didn't take her far."

"Sure, boss." Rebecca headed to the open doorway.

His gaze moved to Linda. "Are you ok with turning?"

She nodded. It had been a long time since she'd shifted but she would do it for Paige.

Rebecca and Linda headed out the door.

Eli looked at Ryan and Paul. "Would you do a thorough sweep of Paige's street? Knock on doors. Talk to neighbors. Maybe someone saw a car that didn't belong or someone near her house."

"We're on it." The two headed out.

Rosemarie had been sitting in the corner as quiet as a mouse and Eli hadn't noticed her until his office was almost empty. "Rosy!"

"You have to find her, Eli. She must be so scared." A tear slipped down her cheek and she brushed it away.

The sad look of concern on the receptionist's face clenched his heart, the sting of tears burning the backs of his eyes, causing him to blink. He stood up, walked over to her, eased her off the chair and wrapped his arms around her cuddly form. "We will, Rosy. I give you my word."

Bobby cleared his throat. "What do you want us to do, boss?" He and Cooper were the only team members left in the room.

"Take the cruiser out and search the town and its outskirts, especially out of the way places like abandoned buildings, the old mill, the cabin my father was staying in… anywhere you can think of where they might've taken her."

His deputy nodded. "I really am sorry I didn't say somethin', Eli." A pained expression crossed his face. If he'd had any idea something like this was going to happen he would have told Eli right away.

"I know."

Cooper headed for the door, Bobby behind him.

"Who would do this?" Rosemarie asked, staring up into his sad, honey colored eyes.

"Whoever's arrived in Moon Grove to start a war. We're in deep trouble, Rosy." Dread washed over him for the first time in a long while and he wasn't sure how he and his pack were going to stop what had come to their town.

Eli pulled his Jeep up behind Paige's sedan and climbed out. Rebecca and Linda were finished inside and the house was empty. He still had the key Paige had given him when he'd stayed over for a few days after the attempt on her life out at her abandoned childhood home. He slid his hand into the front pocket of his jeans, slid out the brass key and frowned at it. How had things gotten so messed up between them? It had been because he'd freaked out about her becoming Lycan and couldn't bear the thought of being the one to take away her humanity. He wondered now if his decision had been a mistake. Rather than keeping her safe, he'd put her life at risk.

His heart rumbled against his ribs as he climbed the front steps and slipped the key into the lock. What did he hope to find by coming here? Rebecca had called in telling him there was no scent in Paige's home. So who took her? He pushed the door back, stepped across the threshold and inhaled a deep, Lycan breath through his nostrils. Rebecca was right. Nothing. Without any kind of lead how would they find Paige? Time was running out. The thought flashed across his mind and he dislodged it as quickly as it had come. He would not give up on her now. She *was* still alive – somewhere out there – and they *would* find her.

The creak of a floor board made him swing around. His grandmother stood at the open doorway.

"Clary?"

"She was taken by a vampire, Eli."

He frowned into her eyes. "How can you be sure?"

"It was in the cards. I tried to find them but they must be cloaked."

Eli rested both hands on her shoulders. "Gran, do you have any idea where Paige is?"

The old woman shook her head, a sad grimace on her face. "If I did I'd tell you, my boy."

"Can you consult the cards again? See if anything else turns up?"

She looked up at him, tears welling in her eyes. "I'll try. But…"

"Please, Clary, please try. For Paige's sake."

As Bobby cruised down the main street he spotted Archer Hamilton heading into the Tribune office. He pulled the cruiser into the curb, climbed out and called his name. The editor turned around. Bobby crossed the sidewalk and stepped into the alcove beside him, standing with hands on hips. "When did you get back?"

Archer's left eyebrow rose. How had the deputy known he'd been out of town? Only Paige knew he'd be in New York for a few days. He had told his crew he'd be taking some research time off and spending it at home. "Just now. My car's in the parking lot and my luggage is still in the trunk. Why?" He sensed anxiety in the man. Something was wrong. He attempted to slip into the wolf's mind but discovered a solid barrier. Why couldn't he penetrate Lycan minds? They were part human, after all. "What's going on, Officer?"

"We're checking to see who's been in town the last few hours." He turned to head back to the patrol car.

"Why? What happened? Does it have something to do with Paige?"

"Talk to Eli if you want to know." Bobby climbed back into the cruiser and drove off. He had no time for the vampire and didn't like him muscling in on his boss's territory, especially where Paige was concerned. The pack needed their union whether Eli wanted to accept it or not.

Archer whipped his cell phone from the pocket of his jacket and keyed in the sheriff's number. Voicemail kicked in. "Dammit!" He rounded the corner, stalked along the sidewalk to the parking lot behind the building and climbed into his car. If he couldn't get any information out of the deputy he'd go to the source. But before he did, he'd head to Paige's.

When the editor pulled his Mercedes into the curb outside Paige's house he could sense vampire. He stepped out of his car, spotting Eli's police Jeep, stalked along the front path and climbed the steps. The front door was open. "Paige?" he called out.

Eli came through the kitchen doorway with a scowl on his face and walked up to him. "What are you doing here, Hamilton?"

"Your deputy quizzed me earlier but wouldn't tell me why so I thought I'd find out for myself. Is Paige here?"

His gaze moved past the sheriff, roamed the entry hall, then returned to him.

"No, she isn't here."

Archer Hamilton folded his arms. "Where is she?"

Eli contemplated whether or not to tell the editor. Could he be of some use in finding her?

"I picked up vampire scent when I pulled up." Archer thought a small piece of information might prompt the sheriff into letting him in on what had happened to Paige.

"Do you know who?" Eli mirrored the editor's movements. They both stood, arms folded, staring at each other.

"No. Sorry. I don't." He glanced over his shoulder. "Have you thought about asking the witch across the street?"

Eli's right eyebrow arched. "How do you know about her?"

"She was here the night I took Paige to dinner. It's not difficult picking up a witch's vibration." He gave a thin smile. "Maybe she can help."

"Already asked her. She can't."

Archer pursed his lips and thought for a moment. "Could she perform a location spell? Assuming Paige is missing, of course."

Eli hesitated before nodding. "Yeah, she is."

"I can help. I'll drive around and see if I can pick up the scent I sensed out here."

The sheriff's forehead wrinkled even more. "Why would you want to help me?"

"I'm helping Paige. I'll let you know if I find anything." He turned on his heel, strutted down the path, climbed into his convertible and drove away.

Eli's gaze moved to his grandmother's house. *Could Clary find Paige with a spell?*

TWENTY SIX

Ross Redmond sat behind his desk, hands clasped in front of him on the brown leather blotter, eyeing the council members sitting opposite him. Why had this meeting been called so late at night? What did they want from him now? Hadn't he already sold his soul to the devil? Six pairs of pale immortal eyes stared back at him, the stillness in the room palpable. The mayor swallowed the thick wad of nerves lodged in his throat and waited for Remus, head vampire, to speak. The others: Julius, Alistair, Ophelia, Leonardo, and Elisha sat in silence behind him.

"We are here as a courtesy to you, Mayor Redmond. As head of the governing body of Moon Grove I thought it my duty to inform you we have taken matters into our own hands with regard to the Lycan population of this town." A long, uncomfortable pause ensued.

Redmond cleared his throat as quietly as he could. Was it his opportunity to speak? He waited for clarification not wanting to infuriate his host, knowing what could happen if he did.

Remus's right eyebrow arched and he tilted his chiseled

jaw, indicating the mayor could respond to his statement.

"May I ask what you mean by 'taken matters into your own hands'?" Ross didn't appreciate being left in the dark. If something significant was going to happen in his town he wanted to be in the know and not look like a complete ass when it all went down and he had no explanation.

"All you need to be aware of is a new law enforcement faction is being instigated which will do *exactly* what we tell them. Not one that impersonates loyalty."

"Eli Blackwood and his pack have done everything you've asked of them, including things that go against the sheriff's moral code."

"Perhaps, but they are not dedicated to our cause."

"What cause?" Beads of perspiration dotted the mayor's brow. The extent of power the council wielded was out of control and there was nothing he could do about it, unless he wanted to end up like Jake O'Connell and the journalist. Up until now the town had functioned perfectly fine under the current laws and enforcement so why change it? What was the motivation behind the council's decision to enlist a more ominous task force?

"That is on a need to know basis and for now you do not need to know. You will be informed at the appropriate time."

Redmond jerked out of his seat. "I'm mayor of Moon Grove or have you forgotten that? I have certain obligations to the town and its residents and I need to be kept in the loop."

"Enough." Remus raised his left hand and Redmond felt the tightening of his airway. He poked his index finger beneath the collar of his white business shirt attempting to alleviate the pressure on his windpipe. The vampire continued. "Things have already been set in motion. There is nothing for you to be concerned about." He lowered his hand and the mayor sucked in a strangled breath. "We will be in touch."

In one fluid movement, the immortal group stood up and followed Remus out.

Redmond loosened his tie and unbuttoned his collar, his throat feeling as though firm fingers were still blocking the passage of air to his lungs. He couldn't continue to play the council's game any longer.

Eli drove along the dirt track to Paige's parents' home, pulled up at the perimeter and ran his eyes over the shadowed, crumbling remains. The night gave the place an eerie vibe and as he stepped from his four wheel drive an owl hooted overhead, causing his Lycan hackles to rise – his senses on high alert. The house looked deserted. No sign of light or movement. Even so, it was the perfect place to bring someone if you didn't want them found. No one came out here.

The three quarter moon hung low in the blue-black sky, its milky aura blanketing the extensive property in a ghostly glow and giving off enough light to allow Eli to cast his wolf gaze over it before making his way to the front door through the waist high grass. You can never be too careful where supernatural creatures were concerned and he wasn't prepared to be caught off guard.

Archer had mentioned he'd caught a trace of vampire scent at Paige's house earlier. How was it possible for a vampire to smell other vampires, but a Lycan, who had heightened canine senses, couldn't? He drew his weapon, checked the clip, and headed for the lopsided front porch, his pistol loaded with sanctified silver. As long as someone didn't wrestle him for his gun and shoot him with it he'd be fine.

Leaping across the rotting step treads and deck onto the threshold, Eli landed without a sound, despite his size, and stood motionless, his ears taking in any noises around him. He slowed his breathing to lower his heart rate so he could pick up the faintest sound. Nothing. He crossed the entry hall to the cellar door, eased it open and descended the stairs into the bowels of the old home, running his nocturnal gaze around the pitch black underground space. It looked like no one had been here since he and Paige had.

Eli gave a heavy sigh, turned around and made his way back up the staircase. Where would they have taken her? The others hadn't found any indication of disturbance at any of the locations they had searched, so where was she?

TWENTY SEVEN

The following morning, Archer pulled his Mercedes convertible into the empty driveway, turned off the engine and ran his gaze over the two-story, cream and white colored house with shuttered windows and full-length front porch. *Will she help me find Paige?* He pulled the keys from the ignition, stepped out, and before he had a chance to cross the lawn the front door flew open and she appeared on the verandah. "You have no business being here, vampire. Get off my property before I end you," the old woman warned, pointing a double-barrel shotgun at him. "And, yes, this thing's loaded with silver."

The editor raised defensive hands. "I'm not here to harm you. I came to ask for your help to find Paige. You can do a location spell, can't you?"

Clarissa kept the weapon aimed at her uninvited visitor while she contemplated the idea. "It might work, unless they have her cloaked. The darkness in Moon Grove is hidden from me. Maybe they've done the same to Paige so we can't find her."

Archer lowered his hands but remained where he stood.

"There's only one way to find out. What other choice do we have?"

"I'm not inviting you in." She lowered the weapon, turned around and disappeared into the house.

"That's fine. I can wait out here," he called after her, crossing the lawn and stepping onto the porch.

Clarissa entered the living room, spread a map of the town and surrounding area across the coffee table and sat down in the middle of the sofa. She closed her eyes and inhaled a deep breath and blew it out. She called on the goddess of light to guide her. She'd need all the help she could get. Afterward, she got up went to the dining room sideboard and took out her box of spell accoutrements. She placed four blue candles around her, representing north, south, east and west and a glass of purified water in the center of the map. She swirled her fingers in the water while repeating, "Let the water be my guide and allow me to find Paige O'Connell. The water will show me where she is." She dripped droplets of water off her index and middle fingers onto the map expecting them to roll to Paige's location, but instead the drops evaporated into the paper. "No, no, no!" Clarissa brought her hands up to her face and let out a frustrated sigh.

Archer's voice echoed into the room from the open front door. "Any luck in there?"

Clarissa stood up and walked into the entry hall. "No, and I don't understand why it didn't work. It's the best spell for locating people."

"Maybe it's like you said. They may have her cloaked or hidden underground."

The old woman's face wrinkled even more. "Then how are we going to find her?"

"Right now, I don't know. But I'll think of something." He turned on his heel and headed for his car.

"Thank you," Clarissa called after him.

Archer turned around. "Let's find her first. Then you can thank me." He climbed into his car and backed out of the drive.

Clarissa realized she'd been wrong about him. He wasn't the darkness that had come to Moon Grove.

As the editor drove toward town, he pressed the Bluetooth button on the console and called the sheriff. "I spoke to your grandmother and she tried a location spell."

"Who gave you permission to go to my grandmother's house, Hamilton?" He waited a beat then asked, "Did it work?"

"Unfortunately, no."

Eli sighed into the phone. "Then I'm out of ideas and options. The clock's ticking. If Paige is still alive, and I'm praying she is, there isn't much time left."

"I know. I'm going to do a drive around and see if I can pick up any residual vibrations from Paige. Nervous energy, fear in other words, tends to linger in the atmosphere longer than any other kind. I'll start outside her house and see if I can follow the trail. If there is one. I'll let you know if I find anything." He was about to ring off when the sheriff spoke.

"Hamilton? Thank you. I appreciate your help."

A smile crept across the editor's handsome face. "We need to work together right now to find Paige. Nothing else matters." He ended the call.

He'd traveled from the witch's house out along the highway, heading north, but hadn't picked up anything out there so he turned around and headed back to Moon

Grove. Paige had to be somewhere nearby. Whoever took her would have chosen a location close to the town. It had to have something to do with the new threat. Archer decided he might have to dig deeper and find out who or what that threat was. It might be the only way to find Paige before they killed her.

He pressed the accelerator down and sped along the highway toward the township. Time may have already run out.

Eli turned his Jeep around and headed back to the station. Ross Redmond had called telling him he needed to speak with him about an urgent town matter. It wasn't like the mayor to come to him. Usually, he was summoned to city hall for their meetings so the reason had to be serious.

He swung into the gravel parking lot beside the red, wood clad station house and as he climbed out Redmond's personal sedan pulled in alongside him out of sight of the street. Eli took the keys from the ignition, closed the door and rounded the back of his four wheel drive. "Ross. What brings you to this side of town?"

The mayor's nervous gaze roamed the intersecting streets. "Can we talk inside?"

Eli could see the anxiety on the man's flushed face. "Sure." He motioned for Redmond to go ahead of him and followed him along the front porch, opened the door, and stepped inside after him. "What's this all about, Ross? Why the sudden secrecy?"

Rosemarie, Bobby and Cooper stared at the mayor. It was out of character for him to come into the station.

Redmond's gaze traveled around the curious faces in the room then back to the sheriff. "Can we speak in private? What I have to tell you is sensitive information."

"Sure. Let's go into my office." Eli motioned for Redmond to step through the barrier, followed him into his office and closed the door. "Have a seat." He moved around his desk and sat down. "Can I get you anything... coffee?"

Ross waved it off. "No, no thanks." He scanned the office. "Is this room secure?"

Eli's eyes roamed the four walls before returning to Redmond. "As far as I'm aware." He frowned. "Why?" He could sense the mayor's discomfort.

"Because what I have to tell you could potentially get me killed."

TWENTY EIGHT

Bobby and Cooper were out on patrol, cruising the tree-lined streets of Moon Grove and keeping an eye out for anyone or anything that might appear suspicious. The thought consuming the deputy's mind, apart from the fact he should've told Eli in the first place, was that Paige had to be somewhere close by. But where? Cooper was behind the wheel and as they turned the corner onto the main street Bobby spotted a man outside Paige's office peering through the door. He pointed through the windshield and motioned for Cooper to pull the black and white into the curb then climbed out and walked over to the guy. "Do you need some help?"

The tall, leather-clad man turned around. "I have an appointment with Dr. O'Connell today." Which was a lie. His appointment was set for Friday and it was Wednesday, but he'd hoped to coerce the doctor into seeing him earlier so he could check to make sure the trigger he'd implanted in her subconscious would activate on his command.

"Well, as you can see, the office is closed. Maybe you can give them a call and reschedule."

"Do you know why the office is unattended?"

"Sorry, I don't." Bobby didn't know who the guy was and he wasn't about to offer up any information regarding Paige to a stranger. "Can I ask your name?"

"Why do you people keep asking me my name?"

"We're just tryin' to be neighborly." He forced a pleasant smile.

"I do not think that is the reason, *Officer*. You want to know who I am so you can check to see if I have a criminal record. I can assure you I do not."

Bobby felt a rush of heat to his cheeks, not from embarrassment but frustration. Why was it people didn't want to give their names? Was it to avoid detection? "Well now I'm asking under an official capacity." He stood with hands on hips. *Who is this guy? And what does he want with Paige?*

"Very well. My name is Greg Petrov."

"Wasn't so hard now, was it?" Bobby gave him another thin smile. *So this is Greg Petrov.* "Like I said, maybe you can reschedule your appointment. Or if you need to speak to someone sooner we have another psychiatrist just up the road." He pointed in the direction of Doc Taylor's.

"Thank you, but no. I would prefer to stay with the doctor I am already seeing." His eyes moved to the office door.

"Sure. It's your choice. Are you staying at the inn?"

Petrov's dark gaze returned to the deputy. "No. I have a place out of town."

"Oh? Where?" *Could this guy have something to do with Paige's disappearance?*

"It's off highway fifty seven."

"How far out are you?"

"About forty five minutes. Why do you ask?"

"No particular reason, just curious."

"Am I free to leave now, Officer?"

"Absolutely. Appreciate your time." He tipped the brim of his fawn Stetson. "You have a nice day now." Bobby could sense something supernatural about the guy, subtle, but noticeable. Vampire for sure. And he had just become a person of interest. *Greg Petrov, who are you and why are you in Moon Grove?* He made a mental note to look the guy up once he was back at the station. He knew Eli hadn't been able to find anything on him so now it was his turn to see if he could come up with anything.

Eli's frowning gaze remained on the mayor as his mind tried to absorb what he'd just been told. The council had plans in place to exterminate his pack and take over law enforcement of the town, and they were keeping Redmond out of the loop so he couldn't tell him the specifics of who was in Moon Grove and where they were located. His gut tightened at the thought of whoever they had delegated having access to their Book of Laws, which would give them a clear advantage.

"I'm sorry, Sheriff, I wish I had more to offer you but they've decided to exclude me from whatever it is they have planned until I absolutely need to know."

"There's no way you can find out? You don't have a rapport with any individual member?"

Redmond gave a heavy sigh and shook his head. "None at all, I'm afraid."

"Ok. I appreciate you giving me a heads up." Eli stood up.

"What I told you means nothing except now you know something's coming."

"Something's already here, Ross. I just wish I knew who and where." He had his suspicions but couldn't prove it.

The mayor stood up. "Anything on Paige's whereabouts?"

"Not yet, but we're working on it."

"I hope you find her." He headed for the door. "Should anything happen to me…"

"I won't let it." Eli came around his desk.

"You may not be able to prevent it." He gave a wry smile. "There are certain documents in a safety deposit box at the Federal Reserve Bank in Chicago." He pulled a chain from around his neck underneath his shirt and tugged at it. The links snapped and he handed the key to Eli. "You'll know what to do with it when you see what's inside."

"Don't give up. Get out of Moon Grove if you think your life's in danger."

"I plan to. I can't sit back anymore and watch the council destroy our town. But this is in case something happens to me before I can get away. Keep it in a safe place, Eli, and don't tell anyone you have it. And I do mean *anyone*."

"You have my word. Thank you." He slipped the key into the front pocket of his jeans and would transfer it to his hidden floor safe once he was home.

The mayor rushed out of the station, hoping he hadn't been seen or followed.

Eli crossed his office to the open doorway.

"What was that all about?" Rosemarie asked, a curious

frown crossing her plump, rosy-cheeked face. "The mayor looked awfully nervous and it's not like him at all."

Eli stood with arms folded, his eyes on the back of the station door. "We need to call everyone together." He turned to see his deputy walking through the door. "Bobby, has the church been cleaned up?"

"Sure has. No one would know it was ransacked."

"Let's call a meeting for tonight at nine. There's something you all need to know." Eli turned around, went back into his office and closed the door. He needed some time to think.

"I knew it." Bobby folded his arms. "The feeling of dread hanging over Moon Grove is rising to the surface."

"What do you mean?" Cooper asked, a nervous tremor in his deep voice.

"The battle has come sooner than expected."

Archer Hamilton entered the police station later in the afternoon. He'd done a thorough sweep of Moon Grove and its borders and wanted to tell the sheriff what he'd found. All eyes were on him as he crossed reception and stopped in front of Rosemarie's desk. He felt like an insect under a microscope. The receptionist gave him an uncertain smile and clasped her hands on the desk. "Can I help you, Mr. Hamilton?"

"It's all right, Rosy, he's here to see me." Eli poked his head around his office door and waved the editor through.

"Oh. Sure." Rosemarie's frowning gaze followed the man dressed in black all the way to Eli's office. Once the door closed she turned her head and said, "Well what do you make of that?"

Bobby was still staring at Eli's closed door. "Don't

know. I spoke to him a couple of days ago and he said he didn't know anything."

"Well it looks as though he does now." Rosemarie glanced over her left shoulder then returned her gaze to the deputy.

"Yeah. So it would seem."

Eli sat down at his desk and Archer took a seat opposite, crossing one leg over the other.

"So what did you find out?" The sheriff closed the lid of his laptop and folded his arms.

"Nothing." He mirrored Eli's movements. "I traveled to the outskirts of town and took the highway north and didn't pick up any residual vibrations. But the one thing I am sure of is it had to be a vampire or vampires."

"What makes you so sure?" He remembered what the editor had told him the other night and what his grandmother had said.

"The scent I picked up outside Paige's house for one thing."

"Yeah, I remember. Reasoning like a vampire, where do you think they might have taken her?"

"Somewhere out of the way but not too far from Moon Grove. I was thinking possibly underground."

"My guys have been to most of the abandoned buildings in the local and outlying areas and haven't found anything."

"Is there anywhere else you can think of... an old mill, factory, hospital?"

"We've covered everywhere that we know of at this point. It's been over forty eight hours; we're running out of time."

"I'll head back to the Tribune and do some research on

the area. Maybe there are places your team hasn't looked at yet." Archer stood up. "I'll call when I have something."

"Thanks."

"Anything to find Paige and get her back safely."

TWENTY NINE

Brent stalked along the sidewalk, hands pushed deep into the pockets of his black hoodie, and stopped at the edge of the lawn. He walked up the front path, climbed the steps, and knocked. He'd given Paige some time to digest what he'd told her and wondered what kind of reception he'd get when she opened the door. No answer. Maybe she was still at her office.

He leaped off the porch and marched down the path to the street, gazing along the road in both directions. Then he noticed it. Paige's car was in the drive. His brow creased into a deep frown and he walked over to it, circling the sedan and peering inside. *If her car's here where is she?* Brent crossed the lawn, climbed the steps and knocked again. Louder this time. He pressed his face to the living room window but couldn't see inside.

Wandering along the porch, he jumped the railing and sprang up and over the side gate. Once in the back yard, he leaped up and gripped the window ledge, peering into Paige's room. No one. He dropped to the ground on all fours, stood, and followed the path back to the gate. Before opening it, he listened for a heartbeat or some other sound inside the house. Nothing.

Where was his sister?

Brent closed the gate behind him and headed for the sidewalk and as he did he heard someone call out.

"Young man, young man," the old woman called from across the street.

His scrutinizing gaze moved to her and he could sense her powers right away. A witch. *What does she want with me?* He pushed his hands into his pockets and crossed the road. "Yeah?"

"You're Paige's brother, aren't you?"

"How'd you know?" His intense wolf eyes remained on her wrinkled face.

"I'm Eli Blackwood's grandmother."

"What do you want?"

"You need to go see Eli. Paige was taken from her house a couple of nights ago and he could use your help in trying to find her."

"What?!" The young man's face paled and his eyes widened.

"Go talk to him and work with him to locate her. They're not making any progress and time is of the essence. You might be able to pick up her vibration or scent, being related."

Brent turned on his heel and stalked down the woman's front path. He pulled his cell phone from the right hand pocket of his jacket, checked the internet for the station's number and keyed it in. "I want to speak to Sheriff Blackwood. Tell him it's Paige's brother."

About ten minutes later, Eli pulled into the curb and threw the passenger door open from the inside. "Get in."

Brent climbed into the idling four wheel drive. "So Paige has been missing since Monday?"

"Yeah, she has. We've covered everywhere we can think of but haven't found anything so far."

"Maybe I can track her."

"After two days?"

He shrugged. "All I can do is try. Being blood related might help."

"Are you planning on turning to do it?"

Brent nodded. "Yeah. I figure it's my best option. I'll be able to travel faster and cover more ground."

"I'll take you back to the station and show you where we've searched so you don't double up. There aren't many more places to look, unless they have her somewhere in town. There are some empty buildings along Main Street we haven't searched yet, only because they're too close to other businesses and didn't seem like a place someone would hold someone captive."

"Have the other pack members gone out searching as wolves?"

"Yeah."

"And nothing?"

"No."

"Ok. Let's get going. I want to find my sister. I didn't let her know about me to lose her now."

"Have you told your mom?"

"Not yet. I want to find Paige now before I tell her anything."

Eli stepped on the gas and headed back to the station.

Once they arrived, the sheriff ushered Paige's brother into the briefing room. Maps and photos were tacked to a white pin board and he pointed out the areas they had already covered. "We assumed the abductor would have kept the location close to Moon Grove. Maybe we've been wrong all along." He stood with hands on hips.

"What about the old abandoned medical center off the highway about ninety minutes out of town? Did anyone think to look there?"

Eli ran his gaze over the pinned locations on the map. "Doesn't look like it." Why hadn't they thought of the old medical center before? It would be the perfect place to hide Paige. Far enough away but not too far.

"I'll head over there first and do a thorough walk through."

"Do you want one of my pack to go with you?"

"Nope."

"You're sure? What if there's more than one abductor?"

"I can handle it."

The sheriff was impressed by the young man's courage, remembering how he'd held off Elijah outside his house when his father had come for Paige, but didn't think it was safe to go out to the deserted hospital alone. "What if I come with you?"

Brent ran the idea around his mind for a moment. Maybe he could use the sheriff's help. "Ok, sure. If Paige *is* out there she'll be glad to see you."

Paige's eyes roamed the dark. How could this have happened? What was the point of having Lycan blood pulsing through her veins if it didn't offer any kind of protection or foresight? The warmth of a single tear slipped down her left cheek and she blinked back the urge to cry. Where was she? Somewhere underground she imagined. A wave of nausea rolled around her belly. Would Eli find her before it was too late?

She knew she was in serious trouble. Her life was in grave danger. What if her abductor left her here and didn't come back? She would die a slow, painful death without water or food. The surrounding darkness pressed in on her and Paige's throat tightened into a thick knot of nerves. Her nostrils flared as she tried to inhale a deep breath, her racing heartbeat thudding against her ribs. She wanted to scream but even that had been taken away from her by the foul-tasting cloth wedged in her mouth and secured with a strip of duct tape.

She'd been told it was only a matter of time. How much time?

A rush of adrenalin burst through her body and she writhed and twisted her wrists caught in the restraints feeling the skin graze beneath the tight, plastic zip ties and the warm trickle of blood run down her hands. She had to get free. The choking sense of panic rose in her throat and she couldn't hold the fear in any longer. A stream of tears rolled down her face and she sobbed and sobbed until her throat ached. How had this become her life? Paige wasn't ready to die. She wanted to tell Eli her feelings hadn't changed. Wanted to convince him they still belonged together, wanted him to make love to her in the way she'd imagined he would so she'd no longer be the scared, helpless human she was.

A thought dashed across her terrified mind and a feeling of calm washed over her. Maybe she could maneuver her tied hands underneath her bottom and push her legs back through her arms so her hands were in front of her. It would be a difficult stretch but anything was worth a try. With her hands free she'd be able to feel around the floor for some kind of weapon to defend herself with. And try to loosen the ties on her ankles as well. Even though she was unable to see in the dark, she had to do everything she could to stay alive. She would not give up without a fight!

THIRTY

Eli revved his Jeep up over the cracked, concrete curb, steam-rolled the tall, dry grass and skidded the four wheel drive to a stop outside the boarded up front entrance of the abandoned medical center. He and Brent threw open the doors, climbed out, and scanned the outside of the weathered, red brick building before heading over to the twin set of double doors. Using his Lycan muscle, Eli gripped the edges of the board on one door, ripped it off, tossed it aside and climbed through the jagged glass hole, Paige's brother close behind him.

The dim, rubbish-strewn lobby was dank, the musty stench of rotting paper and stagnant water drifting into their nostrils as they trod through the dampness. Waiting room chairs were turned upside down, patient files strewn across the linoleum floor soaked in muddy pools of rainwater, and colorful spray-painted tags: Dragon, Wolf and Lizard were splashed across the walls and reception desk. Their eyes roamed the gloom.

"Maybe we should see what's underneath this place," Brent said. "There's always a morgue and storage areas down below. Would be the perfect place to hide someone so no one could hear them."

"What about checking up here first? She could be on an upper level." Eli stalked through a pair of broken wooden doors and along the right-hand corridor in search of stairs.

Brent sighed and shrugged. "I doubt they'd hide her somewhere she could scream or call for help." Although, he realized, it would be difficult for anyone to hear her out here as the building was far removed from the nearest town district and residential zone.

The stairwell was midway down the hall and when Eli turned around Brent was gone. "Dammit." The sheriff spun on his heel and marched back along the corridor into reception. No sign of Paige's brother, and he didn't have his cell phone number. "Just great." He thought it best not to call out in case it alerted anyone already in the building, so he crossed the lobby, took the left-hand corridor and followed it to a staircase with red metal railing that descended into the dark abyss beneath ground floor level. He hesitated before taking the stairs, his ears straining to hear any sounds below. Why had Brent taken off on his own? Safety in numbers, he believed. They were pack animals, after all.

Climbing over broken chunks of concrete, filthy, blue operating scrubs and other rubbish creating a rough obstacle course on the stairs, Eli made his way down into the pitch black bowels of the hospital.

His nocturnal Lycan vision kicked in once in complete darkness but it still wasn't enough to gauge the distance of the lower level corridor nor what could be waiting at the other end. *Paige's brother has to be down here somewhere.* "Brent?" he whispered, knowing if the young man was anywhere within hearing range, which covered a fair distance in wolves, he'd know Eli was in the basement. He eased his tall frame, back close to the wall, weapon in hand, through the gloom. "Brent?" He peered into blackness through the open morgue doorway. Nothing. Eli's agitated gut churned beneath his belt. He wasn't fond of dark places with only one escape route.

The sheriff continued down the hallway with caution, ears pricked, his senses on high alert. He tugged a small flashlight from the back pocket of his jeans and flicked it on, holding it beneath his raised weapon. The stark, white circle of LED light lit up the dark space, fanning the grimy, green tiled walls and several feet ahead of him. Broken wheelchairs, upturned gurneys, rusting medical equipment, and fallen plaster ceiling tiles littered the corridor. A noise behind him caused his hackles to rise and he spun around.

"I've been right through this place and there's no one here," Brent told him.

"Why'd you disappear on me?" Eli lowered the light.

"I thought we could cover more ground that way. Did you find anything upstairs?"

Eli let out a frustrated sigh. "No, because I came looking for you."

"Why? You knew I'd be ok." He rammed his hands into the pockets of his hoodie and scowled at the sheriff.

"Did I? Neither of us knew if the abductors had brought Paige here or not. What if you'd run into trouble?"

"I can take care of myself. Been doing it for long enough." He turned on his heel and stalked back down the corridor to the stairs. Eli glanced over his shoulder along the dark passage behind him before following Paige's brother out. *If she isn't here where else could she be?*

Gregor stood at the multi-pained window, a mug of microwaved blood in his hand, gazing out at the impending night. The springtime sun had almost set, the last of its shimmering, orange rays streaming through the trunks of the tall pine trees surrounding the property and gradually receding into the legion of wood. His plan had come to a grinding halt. Where was Paige O'Connell? He swallowed the last of the warm sanguine fluid, crossed the living room and walked into the kitchen. Without her blood the fight would be on a level playing field, something he didn't relish. He craved the advantage over the dogs. Well, that's what they were – canine creatures – inferior to vampires.

His frustrated mind ticked over with ways of solving the current predicament. Perhaps he could enlist one of the witches from the council to try to locate the woman. He'd seen the sheriff speeding out of Moon Grove earlier in the day, siren blaring, and wondered where he was heading. Could they have found Paige? His cell phone vibrated in the pocket of his black, figure-hugging jeans and he whipped it out to check the caller ID. He gave a throaty groan and pressed the green circle. "Yes?"

"Any word on the woman?" Remus asked.

"Not yet. But I am looking into ways of finding her." He slid his mug onto the kitchen counter then headed for the front door and stepped out onto the porch.

"What were your thoughts on the matter?"

"Would one or all of your witches be willing to try a location spell?"

Silence.

"Remus?"

"We have already tried and have been unsuccessful."

Gregor ran a hand over his stubbled face. "Apart from searching for her myself I am out of ideas."

"Let me look into it and I will get back to you soon." The line died.

Gregor pulled the phone from his ear and frowned at the screen. "Was Paige's abduction one of the council's games? Could they have her hidden away somewhere?" They wanted him to drink from her so why would they hide her from him? Perhaps he *should* go in search of her himself.

When he reentered the cabin, Yana was leaning against the kitchen counter, arms folded, a scowl on her face. Gregor's curious gaze met hers and he wondered what she was angry about. He knew that look. He crossed the living room and stopped in front of her. "What is wrong, my sweet? Why the sullen expression on such a pretty face?" He reached out to grip her chin and bring her closer to him for a kiss but she jerked her face away. "Tell me what is wrong, Yana. I am not a mind-reader like some of us."

"Why are you so concerned about the O'Connell woman?"

"She is part of the plan to remove the wolves from the town. You know that."

Yana shook her head, her scowl deepening. "I do not think it is the only reason for your interest in her."

Gregor grasped her chin and yanked her face toward him. "Be careful what you say, my love. Let us not fight over a woman I have no further interest in than to use her to my advantage."

A single, crimson-stained tear slid down Yana's cheek. "Are you telling me the truth, Gregor? You are not interested in her for any other reason than to drink her blood?" She knew he was lying. She could sense it.

"Why would I lie to you?"

She leaned her head against his chest and sighed. "I do not know. Why would you?" Yana had come to a decision about what she must do.

The cloying darkness pressing in on Paige suffocated her and she inhaled a deep breath and blew it out slowly to calm her racing heartbeat. How long had she been trapped in here? At least with her hands in front of her and her feet untied she could move around the bleak space, feeling for any covered windows or another door in the wall that could lead to escape. If only she could find a way out of this nightmare.

Paige stood up on shaking legs and pressed her hands against the wall to steady herself before taking a step. With her tied hands stretched out in front of her, she moved through the gloom with caution, bumping into something solid in front of her. She frowned and felt around the object. Oblong, wooden, drawers. A desk? She eased herself around it and continued forward, kicking something that gave a rusty squeal as it rolled across the floor. *What was that?* Her breathing quickened. She felt to her right, her hands roaming what appeared to be stacked storage containers. They seemed full, heavy and high.

She sidled past the wall of cardboard and continued moving ahead.

Another desk. She ran her hands over its surface, knocking something off of it. The object landed on the hard floor with a clacking thud and a clang. A telephone? *Where am I?* She moved to her left to get closer to the wall but it was blocked with filing cabinets – metal filing cabinets. Paige tugged at the drawers. Locked. She sighed, turned around and felt her way around the desk.

There didn't appear to be any covered windows or doors in the walls which led her to believe she was in an underground storage area or basement. The space was larger than she had first anticipated and extended along to the left by about a hundred feet, to her right, though, only several feet from where she had been sitting.

She could be in an old bank or office building for all she knew. Would anyone hear her if she called for help? Paige didn't think so.

Bobby ran Greg Petrov's name through the International Crimes Database, sat back in his office chair, arms folded, and waited for a file to pop up on the screen. His gut told him the guy had to have some kind of criminal history – even if it was only a parking ticket. After several minutes a box popped up with No Match Found. The deputy frowned at the words for a moment before trying another variation of the name. He keyed in Gregory Petrov, hit enter and stared at the screen. Again, nothing. He sighed. What else could he try? Pulling up Google search, he typed in Russian male names. He figured the guy was European by his accent so why not start with Russia? It seemed the likely choice.

A list of sites came up and he hit one. When the list loaded he clicked on the G tab and waited for the names to appear. He ran his gaze down the list and scribbled down similar names to Greg. He typed the different names into the database one at a time hoping something would show up. Nothing did. Bobby leaned back in his chair and ran a hand over his face. The guy couldn't be that squeaky clean.

"Anything?" Eli asked, poking his head around his office door.

"Not so far, boss. I don't know what else to try."

Eli stepped into reception. "Maybe he doesn't have a record."

"You didn't think he looked like a tough guy? 'Cause he sure did to me. Probably part of the Russian Mafia or somethin'."

A sudden thought flashed across the sheriff's mind. *Or part of the council's new law enforcement.* "I suspected he's part of what arrived here. Not the Mafia but the council's mercenaries."

His deputy sprang from his chair. "So we need to find out where he's staying and fast. There'll be others with him."

"Yeah, there will be. What if he's got Paige?"

"I had the same thought when I spoke to him. He told me he had a place about forty five minutes out of town on 57. I wonder where."

"He told me he was passing through so he lied about that." The sheriff came through the partition. "Check with the realtors, Bobby. If the property was rented here in

Moon Grove someone will be able to give us a location for the place."

"What if they're too scared to say anything?" Bobby stood with hands on his belt.

"Tell them the town's in danger of being controlled by a new law enforcement."

"I don't know. I think people here are more scared of the council than anything else, at least the ones who know about it."

"You're right." Eli considered his options, which were limited. "Better to go to the source."

"I hope you don't mean what I think you mean." Bobby came around his desk.

"Yep, I'll go see Remus."

"Eli."

The sheriff headed to the door. "It's the only way to find out what we want to know."

Bobby huffed out a breath and raised a hand to his brow. "Do you really expect him to tell you anything? Come on, Eli, you're just putting yourself at risk."

Eli shrugged into his jacket. "They won't touch me, not yet. Have you got a better idea?"

THIRTY ONE

Eli drove along the circular drive and pulled the Jeep up in front of the twin set of curved, ornate concrete stairs leading to the double, black wood doors. Every window in the elaborate home was covered so that no light entered the premises, which gave the house an eerie demeanor. And although the property was well maintained, for some reason it reminded him of the creepy old house in the Psycho movie. He'd been to the council residence on a couple of occasions over the past few years, but never alone. He hadn't called ahead to let them know he was on his way so this would be an impromptu visit the members of the governing body would not appreciate. No one came here uninvited. *What the hell! May as well go out with a bang.*

He pulled the keys from the ignition, stepped out of the four wheel drive, and gazed around at the manicured gardens surrounding the four story Victorian mansion. Spring had brought with it new blooms and the beds were alive with a brilliant display of color: yellow daffodils, vivid pink asters, white tulips and purple blue bonnets swayed in the warm gentle breeze and it was difficult to comprehend that vampires dwelled here.

The sheriff rounded the hood of his vehicle, took the left-hand set of stairs and before he reached the front landing one door swung open and a tall, thin man with graying skin and sunken cheeks dressed in a black suit appeared in the doorway. "Are you expected, Sheriff Blackwood?" He knew Eli had arrived unannounced because he took all calls.

"No, Roger, I'm not but I need to speak to Remus. It's an urgent police matter."

"Urgent or not, Sheriff, I'm afraid you can't."

"And why is that?" Eli climbed the last step and walked over to him.

"Because they are in repose and do not wish to be disturbed."

Eli stood with hands on his belt. "I don't expect you to wake them all, just Remus."

Roger's leathery skin creased even more and he gave the sheriff a skeptical frown. "Remus would be the *least* impressed if I awoke him before sunset."

Eli glanced at his watch. 6:45 PM. "Well it's not far off. Can I come in and wait?"

The older man sighed, realizing the sheriff was not to be deterred. "Do you drink *tea*, Sheriff Blackwood?"

"As a matter of fact I do."

"Very well. Follow me." Roger stepped aside and motioned for him to enter the mansion.

The moment Eli stepped across the threshold into the shadowed entry hall his hackles rose.

Bobby and Rosemarie were worried about Eli going to the mansion alone. As the deputy paced, the receptionist's eyes followed him back and forth with a flushed look of concern. Cooper had been out on patrol and by the time he arrived back at the station a little after nine both Bobby and Rosemarie were in a state. The sheriff hadn't returned.

Cooper sat and watched Bobby pace up to the door, turn and pace back to the reception desk, giving Rosemarie a solemn glance before turning around and repeating the process. "Why don't you call the others?" the young deputy offered.

Bobby stopped, spun on his heel, and gave him a frown. "Because Eli wouldn't want us to get the others involved unless it was absolutely necessary."

The apprentice deputy's Adam's apple bobbed above the collar of his blue denim shirt. "Well, hell, don't you think it's necessary? The sheriff's been gone for over two hours. Has he called in?"

"No, he hasn't," Rosemarie piped up. "And I'm worried, to say the least. I asked Bobby to call the pack but he wants to wait." She wrung her pink floral handkerchief around her fingers, a pained look crossing her face. "I sure hope he's all right."

"Then I'm calling them." Cooper snatched the handset out of its base and started to key in the linked number.

"Wait!" Bobby crossed the office to Cooper's desk. "We can't get everyone here on a whim. Eli could be in negotiations with the council members and can't call. What if we turned up there and forced our way in only to find that was the case? Eli would be pissed at us for not trusting him. And what about Remus? There would be serious consequences for that little faux pas."

"Bobby, I think Cooper's right…"

The door opened and Eli walked in.

"Eli!" Rosemarie and Bobby chorused.

"Yeah?"

"What took you so long? We were worried about you?" Rosemarie rushed around the partition, threw her arms out and gave Eli a big hug. "Why didn't you call?"

"I couldn't. Remus requested my undivided attention during our meeting so I turned my cell off."

Bobby turned to Cooper. "See, what'd I tell ya?"

The young deputy raised defensive hands and grumbled, "Ok, ok."

"Next time trust me."

Rosemarie continued to hug Eli. "Well I'm just glad you're back safe 'n sound."

"Thanks, Rosy." He kissed the top of her head, eased out of her tight embrace, and walked through to his office. "Come in, I want to tell you what I found out."

After the meeting with Bobby, Cooper, and Rosemarie, Eli left the station and headed to the Tribune. He'd spoken to Archer Hamilton over the phone and wanted to fill him in on what he'd found out from Remus. It wasn't like the head vampire to be so forthcoming and the sheriff wondered what his motives were. Did he want Eli and his pack to go out to the cabin and initiate an all-out war? Or would the occupants be lying in wait for him and his wolves? He wasn't about to make any rash decisions where the welfare of his pack was concerned and wanted to run what he knew by Archer to see if he could offer a vampire's perspective. They were cunning creatures, after all, so who better to ask?

When he pulled up outside the newspaper office Archer was on the sidewalk. Eli came around his Jeep and walked over to him. "Can we talk inside?"

"Of course. No one's here." He unlocked the glass door and swung it back. "After you."

Eli stepped into the dark room, Archer right behind him. "Let me turn on a light."

The sheriff turned around. "No, don't. We can see without it and we don't want to alert anyone to the fact that we're here."

"Like who?" Archer crossed the office and sat down on the client sofa.

"Someone whose loyalty lies with the council."

Archer frowned. "You think we're being watched?"

"Yeah, I do." Eli walked over to the sofa and sat down beside the editor.

"For what purpose?"

"To keep track of what we're doing... and find out what we know."

The editor's eyes roamed the shadowed office space and he lowered his voice. "Could this place be bugged?"

"Anything's possible where the council is concerned. I wouldn't put anything past them."

"Then maybe we should talk somewhere else." He motioned with his eyes to the street and the Jeep.

Eli nodded and the pair got up, crossed the office and stepped outside.

"Any word on Paige's location?" Archer asked.

"No. And I'm getting more worried by the minute. If we don't find her soon it *will* be too late." He didn't want to say or believe it could be already.

"I'll do another search of the outer perimeter first thing. Nothing at the hospital?"

Eli shook his head.

"There aren't many more places to try. Maybe they took her further than you thought."

"Remus gave me some information about the team he brought in…"

"Why would he do that?" Archer climbed into the four wheel drive.

Eli eased his tall frame into the driver's seat and closed the door. "Because he wants the war to commence now. He wants us dead."

"Are you ready for the fight?"

"Far from it, and now that they have our Lycan tome we're even more vulnerable."

"What about the moonstone ring? Won't it offer you and your pack some form of protection?"

"Maybe. I don't know." He shrugged and glanced at the ring on his finger. "It seems to have warmed to me." He gave a thin smile. "But it doesn't mean much because I don't know how to use it."

"Maybe when you turn into a wolf? Perhaps it will do its thing then."

"I hope you're right because without its power we're in serious trouble, especially against militant, European vampires, as it turns out."

"Have you tried shifting to see what happens?"

"I haven't had the time. With looking for Paige and the looming threat I've been a little preoccupied."

Archer nodded. "I understand. So what did Remus tell you?"

"He said there's a total of ten vampires on Gregor's team, including Gregor. Some are hundreds of years old, making them more invincible because they've learned how to survive over the time they've been alive. They're in a cabin about forty five minutes from Moon Grove. Some members of his team are still on their way. So right now there are five out there – four males and one female."

"And you have five in your pack, including you?"

"Yeah." Eli gripped the steering wheel with both hands. "Right now it would be a fair fight, but when the others get here it'll be a different story."

Archer folded his arms. "I can help. And I have others who will too."

Eli turned in his seat. "Here in Moon Grove?"

"No. But it wouldn't take them long to get here."

The sheriff let out a long sigh. "We still need to find Paige. I was wondering if they have her at the cabin."

Archer's left eyebrow rose. "It's one place we haven't looked yet."

"My thoughts exactly."

"Want to take a drive out there now and give the place a look over?"

Eli turned the idea over in his mind. "We could, I guess." Was he really about to put his safety into a vampire's hands? A vampire he hardly knew?

THIRTY TWO

The moon cast a milky veil over the shingled, green metal rooftop of the log cabin nestled among the tall pine trees giving it a ghostly aura. No soft amber glow shone out through the windows from inside, the place in total darkness. Eli had parked the Jeep a few hundred feet down the dirt track outside the padlocked gate and he and Archer trudged the distance on foot, keeping to the shadows. The sheriff knew vampires didn't need light to see by, he didn't even need it because of his nocturnal vision, so the fact that there were no lights on in the house didn't surprise him.

Archer, dressed from head to foot in black, blended into the night like a phantom. An advantage in their favor as far as Eli was concerned because the vampire could get close to the property and suss out the location of the five in the cabin without being spotted. The pair moved in, the editor using hand signals to let the sheriff know he was going ahead alone. Although he was cloaked by darkness, Archer was more than aware that if he got too close the other vampires would sense him.

Eli hung back, hidden amongst the pines, his navy blue police attire shielding him in the dark, and waited for Archer to return. So as not to be detected by sensitive hearing, he slowed his breathing to lower his heart rate. Two against five didn't seem a fair fight if the occupants realized he and the editor were skulking around outside. A blur of black hurtled toward him and he drew his weapon, which was now always loaded with silver, and aimed.

"It's me," Archer said, his voice low. He motioned with his head for Eli to move off and followed him through the legion of tall trees back down the dirt track to the sheriff's car.

"I did a thorough sweep of the house. The five are inside but I didn't pick up any human vibrations."

"So Paige isn't here." Eli climbed into the Jeep.

"Doesn't appear so." Archer stepped up and into the passenger seat. "What now?"

"At least we know where they're located."

"Perhaps, but what are you going to do about it?"

Eli released the handbrake, shifted the automatic gear to neutral and rolled down the dirt track without starting the engine. Just in case. "Nothing for the moment. The point is they don't know I know where they are and that's an advantage in my favor right now."

"Do you want me to contact the immortals who can help?"

"Yes. We need numbers. Are they prepared to fight other vampires?"

"They'll do whatever I ask of them."

Eli's right eyebrow arched. "I underestimated you, Hamilton."

"People usually do."

The thought had been on the sheriff's mind for a while and he decided to ask. "Why do you want to help us?"

"Because I don't relish the idea of a vampire enforcement running Moon Grove. Nothing good can come from it as we already know by the council's hold on the town. And, besides, you and your deputies do a fair enough job. Why change anything?"

"I appreciate your candor... and your help." He started the engine, did a dusty U-turn and headed back toward town.

"No problem. Sometimes it's not what you know but who." He gave Eli a self-satisfied smirk, clipped in his seatbelt and folded his arms.

Once Eli dropped the editor off at the Tribune office he headed home. He needed some sleep before the new day began. Well, at least before the sun came up. When he pulled up outside his house a distortion of the shadows on his porch drew his immediate attention. He whipped his pistol out of its holster and eased the Jeep door open. Standing between the door and the vehicle, with his hands resting on the roof and his gun aimed in that direction, he called out, "I know you're there. Show yourself." Why did other creatures keep showing up on his doorstep late at night?

The figure remained hidden in the dark.

Eli moved around the door, leaving it open, and stood behind the left-hand fender, his pistol still aimed in the direction of his uninvited guest. "I said show yourself."

"All right." A woman dressed in a long black cape stepped into the moon's glow, hands raised, her pale skin glistening in the hazy light. "Don't shoot me, Eli. I come in peace."

The sheriff holstered his weapon and rounded the front of his car. "Isn't that what you all say? Why are you here, Elisha?" She was the one member of the council he trusted the least, not that he trusted any of them.

"I can help you locate the O'Connell woman. I know your grandmother tried but couldn't find her."

"How do you know?" He frowned and folded his arms. "What's in it for you?" A price always came with the council's help.

"Witches pick up on spells being cast. It's something we do. And what I want is my freedom."

Eli's right eyebrow arched. "You mean you want to get away from Remus and the others?"

"Yes. If I help you will you help me leave as soon as possible?" She seemed afraid to Eli.

He walked over to the front steps. "If you can guarantee you can find Paige then yes."

The door swung open allowing a bright shock of light to stretch across the dark space. Yana's eyes roamed the gloom. Where was Paige O'Connell? She stepped across the threshold, stood with hands on hips, and searched the dark clutter with her nocturnal vision. The woman had to be here somewhere. She couldn't have escaped. "Paige," she called in a sing song tone. "Come out, come out wherever you are." She stepped further into the underground room. Yana gave an amused chuckle. "I know you're here. Why not come out and stop this charade? It will only be worse for you when I find you."

Paige didn't move. If she could make the woman

believe she'd escaped, get her to move further down the long basement, perhaps she could run.

"Paige!" the vampire roared. "Don't make this hard on yourself." She let out a shrill scream. "When I find you I'm going to *kill* you!" She stalked through the jumble of old furniture, storage boxes and other office equipment no longer required by the town's City Hall, tossing old telephones, upturning boxed files and other loose items around the room. "Where are *you*?"

Holding her breath, her heart hammering against her ribs, Paige eased herself out from behind the open door without a sound, slammed it shut and secured the large padlock on the hasp, tears of fear and joy slipping down her face. She was free. Before the woman had a chance to get out, Paige raced along the dimly lit corridor to a set of metal stairs and climbed them two at a time. She was almost there. When she reached the security door she found it locked. She gripped the handle with both hands and tugged and tugged. The door wouldn't budge. "No, no, no!"

A loud crash from along the corridor below made her swing around. The woman was free and coming for her.

THIRTY THREE

Paige cowered against the door, her back sliding down the gray wood, tears streaming down her dirty, blood streaked face. The woman stalked the last few feet of the corridor toward the stairs, knowing Paige was trapped, a broad, smug grin spreading across her face. "So, you thought you could get away from me, did you?" She climbed the steps slowly. "Run into the arms of Gregor, is that it?"

"I don't know who you're talking about." Paige sniffed back the urge to sob knowing she was about to die at the hands of this crazed woman.

"He is mine, my vampire, my lover, not yours." She gave a sharp poke in Paige's direction.

"I – I don't know who he is."

"Do not play games with me. He came to see you at your office."

Paige frowned and thought for a moment, then it occurred to her. "You mean Greg? Greg Petrov?"

"Who else would I be talking about? His name is Gregor."

"He's a – a client."

Yana let out a high-pitched cackle that echoed around the concrete walls. "Oh, yes." She pouted. "He has emotional issues only *you* can help him with." She tapped her index finger against her lips then pointed at Paige. "Stupid you."

"I don't understand."

She sneered. "Of course you don't. That is what makes the whole situation even funnier."

"What do you mean?" A single tear slid from Paige's left eye.

"Gregor could never have feelings for a weak, pathetic creature like you," Yana spat. "All he wanted was to taste you."

"Taste me?"

Yana laughed again. "Your blood of course."

"But why?" Paige pressed her spine against the wood to steady her trembling body.

"Because you have Lycan genes pulsing through your veins and he wanted to become stronger, different, a hybrid creature."

"He planned to kill me?"

Yana climbed the last step onto the landing. "That was his plan all along. Why? Did you think he would fall in love with you?" She lowered herself to Paige's level. "Ha, you are nothing to him."

"I never thought I was."

"Liar!" She grabbed Paige by her sweater front and yanked her to her feet. "It does not matter anymore, anyhow. I will remedy the problem so you are no longer a distraction for him." She opened her mouth, her razor sharp fangs locking into place, and just as she was about to take a bite the door beside them burst from its hinges outwards. Eli wrenched Paige free, tore the restraints from her wrists, and shoved the vampire backwards down the staircase. He knew it wouldn't kill her but at least it would put her out of action for a while.

Paige's tear-filled eyes met his glowing yellow gaze and she threw her arms around his neck and pressed herself against his firm chest. "Thank you for coming to my rescue."

Eli's heart quivered at her trembling touch. A touch he'd missed. But now wasn't the time. Easing her away from him and said, "Go. Now!" He remained on the landing to ensure Paige got away. Bobby and Linda were waiting outside to take her to a safe, hidden location.

Within minutes, Yana came to in a disheveled heap at the bottom of the stairs and was on her feet in an instant. She flew up the staircase at Eli, arms outstretched, black painted claws ready to scratch his eyes out. He grabbed her around the throat and gave her a solemn warning. "I'm letting you live... this time. If you go near Paige again I *will* finish this."

"You are a fool, Eli Blackwood. You should finish me while you have the chance because you may not get another opportunity to diminish Gregor's army."

"And start an early war? I don't think so." He held her at arm's length, the toes of her black combat boots hovering over the top step. "I'll wager Gregor doesn't know you held Paige captive down here. What would he do to you if he found out what you've done?" He released his grip and she teetered on the edge of the metal step before regaining her balance.

Yana raised her defiant chin. "How do you know *he* didn't organize it?"

Eli knew she was bluffing. Gregor had been looking for Paige at her office. "Why would he look for her if he knew where she was?"

Her eyes widened. She hadn't known Gregor had been in search of the O'Connell woman.

"That's what I thought." Eli motioned to the damaged doorway. "You're free to go. But if you come after Paige again I won't hesitate to tell your leader you were the one who abducted her."

Paige stood beneath the hot shower spray allowing the water to roll down her back, her head bowed, warm, silent tears streaming down her face. Once again, she had almost died and Eli had saved her. He was her knight in shining armor, her soulmate, the man she should be with. Would her abduction make him see the truth? Would he realize the only way they can be safe is together?

A knock pulled her thoughts back to the present, her red eyes darting to the closed door. "Yes?"

"Eli's here. He wants to talk to you. Are you gonna be much longer?"

She had been in the bathroom for almost an hour. "I'll be out in a minute."

"Ok. I'll let him know. There's coffee and donuts if you're hungry." Bobby headed back down the hallway.

Paige lifted her face, letting the water wash away her tears before turning off the shower, wrapping a towel around her and stepping out of the frosted glass cubicle. Eli was here to see her. Her heart gave a little stutter and she hurried to dress.

When she stepped into the hallway she couldn't hear any voices coming from the living room. A frown creased her brow as she made her way to the doorway and peered inside. Eli was at the kitchen counter drinking coffee but Linda and Bobby were nowhere to be seen. Paige crossed the room to the kitchen. "Where's Bobby and Linda?"

"I sent them home. I'll keep watch tonight." His eyes met hers and there was something in them. Something she couldn't quite make out.

"You don't have to, Eli. It would've been better for Linda to stay here with me."

He turned toward the counter, picked up the coffee pot and a mug. "Coffee?"

Paige nodded. She hadn't eaten or drank anything during the time she'd been gone. She pointed to the bakery box on the table. "Can I have a donut?"

"Help yourself." Eli brought the coffee over to the table and sat down opposite her. "You must be starved."

"I am." She lifted the lid, reached in, took out a jelly donut, broke a piece off and popped it in her mouth. "Mm." She closed her eyes, sighed, and smiled. "I don't usually eat these."

"I remember." He swallowed a mouthful of coffee.

Paige picked up her mug and sipped the black brew. "Thank you for saving my life, Eli. You always seem to be doing that."

"You don't have to thank me, Paige. It's my job."

Tears stung the backs of her eyes and she realized how vulnerable she felt right now. Was that all it had been to him? His job?

"Why did you want to stay here tonight?"

"To make sure no one found you."

"As I said, Linda or even Bobby could've stayed." She set the coffee mug down on the table. "Why you?"

"I…" His honey colored eyes moved to her beautiful, pale face. "I wanted to be sure you were safe."

"You could've accomplished that through phone calls or text messages."

Eli leaned back on his chair, folded his arms, and frowned. "I had to be here."

"But why?"

THIRTY FOUR

Remus stood at the window, hands clasped behind his deep maroon, calf-length tunic, gazing out at the still, clear evening. The afternoon breeze had died down to a whisper and not even the leaves on the trees were rustling. He appreciated the night. It had been his immortal playground for more than a thousand years and he much preferred the shadows. Now that Paige O'Connell had been rescued his scheme to rid Moon Grove of Eli Blackwood and his pack would move ahead as planned. Once the psychologist regained her strength and was back in her office, Gregor could continue to groom her for the task ahead. She had no idea she was the key to winning this war. Well, her genes were.

Gregor partaking of her blood was an experiment of sorts because Remus was uncertain as to the effect it would have on a vampire. It was believed that if such a creature drank from a human carrying Lycan DNA it would create a hybrid vampire which would be virtually unstoppable, unless, of course, their head was severed from their body. No one survived decapitation. If the potency of the O'Connell woman's blood did offer this genetic anomaly his enforcement team would never be challenged and the council could govern the town unrestrained, preventing any kind of rebellion. What he wasn't aware of was that Yana had handed Gregor's plan to Paige in a fit of rage and his well-orchestrated scheme was about to come unraveled.

A knock echoed into the spacious, high-ceilinged bed chamber and Remus turned around. "You may enter."

Roger stepped inside and closed the door behind him. "My Lord, your guest has arrived and is downstairs in the parlor."

"Good. I will be along in a moment." His manservant nodded and turned toward the door. "Oh, and Roger, have the others gather in the library. I wish to speak to them after my visitor departs."

"Very good, Sir."

Remus opened the large, recessed, dark wood paneled door and entered the room which resembled something out of the 1920s with its lavish, ornate cream mantel, rich Persian rugs overlaying the polished wooden floor, patterned wing backed armchairs, multiple oak tables, and floor lamps with tasseled shades adorning the generous space. His guest sat in a high-backed chair beside the unlit fireplace and stood when the older immortal entered.

"Sit. Is everything going according to plan?" Remus asked, crossing the room and seating himself opposite his visitor in a matching armchair.

"As far as I am aware, yes, my Lord." He crossed one leg over the other and eyed his companion with reverence.

"Excellent. And he is unaware anything is amiss?"

"He doesn't suspect a thing." A broad smile crossed his handsome face.

"Good, good." Remus' tight, angular features loosened into a satisfied grin. "I am most pleased with your efforts."

"Thank you, my Lord." The younger vampire stood. "I will keep him occupied with other matters so he doesn't have time to prepare for the impending assault."

"Make sure nothing goes wrong... and keep me informed. We *must* win this war." Remus remained seated.

"Nothing will. I give you my word." He headed for the door and Roger showed him out of the mansion.

Paige lay on her back in bed, the soothing wave of sleep eluding her. She plumped her pillows and dropped back onto the cotton covers with a heavy sigh. Why wouldn't Eli tell her he was still in love with her? His being with her now proved that so why couldn't he just admit it? She turned onto her right side and gazed out the window at the clear, blue-black sky with its myriad of twinkling stars. She'd wanted to tell him she was still in love with him, despite seeing Archer. If only Eli would open up to her the way he used to and tell her he felt the same, things could be so different. She needed him in her life and knew he needed her, too.

She turned over again and plopped onto her back, staring at the ceiling. She would give herself a few days to fully recover from her ordeal and then go back to work. It was the only distraction she had, and she needed to continue the sessions with Zach to get to the bottom of the night Charlene died. His mind seemed protected, inaccessible. Why? Maybe it was a vampire defense. Perhaps she had to delve deeper. Paige wanted to help him remember to assist Eli in finding out what happened. Had Zach been party to the blood ritual? If she could crack the combination to that lock in his mind she knew she'd be able to get to the truth.

A knock on the door startled her. She picked up her cell phone to check the time. 4.08 AM. *What could Eli want at this hour?* "Come in."

The door swung back and Eli stood in the opening still fully clothed. "I have to go out for a while. I've called Linda and she should be here any minute."

Paige sat up in bed. "Why, what's happened?"

A body's been discovered in the woods behind the church.

"A body? Whose body?" She threw off the covers and scrambled out of bed.

"Mayor Redmond."

"Oh, my God. Do you know what happened to him?"

"Looks like the work of vampires. He's been drained of blood and has bites all over his body."

Paige brought her hand up to her mouth. "It had to be Gregor's team. Who else would it be?"

"Yeah, I figured as much. Ross came to see me with sensitive information about what the council had planned. Someone must've been following him." He stood with hands on his belt. "I'd say it was payback for his betrayal. The Mayor was leaving Moon Grove and this was the only way they could stop him."

"None of us are safe here now." An icy chill ran through Paige and she shivered.

Eli noticed and felt the urge to pull her into his arms but didn't. "We're going to win this war. I won't let anything happen to you or anyone else."

"You can't make that kind of promise. Look what's happened so far since Gregor and his vampires arrived here. How are you going to stop him?"

"With this, I hope." He held up his left hand, revealing the ring to her.

Paige gasped. She hadn't noticed it before. "Are you ok? Do you feel any different? What does it do?" Her surprised gaze moved from the ring to his handsome face.

"Yes, I'm ok. I did feel different for a while but Clary made me something to take the edge off. And to answer your last question, I have no idea what it does. It hasn't shown me yet."

"What if all the danger associated with the ring was for nothing? What if it's lost its power?"

"I've been thinking the same thing." His ears pricked up. "I have to go. Linda's here."

Paige crossed the room to him. "Be careful, Eli. Please."

"I will." He gave her a thin smile and touched her arm. "Promise."

When Eli arrived, Bobby and Cooper were waiting by the Mayor's body while Paul did a thorough sweep of the surrounding area searching for evidence. The sheriff had parked his Jeep at the end of the church parking lot on the edge of the woods and made his way through the army of tall pines to the crime scene. "Who found the body?"

"I did." Paige's brother appeared from behind the trunk of a tree wearing Bobby's police jacket, naked beneath. "I was out for a wolf run and almost fell over it – I mean *him*."

Eli frowned at the young man. "How'd you call it in?"

Brent reached inside the open collar of the dark blue anorak he had on and pulled out his cell phone attached to a chain around his neck.

Eli nodded. "I'll need you to come into the station to make a statement later in the day. Why don't you go home?"

"Ok. I'll see you later." He threw off the jacket shifted into wolf form and bounded through the trees.

"Wow!" Cooper said, eyes wide. "*That* was awesome!"

"Yeah, it is, but not so much fun while it's happening. It does hurt, ya know," Bobby told him.

"How bad?" The deputy's eyebrows knitted together in a frown.

"Not too bad. You get used to it after a while."

Eli lifted the gray tarp off of Ross Redmond's body and studied the extent of the injuries. The Mayor's pale, staring face was distorted in an agonized grimace. The bites were extensive and would've drained him in seconds. He crouched beside the body, reached over and closed Ross's bloodshot eyes then turned to his deputy. "We can't risk him coming back," he said. "We'll have to perform the ritual."

"That's what I thought so I came prepared." Bobby moved to a long, metal case leaning against a tree trunk and picked it up.

"What's the ritual?" Cooper asked.

"You're about to find out," Bobby answered. He opened the case and passed the ancient axe with its etched, sanctified silver blade to Eli, the inscription on the wooden handle a protection for any Lycan who wielded it.

"Wait. What are you going to do with that?" Cooper's complexion turned a pale shade of green.

"The only thing we can do to prevent him from returning as a vampire." Eli raised the artifact into the air and brought it down in one swift movement. The Mayor's head rolled away from the body backwards and bumped against the root of a tree.

Cooper rushed over to the tree trunk behind him, his clammy hand pressed against the rough bark, and hurled the contents of his stomach against it. Turning around and wiping his mouth on the back of his hand he said, "Was that really necessary?"

"You bet. Otherwise it would be only a matter of time before he woke up hungry and looking for blood." Bobby stepped across the body and picked up the head. "A new vampire is like a crazed animal. They'll tear their victims to shreds while they feed and still won't be satisfied." He bagged the head and set it down next to the body.

"Jeez – us." The green color in Cooper's face began to subside and his cheeks showed a slight tinge of color.

Paul joined the group in the small clearing. "Not a footprint, DNA sample, nothing."

Eli sighed. "Of course not. Ok. Let's wrap this up and head back to the station." He passed the cumbersome axe back to Bobby and headed to his car. This murder was only the beginning. He could feel it. The council was out for blood.

THIRTY FIVE

rcher arrived at the police station the next morning to speak with the sheriff. He'd had a call from Paige telling him she was ok, but wouldn't give him the location of her whereabouts. He wanted to see her. Make sure she was as fine as she professed to be. When he came up to the reception desk, Rosemarie's scrutinizing gaze moved from her computer to him. "Can I help you, Mr. Hamilton?" She didn't smile, which was not like her but she didn't like the man or vampire or whatever he was. And she also didn't like the fact that he was seeing Paige. In her opinion he should butt out of Eli's business.

"I'm here to see the sheriff. He asked me to stop by." His eyes moved to the windowed office. Eli wasn't at his desk.

"Well, as you can see, he's not here. Maybe you could come by later. I can take a message for him, if you'd like." She gave him a forced smile, picked up a ball-point pen from off her desk and a thick writing pad and poised the nib on the sheet of white, blue lined paper ready to write.

"That's ok. I'll give him a call and see if he can meet me at the Tribune office later on. Thanks for your time."

Archer turned and headed to the door and was about to reach for the handle when Eli pushed the door open.

"Leaving?" Eli stepped inside, removed his Stetson, and closed the door. "I thought you wanted to talk to me."

"Yes, I do. Your receptionist wasn't sure when you'd be back so…"

"Is that so?" Eli gave her a curious frown. He'd told her he wouldn't be long and to tell Archer to wait in his office. Rosemarie's cheeks flushed and she returned her gaze to the computer screen. "Come through." He crossed the office and held the partition gate open for the editor.

Both men entered the sheriff's office and Eli closed the door. He'd have a word with Rosy later about client relations, regardless of who they were.

"Have a seat," Eli said, motioning to the chair in front of his desk as he walked around and sat down, placing his cell phone in front of him on the blotter. "What can I help you with?"

"Paige called me a while a go to tell me she was ok and I wanted to ask you where she was so I could go see her."

Even though Archer had been helpful and cooperative with his department, Eli still wasn't comfortable with the vampire dating Paige. He'd come to realize he wasn't comfortable with any man seeing her. "She's in a safe location. That's all I can tell you."

"Come on, Eli, help me out here. I had the feeling Paige wasn't as ok as she said she was and I'd really like to see for myself. She's been through a harrowing ordeal. I'm sure she could use a friend."

"Yes, she has been and right now what she needs most is time to get over what happened to her."

The editor folded his arms. "And how does my wanting to see her change the outcome?"

"I just think it's best for her to have some alone time to sort out how she feels…"

"Feels about what?"

"What happened to her, of course." Eli mirrored Archer's movements. He hoped she'd realize that Hamilton wasn't the right man/vampire for her.

"That still doesn't answer my question, does it? Perhaps you could call her and ask her if she'd like to see me." He pointed to Eli's phone lying on the desk.

"I could but I'm not going to. She's resting."

"How do you know she's resting?"

"Because I had a call from the person who's with her before I came into the office."

"I want to see her, Eli." The editor stood up.

Eli moved to his feet. "You can't right now. It is what it is. I'll let her know you're concerned about her and if she wants to see you she can call you herself."

Archer gave the sheriff a dark stare. "If I didn't know better, I'd think you were trying to prevent us from seeing each other." He walked across the office. "I'll expect that call." He swung the door back and stepped out, leaving the door open.

The cell phone on his desk buzzed and he snatched it up to answer the call. "Hi, Paige, everything all right?"

"I was wondering if you'd bring Archer with you when you're heading back. I'd really like to see him."

Eli sighed inwardly. "He was just here and I told you needed some time to work through what happened before you had any visitors."

The thought crossed Paige's mind, *Is Eli jealous?* "Why? I'm fine."

"The dream you were having last night didn't seem fine."

"What do you mean?" She frowned and bit her bottom lip.

"You were calling out in your sleep. Something about Gregor."

"What did I say?"

"I guess it's whatever the woman told you about him."

"He wanted to drain me, Eli. He wanted to drink my blood."

"I know and I'm sorry you had to find out like that, but it's better than not knowing. Now you can keep your distance."

She shook her head. "No. I want him to continue coming to see me so I can find out what his plans are."

Eli gripped the phone so hard he felt it flex in his hand. "Paige, I won't let you do that. It's too dangerous."

"I want to help you win this war and the only way I can do it is by getting information straight from the horse's mouth. That woman isn't about to tell him not to see me otherwise she'd give herself away. Trust me, I can do this."

"We'll talk about it later."

"I want to see Archer so bring him with you." She hung up.

Eli snatched the phone from his ear and glared at the screen. If he had anything to do with it, Paige would not see Gregor Petrov again.

THIRTY SIX

Zachary Ridgeway listened to the continuous ring on the other end of the line. He knew it was late and that the sheriff might be in the middle of dinner but that still didn't account for why Eli wasn't answering his phone? Zach wanted to find out how Paige was doing and also when they could resume their sessions. He knew it wouldn't be right away, not after everything the psychiatrist had been through, but if he had some indication of a timeframe it would give him a sense of how things were traveling. The thought crossed his mind: *Do shrinks know how to deal with their own trauma or do they get professional help too?* The right corner of his mouth twitched and he almost smiled at the idea of a shrink being analyzed by another shrink.

But then again, that would make sense. How much of other people's crap could a person store in their mind before going completely mad themselves? A knock echoed into the room and he got up off the bed to answer it, peering through the peephole before opening the door. No one. He eased the door back, stuck his head out, ran his gaze along the hallway, and frowned. *Where did they go?*

He was about to close the door when something near his feet caught his eye. A medium-sized, black leather box with gold hinges and clasp.

Zach studied the obtrusive object for a moment, then his suspicious gaze roamed the passage in both directions once more before he picked it up and closed the door. Setting it down on top of the dresser, he folded his arms and studied the box in more depth. Why had it been left outside his room? He reached out to unhook the catch but pulled back, wondering what was inside. Was it dangerous? He leaned closer and listened. No ticking. At least it wasn't an explosive device. He huffed out a humorless chuckle. *Stop being a pussy and open the damn thing.*

Flipping the lid up, Zach stood speechless.

Paige sat at the table pushing food around her plate, unable to look at Eli. Why hadn't he brought Archer with him as she'd asked him to? If he didn't want her in his life anymore then why try to prevent her from having a relationship with someone she had grown to care about? It wasn't fair. He didn't get a say in who she could see or what she could do anymore – his choice. Her eyes moved surreptitiously from her dinner to him and back again.

"I'm doing what I think is best for you right now, Paige. I know you don't appreciate it but I'm only looking out for your well-being and safety."

Paige's frowning gaze moved to him. "And you think it's in my best interest to keep Archer away?"

He nodded. "Yeah, I do for now."

"Why?" She dropped her fork onto the plate, leaned back on her chair, and folded her arms.

Eli sighed. "For one thing he's a vampire."

"You're a werewolf. What's the difference?"

"A lot." He mirrored her movements. "You don't mix bloodlines. You can't mix them."

"And you can't protect me from everyone, Eli. I'm a grown woman who has the right to see whomever I please."

"I'm not disputing that. I just want you to be safe."

"I don't think that's the only reason."

"What do you mean?"

"You tell me. You told me it was over between us and yet you're still trying to manipulate my life and I want to know why."

Eli's frown deepened. "I told you. To keep you safe."

Paige leaned in and rested an elbow on the table. "And you believe Archer is a threat to my safety, is that it?"

"He's a vampire."

"You said that already. There's more to it though, isn't there?" She wanted him to tell her the reason he was doing it was because he was still in love her. She wanted him to say he was the only man she should be with. "Well?"

Eli jerked out of his seat and dropped his plate into the sink. "Do what you want. You will anyway." He walked through the kitchen door, crossed the living room and stepped out onto the front porch. He had to get away from her before his resolve let him down.

Paige remained seated at the table, her eyes on his empty chair. Perhaps she needed to try a different approach.

Clarissa snatched the receiver from its cradle on the second ring. She knew right away it was her grandson. She always got a particular feeling when he called. "Hello, my boy, everything all right?"

Eli descended the front steps, walked over and leaned against the right-hand fender of his Jeep. "Not at the moment. No."

"Still having problems with the ring?" She frowned as she eased a chair out from under the kitchen table and sat down.

"The ring seems fine, at least as far as I can tell. It hasn't offered anything yet." Should he talk to his grandmother about his feelings? He already knew what she'd say. "No, it's not the ring, it's Paige."

Clarissa's eyebrows shot up. "Oh? Is she all right? Has something else happened?"

"No, nothing's happened, she's ok. I want to know if there's anything you can give me to stop the way I feel about her?"

"Hon, I'm sorry, you know I can't do that. It goes against our laws. What you feel is written in the stars. No one can change what fate has in store for you both." She waited a beat then said, "You belong together, Eli. Look what's happened already. You almost lost her. Don't you think it's time to be honest with her about how you feel and allow her back into your life?"

Silence.

"Eli?"

"I'm here, Clary." He ran his hand over his face as the idea circled his mind. "I don't want to destroy her life."

"You won't be destroying her life, you'll be protecting it."

"Will I? If we get back together I'll be taking away who she is now."

"Why don't you talk to her? Listen to her? Find out what *she* wants."

"I know what she wants."

"Then you have your answer."

Eli stepped through the front door only to find the living room and kitchen empty. He hated that Paige was angry with him for not doing as she'd asked, but he had to make her see that Archer Hamilton, a vampire, was not the man she should be with. He wrestled with the idea of telling her how he felt but couldn't bring himself to say the words out loud for fear it would begin a chain of events that couldn't be undone. He'd wanted her from the moment he'd first laid eyes on her, that is, until he discovered at what cost. The thought of taking away her humanity was the reason why he couldn't say those words now. It wouldn't change the way he felt about her but it would change her.

Paige came into the living room dressed to go out.

"Where are you going?" Eli frowned as his eyes roamed her body from head to toe. She looked amazing.

"I called Archer and told him I'd meet him at the Jade Dragon for a late dinner."

Eli rushed across the room. "Paige, you can't it's too dangerous."

"I need some kind of normal in my life right now and sitting down to dinner with an attractive man who just happens to like me would be a nice distraction."

"We already had dinner."

"You might've noticed I didn't eat much." *If you'd been paying any attention at all.* She hoped a twinge of jealousy might prompt him to open up to her.

"I thought, maybe, you were still adjusting after…"

"I'm fine. I wish you'd stop treating me like a baby." She held out her hand.

His right eyebrow arched. "What?"

"The keys to your Jeep, please. I can't get to Moon Grove without a car."

Eli shook his head. "I'm not giving you the keys to the wagon, Paige."

A scowl crossed her pretty face. "Why not?"

"Because you can't go." He folded his arms.

"I what?!" She stood with hands on hips. "You don't get to tell me what I can and can't do, Eli Blackwood. You gave up that right when you…"

Eli rushed across the room, pulled her into his arms, and kissed her hard on the mouth.

Paige tugged free, tripping backwards in her high-heeled shoes but maintaining her balance. "Why – why did you do that?" she said, breathless, a tear slipping down her left cheek.

"See reason, Paige. Please. It's not safe for you out there right now."

"Is that all you have to say to me? Why did you just kiss me?"

His eyes moved to the floor then back to her. "I guess I overreacted."

219

Paige's shocked expression darkened. "That's it? You kiss me and then tell me you overreacted. What are you doing, Eli?" She turned on her heel and marched over to the front door. As she got closer she noticed the keys for the four wheel drive sitting on the small table so she snatched them up, threw the door open, climbed into the car and was gone before Eli made it onto the porch.

"Dammit." He stood with hands on hips, watching the red taillights disappear into the distance, knowing that if he continued doing these things to Paige he'd push her away for good, and he didn't want to do that. But he also didn't want to ruin her life.

As Paige pulled into the curb she spotted Archer waiting on the sidewalk outside the restaurant. He gave her one of his dazzling smiles, came around the Jeep and opened the door for her, taking her hand and helping her out of the car. "It's so good to see you," he said, leading her over to the door of the Jade Dragon.

"It's good to see you, too."

Archer held the door and motioned for Paige to go in ahead of him. She smiled and stepped into the ambience of the Chinese restaurant. She hadn't been here since that first disastrous date with Eli. Well, it hadn't really been a date, just a welcome dinner. She ran her gaze around the almost empty café. There never seemed to be many patrons even though the food was amazing.

"Shall we?" Archer led her to a table in the back corner separated from the main floor of the restaurant by a red floral partition. "I hope you don't mind us having some privacy."

Paige smiled. "No, not at all. Right now I welcome it."

"I thought you might." He pulled out a chair for her.

She sat down, waiting for him to join her. "Thank you."

"My pleasure." He took the seat beside her, shook out a red napkin and placed it across his lap. "What would you like tonight?"

"Could we order some wine first? I feel like a glass of something soothing."

"Of course." Archer set the napkin on the table and wandered down to the counter to ask for a bottle of Merlot and a couple of menus. He didn't often eat but would do so tonight for Paige's sake. He returned to the table. "It'll be along shortly." He passed her a menu. "I thought, in the meantime, we could peruse these and decide on dinner."

"Thanks." She took the menu and opened it. "I think I'll try something I haven't had before."

"Always good to try something new." He smiled.

Paige glanced up from the menu and their eyes met. Now she knew why he had the palest blue eyes, mesmerizing eyes, that drew her in and held her there. But where was there? Her heart gave a small shudder as he raised her wrist to his lips and kissed it.

The evening with Archer was just what Paige had needed. She felt light-hearted and relaxed for the first time in a long while. No thoughts of the situation with Eli had entered her mind until she reached the Jeep – his Jeep – and she realized she'd have to face him again when she got back to their hideaway. She sighed inwardly, gave Archer a smile, and eased herself into the driver's seat. "I've had a wonderful time tonight. Thank you."

"The pleasure, I can assure you, is all mine." He brought her hand up to his lips and kissed it, her blood scent drifting into his nostrils. "Let's do it again soon."

"Yes, let's." Paige started the engine and the editor closed the door, watching her drive away.

He crossed the street and climbed into his Mercedes. Reaching across, he opened the glove compartment and gazed at the silver and crystal necklace Paige had worn on their first dinner date. He couldn't have her being protected when he needed to drink from her, now could he? Tonight had been his third taste, unbeknown to her, and he was feeling the effect her blood had on his immortal anatomy. And it felt amazing.

It was his good fortune to be one of a select few who could heal the bite wounds after consuming the life-giving elixir pulsing through their veins, so the donor, willing or not, had no idea of what had occurred. Paige would have assumed on the two previous occasions that she was hungover, nothing more, because he had consumed a substantial quantity of her blood. Tonight had been different. He could only partake of a small amount because of their location. Archer smiled at his reflection in the rear view mirror, started the engine of his sports car, and headed home. He would need another dose before it took its full effect.

THIRTY SEVEN

Gregor sensed something was wrong with Yana. He could smell the anxiety exuding from every pore of her body and see it in her eyes whenever she glanced at him. What had she done? And where had she been disappearing to so often? He crossed the living room of the luxurious wood cabin to where she sat, arms folded, a pout on her pretty face. "Is everything all right, my sweet?" he asked.

She raised her chin but didn't meet his gaze. "Why wouldn't it be?"

"You seem distracted. Is there something you want to talk to me about?"

Yana's eyes darted to him. Did he suspect her? "No. Of course not." Her defensive response would be sure to raise his suspicions.

He eased his tall frame down beside her. "You know you can tell me anything," he said, his voice low and calm.

She almost laughed in his face. Gregor was the least approachable vampire in their team. He did not have the ability to listen without judgement. If he found out what she had done he would end her undead life without hesitation, even though they were lovers. Anyone who interfered with his plans or defied him did not get a second chance. "I have nothing to say."

"Very well. Do not say I didn't try." He stood up and stalked into the kitchen where his men were sitting, cards in hand, playing a game of Durak. "We need to work on our strategy. Play time is over."

"Come on, Gregor, I was on a winning streak," Alexei told him, raising his cards, a scowl on his unshaved face.

Gregor stepped up to him and whacked him across the back of his head. "Would you prefer to die? Because if we do not get clear in our minds how this war is to be won we will lose it."

The other two vampires on his team pushed their cards into the center of the table, scuffed back their chairs and stood up. "We are ready."

"Alexei?"

"Da. Of course I am ready." He threw his cards on top of the pile and stood up.

"Good. Then follow me to the study." As he strutted out of the kitchen, Gregor's serious gaze moved to Yana. Her mood was unchanged. "Coming?"

"What else?" She shrugged and stood up.

The group followed Gregor into the den which was set up with a map pinned to the wall, a layout of the town spread across the table, and numerous documents and the Lycan tome sitting on a desk in the corner of the room. It resembled something out of a classic war movie.

Paige climbed the front steps onto the porch and stopped, her heartbeat thumping against her breastbone. She had gone out with Archer to try to get Eli to be honest with her and it had backfired. Not entirely. He had kissed her so she knew the feelings were still there locked inside him. She raised her hand to knock but the door swung open before she could.

"Have a nice time?" Eli turned around, stalked across the living room to the kitchen and poured himself a coffee.

Paige could see he'd been brooding while she was gone. She closed the door and walked over to the doorway. "Yes, thanks, I did. It was good to get out of this cocoon and feel normal again."

"Normal?" His right eyebrow arched. "How could you feel *normal* with a vampire?"

"Archer was very accommodating. He even ate with me, which I believe vampires don't often do."

"How thoughtful of him." Eli leaned against the counter sipping his coffee.

"If you care about me at all then why can't you be happy that I had a good time?"

"I do care." Eli slid his mug onto the counter and folded his arms.

"Well you have a strange way of showing it."

"Let's not fight. Ok? You've been through a terrible ordeal and I'm concerned for your safety. I don't want anything else happening to you."

"Why, Eli?" She hoped he'd say the words she longed to hear. Words she'd missed hearing.

"Because…" Eli's cell phone vibrated in his shirt pocket and he snatched it out. "Sheriff Blackwood

225

speaking." His gaze shifted to her as he took the call and he was grateful for the interruption.

Paige let out a frustrated huff, turned around and wandered down the hallway to her room.

Half an hour later a knock echoed into her bedroom. Did Eli finally want to talk? "Yes?"

The door swung open and Linda poked her head around. "Hi. Eli had to go out for a while on police business. Want some coffee? I brought homemade chocolate cake." She grinned.

"Sure, why not." Paige sighed, followed Linda out to the kitchen and sat down at the table.

"How are you feeling? Things getting back to normal?" Linda cut slices of cake, placed them onto two plates, and popped them on the table, then carried the mugs over and sat opposite Paige.

"I'm fine. Really. I wish people would stop making a fuss over me." She could hear the tightness in her voice and offered Linda a small smile. "Sorry. It's just…"

Linda nodded. "I get it. Eli can be stubborn sometimes."

"Do you think he made the right decision breaking it off with me?"

"No, I don't. I think you belong together… for many reasons. And I know the others in the pack feel the same."

Paige sighed. "Why can't he see it then?"

Linda reached across and patted Paige's hand. "I guess he thought it was the best thing for you. I know I agonized over it. He wasn't the same after and still isn't. I'm sure he still loves you."

"I am still so in love with him it hurts to be around him."

"What about Archer?"

"I like him, I really do, but he isn't Eli."

Linda pointed to the cake in front of Paige. "Eat up. Enjoy the decadence. Things have a way of working themselves out. Hold onto that."

"I'll do my best, but it's not easy."

Gregor had decided, after some deliberation amongst his team, the Lycan church on the hilltop was the perfect place for their supernatural battle. Pine trees offered obscurity from the town, the tall, white cathedral spire the only indication the building was there at all. The expansive grassland and parking lot surrounding it where the war could be waged without the residents of Moon Grove being aware would be the location for the town's wolves' demise. A satisfied smile stretched across his rugged features. *They will be outnumbered and easy to finish.*

He would lure Eli Blackwood there on the premise that he would return their tome and hold him captive until the pack arrived. He wondered about the Lycan who had visited Paige at her home. The genetic bond had been unmistakable the night Gregor had waited outside her house. Was he a sibling? But how could that be possible when her mother and father were dead? The father's remains were collected and taken to the coroner's office in Bellehurst but not the mother's. Could she have escaped the council's death sentence and gotten away with a child in her womb? Was the mother a wolf as well? If so, would they join the fight?

The rest of his team was on their way – two arriving in

a couple of days and the other three over the next week from LA, San Francisco and Australia. Ten against six. There was no contest. The wolves would be defeated in moments and he and his vampires would inherit the town. Gregor's thoughts turned to Paige and he hoped she would return to her office soon so he could continue to prepare her for her part in their victory. Her blood would be the key to their triumph.

THIRTY EIGHT

Zach lay on his bed in a euphoric, vampire blood trance, the effect like that of a drug induced high. His half closed eyes met the ceiling, moving in colorful waves above him, and a satisfied smile spread across his handsome, pale face. The black box had contained a gift – a flask of fresh, warm human blood. So fresh, he could have been drinking right from the source. Nothing else could appease the hunger – the incessant craving. He licked his lips, the rich, coppery taste lingering on his tongue, closed his eyes completely and relished the blissful buzz vibrating through his body.

His cell phone vibrated on the nightstand beside him but he ignored it. Whoever it was could call back. He had better things to do right now.

Eli pressed the red dot on his cell phone screen to end the unanswered call. Where was Zach and why wasn't he picking up? He'd called Doc Taylor and made another appointment for a session with him for the following afternoon. Why? Because he needed to get to the bottom of the mystery of Charlene's death and because Paige still needed time to recover from her abduction ordeal, despite her saying she was fine. He could see on her face every time he looked at her that she wasn't. John Taylor owed him, and Eli would keep him to his word of offering help and telling him what he knew.

The sheriff stepped through the door of the station to find all of his pack and Rosemarie waiting for him. *What is this? Some kind of intervention?*

Bobby stood up and came around his desk. "Hi, boss. Thanks for coming in so late."

Eli crossed the office. "What's going on?"

Paul spoke up. "We'd like to know what you're planning to do about the situation with Paige."

"You mean her recovery?"

Rebecca shook her head. "No, Eli… about you getting back together. Without her as our Alpha female we don't stand a chance of winning the impending fight with the vampires. They'll massacre us."

Eli's frowning gaze circled the serious faces in the room. "I'm wearing the moonstone ring, against my better judgement. That should be enough. I don't want Paige involved in any of this."

Rosemarie stepped forward, a slight flush to her cheeks. She wasn't comfortable with ambushing her boss, but what else could they do to make him see reason? The situation had become desperate. "But she is involved, darlin', she always has been. And you need her in the pack."

"No, I don't." He stood with hands on hips. So this *was* an intervention.

230

"Why can't you just let it happen?" Rebecca asked.

"Do any of you understand what you're asking of me? Do you?" He'd gone over it and over it in his mind, debating a logical reason as to why he should, but couldn't justify taking Paige's humanity from her. He loved her too much for that.

"Yes, we do," Bobby told him. "But she's an essential element to the cohesion of our pack, Eli. Without her we're in danger of losing our strength. Then what?"

"If you were in my position and it was someone you…" He stopped himself from saying the words out loud. "Someone you cared about… would you take a selfish stance just for the sake of the pack?"

"Have you talked it over with her? Doesn't she want to be our Alpha female?" Rebecca stood with arms folded.

"Yes, she does but I made the decision to let her go."

"We're in trouble here, Eli, and unless you fulfil her wishes and bring her into the pack we're in danger of being annihilated by those bloodsuckers." Bobby leaned against his desk, arms folded. "You need to get it done, Eli. Just tell her you still love her and make her one of us." It was time for their Alpha to see it for what it was and evaluate their impending demise – because without Paige they were all doomed.

Linda and Paige finished their cake and coffee and Paige sat the dishes in the sink before joining her body guard in the living room. Where had Eli gone at such a late hour? She crossed the room and sat down on the sofa beside her receptionist and decided to ask her what she knew. "Do you know where Eli went?"

"He was called into the station." Linda picked up the remote and turned on the television.

"It's pretty late. Was there some kind of police situation?" Paige's eyes moved to the large, flat screen TV. A commercial about toothpaste and having a whiter smile was on.

"I'm not sure. Eli didn't say." She flicked through the channels looking for a movie.

"Oh." Paige eased her spine against the backrest and folded her arms.

Linda's gaze moved to her. "Why?"

"No reason, I was just wondering."

"Oh, ok." Linda knew the reason but didn't want to raise Paige's hopes that anything would come out of the meeting. She wished she could have been there to lend voice to reason. Deep down, Eli had to know Paige becoming part of the pack was crucial to their survival, now more than ever, and in the future.

Brent walked through the door of the police station and stopped short. His eyes roamed the room and the people in it and he knew right away what it was. The group had instigated an intervention to get their Alpha to fulfil his duty as their leader and initiate Paige into the pack. His sister had talked to him about the reason why she and Eli had broken up and was more than willing to become his Alpha female. She loved him and would do anything to help protect him and his wolves. The young man's eyes rested on the sheriff, who was standing with hands on hips in the center of the office and did not look happy about what was taking place. "I can come back tomorrow if..."

Eli turned around. "No, come on in. Have you come to roast me as well?"

Brent pushed his hood back, let the door go and walked over to him. "I came by to ask if I can see Paige. She's not answering her phone."

"Not right now. The less people who know where she is the better. And the reason she's not answering her cell is because it's turned off. It can be tracked."

The young man shrugged. "Ok, fair enough. Is she ok?"

"As good as can be expected after what she's been through."

Brent frowned. "What does that mean?"

"She says she's fine but I don't think she is. She's putting on a brave face to protect the people she cares about."

"Then maybe I should talk to her. See if I can do something to help her."

"Tell him where she is, Eli," Rebecca said. "He has a right to know, he's her brother."

Eli swung around. "I'm not disputing the fact, but I'm doing everything I can to keep Paige safe. Anyone who knows her whereabouts is a target, so like I said the less who know the better."

Brent raised his hands. "I get it. It's ok, but I want to see her sometime soon."

The sheriff returned his gaze to the young man. "And you will. She's planning to go back to work in the next few days. Go see her at her office."

Paige's brother nodded, pulled his hood over his head, and walked out the door.

Eli turned back to the others, his eyes searching every concerned face in the room. He'd been second-guessing himself ever since he broke off his relationship with Paige and knew deep down not only did the pack need her... he needed her. Even though he'd done what he thought was in her best interest, his heart had been in pain the whole time they'd been apart. Making love to Paige would be the easiest thing in the world and he wanted to, more than he cared to admit, but he still couldn't rationalize being the one to take her life, the life she had now, away from her. Who would she become?

THIRTY NINE

After the so called *meeting* at his office, Eli decided to make a stop at his house before heading back to Paige and Linda at their safe location. His mind was reeling. Yes, he knew the pack needed Paige's strength to survive situations like the one they were confronted with right now but it still didn't make it any easier for him to come to the decision of taking away the person she was – the woman he loved. There was no doubt she would be different, despite what she would tell him because she'd be a wolf and he wasn't sure he wanted her to be. It had nothing to do with jealousy. He had lost one love because of what he was and he wasn't prepared to lose another because of it. One day he'd tell Paige about Michelle, and what happened to her, but not now.

When Eli pulled the Jeep up outside his front porch, he noticed glowing orange embers on the lower trunk of one of the trees bordering his property. His wary gaze roamed the surrounding darkness as he eased the door open and climbed out of his vehicle, his hackles rising the moment he caught a whiff of the smoky odor on the night air. *This can't be good.* Instinctively, as a cop, he knew that smell and his stomach flipped over and tightened beneath his belt buckle. He pulled his pistol, his Lycan senses on high alert, and wandered the area around his house and surrounding woods before moving toward the tree in question standing in a thicket about a hundred feet away.

His nocturnal vision widened allowing him to see into the gloom ahead of him and when he reached the smoldering tree his heart pounded against his ribs as his eyes met the charred remains of a body tied to the trunk. Eli whipped his cell phone out of his shirt pocket and pressed speed dial for Paul Burke, his forensic guy. "Yeah, it's me. I need you out at my place, pronto. I've got a body burned to a tree."

"What?!" Paul pulled the van to the side of the road. He was on his way home.

"You heard me. I want to know who it is ASAP." He ended the call hoping it wasn't Brent or his mother. Was this the work of the council... or Greg Petrov? It was definitely a message of some kind, but what did it mean? More importantly, who was it?

While he waited, Eli called Linda to make sure she and Paige were safe and secure. To his relief they were. He shouldn't have doubted it because they were well hidden, but with a new team of vampires in town you could never be too careful.

About twenty minutes after his call, Paul, Bobby, and Cooper arrived at his property in separate cars with red and blue strobe lights flashing. They'd made it in record time as it usually took over half an hour to get out to his place.

Eli met the trio at the hood of his Jeep and escorted

them down to the crime scene, which it now was. "I want to know who this is as soon as you do. Ok?" His stern, frowning gaze met his colleague's. "Ross Redmond was the first death in this new chain of events and now this one. Who'll be next? We need to get on top of this."

"Yeah." Paul nodded. "You got it. The minute I know anything I'll call you." He stepped over the snipped barbed wire fencing and set his kit down in the long grass at the foot of the tree, stretching a pair of purple latex gloves onto both hands. His eyes roamed the sizzling, flaky black corpse. "I can tell you right now it's a woman." He pointed to the body's mid region. "The pelvic inlet and arch are too wide to be a man's."

Eli's heart rose in his throat. Could it be Abbey O'Connell? He had no way of contacting Brent to find out if his mother was with him. The pair kept their location and their phone numbers secret, and he understood why.

Bobby stood by the fence, arms folded, his gaze turning to Eli. "If it's not Paige's mom then who is it?"

"That's the answer I'm hoping the county coroner can provide."

After gathering samples, Paul removed the gloves and headed to his wagon. "You guys can load the remains into the van while I finish up here," he said, laying out the black body bag on the gurney and unzipping it.

"Sure." Bobby wheeled the portable bed up to the tree and waved Cooper over. "It's not going to be easy getting the body off that trunk."

Paul removed a battery operated, compact circular saw from the dark blue duffel bag he'd dropped next to his kit and held it up. "That's where this comes in."

Cooper pointed to the power tool, the color draining

from his face. "What are you gonna do with that?" His mind conjured up bloody, charred body parts and his stomach swirled.

Paul gave an inward chuckle. The young guy wasn't cut out for gruesome police work. "I'm going to cut a rectangle around the body, pry the bark off the tree with the corpse still attached and put it in that." He pointed to the black, rubber-coated bag.

"Oh. Good." Cooper nodded, the look of relief crossing his pallid features.

Once the body was in the van Paul told Eli he'd be in touch as soon as the coroner had an ID. He'd radioed the guy in Bellehurst and he was on standby, waiting for Paul to arrive.

Eli stood with arms folded and watched his team leave the property before heading into the house, an unsettling thought running through his mind, *It can't be Paige's mother, it just can't be.*

Eli opened the bureau drawer, picked up the picture frame and turned it over. His frowning gaze studied the photo for a long time. Michelle's radiant, beautiful smiling face looking out at him caused his heart to clench. Their wedding day had been the best day of his life. He'd loved her since they were teenagers and had known he would marry her one day. After she'd been killed he'd made a promise to himself that he wouldn't allow anyone else he loved to get hurt because of what he was. Now, he had to face the difficult task of making the decision to pull Paige into his nightmare world for good or leave things as they were and hopefully convince her to leave Moon Grove.

A single tear slid down his left cheek and he swiped at

it and sniffled. "How can I make that kind of decision, Michelle? How can I turn a lovely young woman into a creature?" He gave a heavy sigh, slid the photo back into the drawer and closed it. Paige's life had been turned upside down since she'd arrived in his town. Why would she want to stay? He knew the answer. Because she was in love with him, just as he was in love with her. But was it enough to keep her safe?

FORTY

The following morning, Eli called Zachary Ridgeway to let him know they had an appointment with Doc Taylor. Zach was surprised the sheriff had chosen to go back to the doctor after what he'd learned, but as Paige was still not unavailable to continue his sessions the unscrupulous psychologist was their only option.

When Eli pulled up outside the Moon Grove Inn Zach was already on the sidewalk. He opened the door and climbed in.

"I tried calling you, last night. Where were you?"

"I was otherwise engaged."

"Doing what?" Eli wondered if Zach had been out on the prowl.

"I'm sure I don't have to check in with you every time I have something else on, do I?"

"Of course not. But it would be a good idea to pick up when I call. It could be beneficial to your health."

Zach gave the sheriff a serious frown. "Meaning what, exactly?"

"Meaning there are certain people in this town that

would prefer you weren't here and it could turn ugly. If I get a heads up I want to be able to reach you."

"Ok. I'll answer your calls in future." Zach clipped in his seatbelt and folded his arms. "Do you think you can trust Doc Taylor to continue working with me and not go to the council with the information?"

"At this point, I'm not sure of anything. But as Paige is still unavailable for the moment, and you want to get to the bottom of the mystery, he's the only choice we have. He told me he'd cooperate."

"I hope you're right about him. If he's still in league with the council and whoever else was pressuring him he might just play along."

"That thought crossed my mind, too. But right now we need to get into your subconscious and figure out what actually happened that night. Once we do I'll deal with John Taylor."

Zach shrugged. "Ok. I'll do whatever you think is best."

"Thanks." Eli pulled the Jeep away from the curb and headed down the main street.

"Can I ask a favor?"

Eli gave him a dubious sideward glance. "Depends."

"Fair comment. I'd like to go out to where it happened. See if I can jog something out of my memory there. Would you take me?"

They pulled up outside the psychiatrist's home.

"Let's get through the session this morning and see what comes out of it." Eli nodded and pulled the keys from the ignition. "But, yeah, it's probably a good idea."

"Thanks, I appreciate it."

"No problem. Anything is worth a try. Oh, by the way,

I'll be recording the session, just so you know. That way we can listen to it later and see if anything jumps out at you." Eli climbed out of the wagon.

Zach followed him down the drive and into the doctor's office. He was confident that the impenetrable wall he'd created in his mind would keep certain information hidden from the psychologist and be difficult for him to crack.

Paige awoke to the smell of smoke and the shrill, high-pitched ping of the alarm screaming in the hallway. She hurled herself out of bed, her heart thumping in her chest, rushed across to the door and pressed her palm against the wood to see if it was hot. It wasn't. She threw it open and headed down the hazy passage. "Eli?" She breathed in a lung full of smoke and coughed, her eyes tearing and stinging as the dark, hazy plume connected with her face. "Eli, where are you?" she called frantically.

Linda stepped into her view waving a tea towel around. "It's ok, Paige, I set the alarm off. The bread got stuck in the toaster while I was out back picking a couple of tomatoes from the bush."

Paige's pounding heartbeat and ragged breathing slowed. "There's an awful lot of smoke for burnt toast."

"Yeah, well, I had four slices in it and they're burnt to a crisp."

"I thought…"

"Sorry. I didn't mean to startle you awake." She gave Paige a sympathetic smile. Even though it was after ten in the morning, Linda thought her boss could do with the extra sleep time.

"I'm just glad it wasn't another dangerous situation." She let out a huge, relieved sigh.

"I've got the exhaust fan on and the back door open so the smoke should clear pretty quickly and then we can have breakfast." Linda smiled and headed back to the kitchen.

Paige turned around and made her way along the hall to the bathroom to take a quick shower. After the morning's heart starter, she needed to relax under the hot spray for a while. Once she was showered and dressed, she wandered out to the kitchen. Whatever Linda had prepared for breakfast, or, as it was now after ten thirty, brunch, smelled scrumptious and her stomach growled. "What's that wonderful smell?"

Linda glanced over her shoulder while she plated up. "Hi. Feel better? I'm really sorry about that whole 'scare you half to death' thing a while ago. I made tomato, cheese and bacon omelets with *unburnt* toast." She smiled and motioned to the table. "Sit. Enjoy." She set a plate down for Paige then took her seat opposite.

"Thanks. This certainly makes up for it." Paige grinned, picked up her cutlery, and dove in. "Mm. It tastes even better than it smells."

"Glad you like it." Linda cut into her omelet.

"It's delicious."

"Well, as I said, enjoy."

Paige wondered where Eli was. "Did Eli go out already?"

"Oh, yeah, he took Zach to…" She wasn't sure she should say where they'd gone.

"He took Zach where?" Paige frowned and set her knife and fork down on her plate.

243

"To see Doc Taylor. He didn't want to hassle you with starting up the sessions with Zach again so soon after what happened so he thought…"

"I'm fine. Seriously. And I plan to go back to work next week. Why didn't he talk to *me* about it?"

"Maybe you should ask him." Linda grimaced. "Sorry."

Paige let out a frustrated huff. "It seems he's still making decisions for me rather than asking me what I want."

Zach's session yielded nothing more than what they already knew. He and his friends had been out in the woods drinking and Charlene had been drained of blood. Had it been planned? Had she been a willing participant and it had gone too far? These were questions that required answers. John stepped out of his office with Eli so they could discuss his thoughts. "It seems to me he's put up a barrier that I can't get through," Doc Taylor told him.

"That makes no sense. He says he wants to get to the bottom of what happened out there but you think he's blocking you?"

"I've never met a mind I couldn't penetrate, except for now." John shrugged. "I don't know what else to tell you, Eli."

The sheriff gave a frustrated sigh. "Well, let's do another session sometime this week and see what happens."

Doc Taylor nodded. "Of course." He waited a beat. "Eli, I really am sorry about what happened. I hope you know that. And I plan to make amends."

Eli gave him a serious frown. "I'm putting my faith in you, despite my better judgement, so don't let me down, John."

"I won't." He gave a thin, uncertain smile. "You *can* count on me."

The drive out to the woods took about twenty minutes, time Eli didn't have but time he needed to invest to get to the bottom of what happened the night of the blood ritual. He pulled the four wheel drive off the road under a tree and both men climbed out. Zach stood, hands on hips, and glanced around the area. It had been years since he'd been here.

"It's this way," Eli said, pointing behind him through the tall pines.

"Yeah, I remember." Zach gave him a surreptitious glance and moved ahead of him, forging a path through the knee high grass and low lying branches to the clearing midway. "It's a lot smaller than I remember." His eyes roamed the overgrown space between the trees. It had once been a make out point for teens of Moon Grove. He'd lost his virginity out here.

"You were a lot younger then." Eli stepped up behind him. "Anything jump out at you?"

Zach shook his head. "Not yet." He wandered the circle of creeping vines, weeds and debris, flashes of that night bursting into his head. "We'd been drinking beer and were all pretty drunk. Charlene knew what we were and she wanted one of us to bite her. She said she wanted to be like us... wanted to remain young and never die."

The sheriff frowned and approached him. "Why didn't that come out under hypnosis?"

Zach shrugged. "I don't know." He ran his gaze along the fallen, rotting tree trunk twenty feet away and walked over to it. "She was sitting over here. I remember Riley was with her and they were making out."

Eli followed him over. "Where were Caleb and Joshua?"

"I'm not sure. They wouldn't have been far because they'd planned to drink from her, too. We all did. But I changed my mind. At least I think I did."

"So what you're telling me is Charlene wanted to be bitten?"

Zach turned around, his eyes meeting Eli's unconvinced gaze. "Yeah. She did. She was flirting with all of us, saying 'come on bite me'. She had no idea that our guts were being ripped apart by the hunger inside us. She was tempting fate."

"The coroner said she put up a fight. There was skin under her fingernails that belonged to Riley and Caleb and she had defensive bruising on her arms."

"I don't know about that, Sheriff, but she *was* a willing participant. She wanted to become immortal."

Charlene Brooks had been considered a *good girl*. Her parents were God-fearing Christians who had raised her to be a young lady and maintained a tight leash. At least that's what they'd thought. But going out into the woods with four, horny teenaged boys, who were also fledgling vampires, didn't seem to reflect that kind of persona. Why would she have gone out there with them willingly? Had she been coerced into it?

"Ok. So what went wrong?"

Zach raised his hands and shrugged. "That's just it, I don't know."

Eli let out a frustrated huff. "Well, continue wandering around and see if anything else comes to mind."

"Sure." Zach nodded. "Ok."

Was he telling the truth? Had Charlene wanted them to bite her? It sounded plausible, being a teenaged girl, wanting the thrill of something dark and dangerous. After all, she lived in a time when nothing exciting happened in Moon Grove. John had to somehow delve deeper into Zachary Ridgeway's mind to find out what really happened that night. Eli stood, arms folded, his eyes following Zach around the clearing, his instincts sensing there was something his companion wasn't sharing with him.

FORTY ONE

Paige opened the door to her office and Linda followed her in. The psychiatrist stopped just inside the open doorway, ran her gaze around the unlit space, and sighed. She'd intended to reopen on Monday, which was only three days away, but wondered if she was ready to take on Gregor again. He had been so cunning with his scheme to kill her, inserting himself into her life the way he had, and the thought sent a shiver up her spine. Could she penetrate his vampire mind and find out what his plans were for the ensuing fight? Could she discover where he'd hidden the Lycan tome so that Eli could retrieve it?

Linda rubbed Paige's arm. "You ok?"

She nodded. "Yes, I'm fine." Paige crossed the office and switched on the overhead light.

Her receptionist locked the door and pulled the blind, the CLOSED sign already in place. "Maybe it's too soon to come back."

Paige sat down at the front desk. "I have to find out what Gregor... or Greg Petrov, as he calls himself, is up to. If I can provide Eli with information about the vampire's plans it will help him and the pack prepare for the battle." Battle? Her stomach shrank into a tight, crackling ball of nerves at the thought. The word sounded so ominous. It would mean the difference between life and death, but whose death?

"Paige, you don't have to do it, you know. Eli doesn't want you to put yourself in danger." Linda crossed the room and leaned on the counter.

"I know he doesn't, but I have to do *something*. I can't sit back and watch the pack be annihilated by those creatures. Do you think they'll play fair?" A sudden thought flashed across her mind and she popped up off her chair. "I have to see Clary."

Linda gave her a confused look. "Wait. What just happened?"

"I'll tell you later. Can I leave you here for a while?" She came around the desk.

"Sure. I guess. You're going to Eli's grandmother's house?"

"Yes. There's something I have to ask her."

"Be careful. Text me when you get there."

Paige rushed across to the door. "I will."

Clarissa threw the door open and held out her arms before Paige stepped onto the front porch. "How are you, my girl?" She pulled her into a tight hug. "It's so good to see you."

"I'm ok, Clary, really. I'm not as soft as people think I am."

Clarissa held Paige at arm's length. "I don't doubt that for one second. You've been through so much and have come out of it just fine." She waved the young woman inside. "To what do I owe the pleasure? Want some tea?" The older woman ushered her guest into the kitchen.

"Yes, tea would be nice. Thank you." Paige eased a chair out from under the table and sat down. "I need to ask you a question."

Clarissa pottered around the kitchen placing teaspoons of black tea into the pot, pouring the boiling water, and pulling cups and saucers from the overhead cupboard. "Oh? And what's that, dear?"

"Is there a way to trigger the Lycan gene without me and Eli making love?"

Clarissa's head turned sharply and she stopped what she was doing. "I was wondering when you'd ask me that."

Paige's eyes widened. "Are you saying there is a way?"

"I'm saying I haven't tried it before but there is a spell, yes – a wolf transformation spell."

"Can we try it?" Paige stood up, a look of desperation on her face. "Please, Clary."

Clarissa turned around. "Oh, well… wouldn't you rather enjoy the experience with Eli?"

"Yes, of course I would, if he'd let me. But he's keeping his distance in that regard and we're running out of time."

"The full moon won't rise for another couple of weeks." A look of concern crossed the old woman's face and she raised a hand to her chin. "But we could try it on Sunday. Spells like this work best at the beginning of the week."

"Wouldn't that be Monday?"

"Oh, no, dear, Sunday is actually the first day of the week. Monday is the first day of the working week."

"I didn't know that."

"Traditionally, both the Hebrew and Christian calendars mark Sunday as the first day. See." She pointed to the calendar on the wall above the refrigerator.

Paige looked up at it. "That's interesting. I wasn't aware."

Clarissa's forehead wrinkled into a deep frown. "Are you sure you want to go through with this? It might be painful. And I'm not exactly sure what will happen."

Paige got up and walked over to her. "Do I have a choice? If I don't do this the pack will be in danger of being murdered by those monsters. I can't let that happen, Clary. I need your help."

Eli climbed out of his Jeep and gazed along the main street in both directions. It was seven o'clock and the town seemed overly quiet for a Friday night. Even the movie house had closed early. A place he'd wanted to take Paige on a date so they could neck in the back row like teenagers. The nefarious vibration in the atmosphere appeared to have everyone spooked, even those who weren't aware of the supernatural aspect of Moon Grove. He closed the door and stepped onto the sidewalk, heading to the Tribune office. Archer had sent him a text asking him to come by.

When he walked through the door the editor rose from his seat. "Thanks for coming."

"No problem. What did you want to see me about?" He walked the length of the office and stood behind the chair in front of the editor's desk.

"I've spoken to several of my associates and they're more than happy to come here to help. A couple of them have heard of Gregor Petrov and have taken an instant dislike to him. He's renowned for disassembling supernatural law enforcement in small towns all over the world and instilling teams that work for him so it's no wonder the council called on him to come here. His reputation precedes him."

"Thank you, Hamilton. At least having them here will make it a fair fight."

"You could call me by my first name, you know. I think we're past the whole sheriff, new resident thing, don't you?"

Eli gave him a thin smile and shrugged. "I guess."

"How soon did you want them here?"

"The sooner the better. I think the situation will escalate once the other members of Gregor's team arrive. I've been keeping an eye on newcomers and two arrived today but aren't staying in town, which can only mean one thing."

"They're out at the cabin."

"Right."

"So there's how many more?"

"Three, I believe. Gregor has a team of ten, including himself."

The editor nodded. "Ok. I'll have my guys arrive in the next couple of days."

"I want you know I appreciate this."

"It's all in the name of Moon Grove remaining the way it is, right? No thanks required. I didn't come here to be ruled by rebel vampires, so let's kick their asses." He smiled.

Linda and Paige sat at the kitchen table eating hamburgers they'd picked up at the all night diner beside the bus station before heading back to their secret location. It had been an interesting day, as far as Paige was concerned, because she now knew she could do something significant to help Eli and his wolves. She wished things could have been different: that she and Eli could have shared a night of love and passion together that would have triggered the Lycan gene lying dormant inside her. If only.

The door opened just as the women finished their meal and Eli walked in. "Hi. How was your day?"

"Good." Paige got up from the table and stood in the kitchen doorway. "What about you?"

"Yeah, good. I spoke to Archer Hamilton tonight. He's organizing for some vampires to come and help us out."

"He is?"

"Yeah. It'll give us better odds against ancient vampires with more strength and resilience than we have right now."

"I trust Archer, but how do we know we can trust the vampires he's bringing here? And why would they want to fight their own kind?"

"It seems Gregor Petrov has a reputation in supernatural circles and not all vampires agree with his methods."

"So they're coming here to help because they want him dead, is that it?"

"He's ruined other towns across the globe. I suspect that's the reason why they want to be rid of him."

"We can't let him win, Eli. He has to be stopped. He cannot have Moon Grove."

"I'm going to do everything in my power to prevent that, Paige. I promise."

She pointed to the moonstone ring. "Anything?"

Eli shook his head and raised his hand to look at the milky stone. "Not that I can tell. I wish I knew how to activate it."

"So do I." Paige wasn't about to tell him she had plans of her own to help the pack fight and win.

FORTY TWO

Eli had just showered and stepped into his room, a navy blue bath towel wrapped around his waist, when his cell rang. He closed the door, rushed over to the nightstand and snatched up his phone. It was Paul. "Any news?"

"Do you know Elisha Adelson? She's a member of the governing body."

Eli didn't answer. He knew what was coming.

"Eli?"

"Yeah, I do. Why?" The body burned to the tree on his property was hers. They'd tied her there during the early hours of the morning and let her to fry in the sun. A warning to him not to meddle in council affairs.

"The DNA is hers."

Eli sighed into the phone. "She performed a location spell to find Paige's whereabouts. That's how I knew where she was."

"Man."

"Yeah. These killings are out of control. First Ross Redmond, now Elisha, who will they pick off next? Something has to be done about Remus and his coven once we win the fight against Gregor Petrov and his vampires."

"And you're confident we'll win?"

"I am. We're not going to be subjugated by the likes of him. This is *our* town. There are others coming to help us. I'll tell you all about it at our next meeting."

"I trust you, Eli. If you believe we're going to win then so do I."

"Thanks, Paul. I appreciate your faith in me. So what were the official findings?"

"There was no accelerant found on the body so it appears the sun did its job."

"That's what I thought."

"What are you going to do about it?"

"Nothing for the moment. Like I said, we'll deal with the council once the battle has been won."

"Ok. Well I'm heading home. See you at the next meeting."

"Yeah. Or the next crime scene, whichever comes first." Eli ended the call and dropped his phone onto the bed. Just as he was about to remove the towel and finish drying off a knock echoed into his room. "Yes?"

"It's me. Can we talk?"

He closed his eyes, sighed, and shook his head. *Paige. Why now?* "Can you give me a minute and I'll come out to the living room?"

Paige burst into the bedroom closing the door behind her. "No, this can't wait. We're running out of time, Eli, and you need to make a decision."

"Yes, I understand," Archer replied into the phone. "I only need one more dose and I think that will be enough." He opened the top drawer of his desk, the office empty, and held up a small vile. He had collected the last dose of Paige's blood the night they'd had dinner together, just in case Eli changed his mind and fulfilled his duty as Alpha. "I know. Yes, they'll be arriving over the next couple of days." His eyes moved to the locked glass door. Someone was cloaked in the shadows of the alcove. "I've got an unexpected visitor. Can I call you back?" He set the phone down on his desk, walked the length of the room and opened the door. "I'm sorry but we're closed for the night."

A ruggedly handsome male face peered out from under the black hoodie. "I was hoping you'd say that."

The editor smiled and embraced his guest. "Max, it's good to see you. When did you get here?"

"Just now." He shoved his hands into his pockets and smirked at his older brother. "Gonna invite me in?"

"I'm a vampire I don't need to invite you in. And, besides, this is a public place."

"Got anything to drink in that desk of yours?" He pointed to the back of the office.

Archer gave his kid brother a curious stare, his left eyebrow arching. "You mean of the red variety?"

Max nodded. "I'm dyin' here. Haven't eaten since last night. And what a tasty little snack she was." He smirked.

Archer shook his head. "Come on in. I'm sure I can find you something."

His brother stepped through the door and the editor closed and locked it. "Follow me."

The pair wandered through the Tribune office and out to the back. Archer removed a key from the pocket of his jacket, unlocked a large, solid padlock on a hasp attached to a dark brown wooden door and swung it open. "After you."

Max gave his brother a dubious, squinted glance then entered the claustrophobic space beneath the staircase. "So, this is where you hide your stash."

"One of them." Archer flicked on the dull, overhead bulb, sidled past his brother, lifted the lid on a cooler sitting on a laminated table, and tossed a blood bag at him. "Here, this should do the trick."

Max twisted the blue stopper, stuck the tube in his mouth, and sucked. "Mm. I needed this. Thanks."

"What are big brothers for? Need another one?"

His brother shook his head. "No, this'll do fine for now." He wasn't fond of chilled blood. He liked his sanguine fluids warm, appetizing, and in a curvy, feminine package.

The editor and his brother stepped out into the short hallway and Archer repositioned the padlock before heading back into the main office. Max followed.

"So what does anyone do for fun around here?"

"Not much. There's a movie house just down the street but apart from that the place is pretty... how shall I put it?"

"Boring?"

"You could say that. At least from a human perspective, I imagine."

"What do you mean?" Max dropped his six feet three inch frame onto the chair in front of his brother's desk, clasped his hands across his abdomen and crossed one leg over the other.

"On the supernatural front there's a lot going on in this town. Hence the reason I asked you and the others to come here."

"Ok, so fill me in."

"I'm not doing this with you, Paige, so you might as well turn around and head back out that door." Eli folded his arms across his bare, muscled chest, his stern gaze meeting her serious one. If she'd come in expecting him to give in she was mistaken.

"Well if you won't do what's right to protect your pack then I will." She turned on her heel and reached for the handle.

Eli was in front of her before she could open the door. "What do you mean, Paige?"

"Someone has to do something to prevent you all from getting yourselves killed."

He gripped her upper arm a little more tightly than he'd intended. "What are you going to do?"

Paige's eyes moved to his hand on her arm. "You're hurting me, Eli."

"Answer the question." He wasn't letting her go without an explanation.

"I've made some plans of my own." She frowned up into his face. "Now will you let me go?"

Eli took a step backwards, releasing her arm. "What kind of plans?"

"Nothing you need to be concerned about."

"If it means putting your life in danger then it does concern me."

"No. It doesn't anymore. You made your choice."

He reached out for her. She flinched and took a step back.

"I didn't mean to grab you so hard. I'm – I'm sorry."

"Apology accepted."

Eli frowned. "Why did you come in here, Paige? What did you think would happen?"

She sighed. "I thought you might reconsider your decision to leave me out of your personal life and do what needs to be done in order to keep your wolves safe. But I guess I was wrong." She opened the door.

"Paige. Wait." Eli's emotions were conflicted and it took every ounce of his self-control not to take her in his arms and kiss her. His body yearned for her in ways he could never have imagined but he couldn't allow himself to succumb to his feelings.

"What is it, Eli?" She turned around and folded her arms.

"If things were different…"

"Please, don't. It doesn't help the problem at all, does it? You're the pack's Alpha. You know what needs to be done to prevent a disaster. I'm here. I'm offering myself to you and the pack, but you refuse to take control of the situation. That's why I am." She turned on her heel and marched out the door.

FORTY THREE

Sunday afternoon, Paige drove to Clarissa's house with fluttering butterfly wings in the pit of her stomach. She pulled into the driveway and turned off the engine. Sitting and gazing out of the windshield at Eli's grandmother's house, she wondered what the spell would do to her. Why couldn't he have just given in and did what needed to be done? She knew he still loved her. It was obvious by the way he fiercely protected her humanity. But now wasn't the time to be honorable, it was time to take drastic measures.

As Paige stepped out of her car, Eli's Jeep screeched in behind her. He climbed out of his four wheel drive, slamming the door, and marched up to her. "Don't do this, Paige. Please."

"How did you know I was here?"

"Where else would you go to have a spell cast to make you a wolf?" He'd figured it out.

"You need to understand I have to do this. Unless you've changed your mind about making love to me."

Eli's honey colored eyes met hers and he frowned into them for a long time trying to comprehend the consequences if he did what she asked. Everyone wanted him to but his heart kept telling him not to. "Paige, I…"

She raised her hand. "Before you tell me you don't want to take away my humanity I'm telling you it's the only way." She reached up and touched his handsome face. "I'm still in love with you, Eli, and I know you're still in love with me so let's just go back to the cabin and share that love for the good of us all."

Clarissa came out onto the porch. "Oh, Eli, you're here."

"Yes, Clary. I came to talk some sense into Paige but she seems to have convinced me otherwise."

His grandmother walked over to the railing and smiled. "Then why are you both still here?

Eli closed the door and turned around. Paige was standing beside the bed, her cheeks slightly flushed with color, her eyes filled with love. He walked across the room to her and brushed gentle fingers against her left cheek, his heart beating just that little bit faster, and smiled at her. This moment – this place in time had been something he thought would never come. He'd fought against it because of his love for her but now knew she was right. He had no other choice, they were out of time. "Are you sure about this, Paige?" His voice was almost a whisper.

Her glistening gaze met his. "I couldn't be more sure. I've longed for this moment." She reached up and wrapped her arms around his neck, drawing him close. Their lips came together in a feather soft kiss as he fumbled with the buttons on her shirt and felt her tremble at his touch.

"You mean everything to me, Paige. I'm sorry for the time we've wasted being apart. If I could take it back I would. I am so in love with you." He slid the shirt off her shoulders and let it drop to the floor.

"And I am so in love with you." A single tear slid down her right cheek and he brushed it away with his thumb before his lips met hers again.

Paige unclipped the snap front buttons on Eli's denim shirt and he shrugged out of it. Her eyes roamed his muscled chest and washboard abs and she ran her index finger down the crevice in the center of his six pack. She had dreamed of this moment.

Eli leaned in, raised her face up to him and planted a firm kiss on her lips as his expectation of what they would share grew. Lifting her into his arms, he eased her down onto the bed covers and climbed over her. "My heart is yours, Paige, and always will be."

She reached up and drew him closer. "My heart belongs to you, too, Eli. I've waited for this moment, never expecting it would ever come, and now it's here." She smiled up at him with tears of joy in her eyes. "Make love to me."

When Eli woke up Paige wasn't beside him. He ran his eyes around the room before climbing out of bed and pulling on his jeans. *Where could she be?* He opened the door and wandered down the hallway to the living room. She wasn't there. He padded across the carpet and peered into the kitchen. Not there either. He frowned. "Paige?"

No answer.

Eli walked back along the hall opening the doors and checking the rooms. Nothing. His heart rate ticked up and an anxious adrenalin rush surged through him, the nerves in his gut tightening. "Paige, are you here?" He hadn't thought to check the bathroom. He threw open the door. Not there either. He rushed into his room, shrugged into his shirt and pulled on his boots, then headed for the front door. Just as he reached it, it opened and Paige stepped into the room. Eli breathed a relieved sigh. "I was starting to worry about you. Where did you go?"

Paige smiled and her honey colored eyes met his. She raised the bunch of wild flowers in her hand. "I wanted to put these on the breakfast table."

Eli eased the bouquet out of her hand and kissed her forehead. "Shouldn't I be making you breakfast?"

Paige gave him a cheeky grin and closed the door. "Yes, you should." She came up to him and pressed her lips to his. "Last night was wonderful."

He felt a pang of sadness as he gazed into her new Lycan eyes. He missed her beautiful, pale blue ones looking back at him. He gave her a smile to cover his feelings. "Yes, it was." His eyes roamed her face for a moment as he remembered their heated lovemaking. "Why don't I make those famous scrambled eggs you love so much?" He turned around and headed to the kitchen.

"Yum. Yes, please. Want me to help?" She followed him across the living room.

"Do you mind making the toast?" He found a crystal vase in one of the cupboards, filled it with water, dropped the flowers into it and sat it in the center of the table.

"Not at all. In fact I think I'll make double the amount. I'm so hungry I could eat a horse."

Eli glanced over his shoulder at her. "That's the wolf inside you. It can be pretty fierce at times."

"Oh? It will settle down though, won't it?"

He walked over to her and rubbed her arm. "Of course it will. You're a pup right now. It'll just take time to adjust. That's all."

Paige wondered how much her life would change now that she was a wolf.

When Paige arrived at her office, Gregor was milling around outside. She pulled her car into the curb on the opposite side of the street and sat watching him pace in front of the window, his hands pushed deep into his pockets. She swallowed the nerves lodged in her throat, glanced in the rear view mirror at her blue contacts hiding her honey colored eyes, stepped out onto the road, and put on her professional smile. As she crossed the street he spotted her and walked across the sidewalk. "Dr. O'Connell, it's good to see you." He tugged his hand free from his leather jacket pocket and extended it to her. Paige didn't want to take it but what choice did she have? She had to continue the charade.

"Thank you, Greg. I appreciate that."

"You've been away for a while. Have you been ill?"

"Yes, I have. But I'm feeling much better now."

"That is good to hear. Do you have some time for me today? I really need to see you after such a long time."

It had only been two weeks, but he was playing the 'emotionally in need' patient to perfection.

"Uh, let me check with Linda and I'll let you know. Can I call you later?"

"I am here now. So if you wouldn't mind checking I can wait."

Paige thought he sounded desperate. And he probably was. He hadn't had a chance to drink any of her blood yet and needed the strength it would offer for their impending battle. Unfortunately for him, her blood would no longer perform the way he expected. It might even kill him, which would be a blessing. She wondered if he would be able to sense the change in her and hoped he couldn't. He hadn't seemed to so far. She knew very little about the abilities of vampires, except for what she had read on the internet.

"Oh. All right. Do you need to talk something through with me?"

"Yes, yes, I do." He gave her a fake uncertain smile. "I've been having some troubling dreams and I want to know what you think about them."

"Ok. Come on in and I'll see what I can do." She pushed open the door and motioned for him to have a seat. "Why don't you sit over there while I find out my schedule for today?"

"Of course." He gave her a slight bow and took a seat near the front window.

When Paige reached the reception desk Linda's eyes roamed her face. "There's something different about you this morning. What is it?"

"We don't have time for that right now. Greg wants to see me... now."

"Oh. Well, you don't have any appointments so..."

Paige sighed. "That's what I thought." She turned and smiled. "Come on through, Greg."

Gregor stood and crossed the room, eyeing both women as he stepped into the small hallway and made his way to Paige's consultation room.

Paige picked up the iPad from off the desk, scrolled through to his file and opened it. Her eyes moved from the screen to her receptionist and she whispered, "Eli and I made love last night."

Linda's mouth dropped open as Paige followed Gregor into her office and closed the door.

After a quiet forty five minutes, the door to Paige's consultation room burst open and she rushed into reception, her startled face pale. "Call 911!" she said, breathless, glancing over her shoulder along the hallway.

Linda swiveled around on her office chair. "Why? What's happened?"

"I – I don't know. Gregor is having some kind of seizure. He – he's frothing at the mouth. Hurry!" She raced back along the hall and into the room. She couldn't have him die at her workplace. What would prospective clients think?

Doc Hoskins and Eli arrived ten minutes later and hurried into the office. "Where is he?" the doctor asked, medical bag in hand.

"Second door on the right," Linda directed, her eyes meeting Eli's in a plea to stay behind.

The doctor disappeared into the consultation room.

"What happened?" Eli asked, standing with hands on hips.

"I don't know. Paige came rushing out here saying Gregor was having some kind of seizure."

Eli's frowning gaze moved to the hallway. "I think I have a feeling I know why."

"Tell me exactly what happened, Paige?" Doc Hoskins asked as he knelt beside Gregor Petrov.

"We were in the middle of a session when his eyes rolled back and he started convulsing."

The doctor got up, crossed the room, grabbed her arms and examined her wrists then tugged down the collar on her shirt and checked her neck. No bite marks.

"What are you doing?" She frowned at him.

"Checking for puncture wounds." He stepped back. "Paige, this is important. Are you sure you remember everything correctly?"

She frowned into the older man's eyes. "Of course I do."

"Could you be mistaken? Could he have mesmerized you and drank your blood?"

Paige stopped to think. As far as she was aware she had been at her desk and he had been lying on the sofa. "I – I don't think so." Her frown deepened. "Why?"

"Because I think he's been poisoned."

"Poisoned?!" She popped up off her chair. "You think he actually did mesmerize me?"

"How else could he be poisoned, Paige? Unless you slipped something into his glass of water, which I doubt."

Eli stepped into the room. "What's the verdict, Doc?"

The doctor turned around. "I think he mesmerized Paige and drank her blood. Now that she's Lycan it's had an adverse effect on him. I've injected him with an antidote but I can't guarantee it'll work. He could die."

The sheriff gave a heavy sigh. "You need to do everything you can to keep him alive. If his team finds out about this there *will* be an all-out war."

"I'll take him back to my surgery and do what I can, but I can't promise anything, Eli."

"Just do the best you can, Doc. What happened here cannot leave this room."

Doc Hoskins called for an ambulance to meet him out the back of Paige's office and once it arrived they loaded Gregor into it and drove away. No strobe lights flashing. No sirens screaming. If this incident got back to the other vampires all hell would break loose.

FORTY FOUR

Zach knew it would be only a matter of time before Doctor John Taylor penetrated the wall he'd created in his mind and ventured inside his head to those dark corners he kept hidden. He'd felt the first sign of erosion at their last session and wasn't sure how much time he had before the psychiatrist discovered what had actually taken place that night. He paced his room at the Moon Grove Inn wondering what the best course of action would be. He'd attempted to solidify the barrier but it no longer seemed to rebuild itself. Time was running out. And once Eli Blackwood knew the truth the consequences could be catastrophic for him and he couldn't allow that to happen. He was involved in something far greater.

His hunger had also increased and it wouldn't be long before he'd need to feed again. Would he receive another gift from his benefactor? He hoped so, because without it he would go rogue and couldn't be held responsible for his actions, just like the night Charlene had died. His gang had drank from her and she had still been alive when it was his turn but once he tasted her he couldn't control himself. He had drained her to the very last drop and enjoyed it. He huffed out a silent chuckle. His friends had been sentenced to death by the council while he had gotten away scot-free. His charade of wanting to find out the truth was just a ploy to keep Sheriff Blackwood busy so that he didn't have time to form conflict strategies for the impending war. And it had worked.

A knock on the door startled him back to the present, his vampire senses distracted by the past, and he spun around. "Who's there?"

Rebecca's voice echoed through the door. "It's me. I have clean towels for you."

Zach stalked across the room, unhinged the security lock, opened the door, and held out his hands. "Thanks. I'll take them."

Rebecca dropped the towels onto his outstretched arms and studied his pale face with a frown. "Are you ok? You don't look so good."

He stared at her for a moment before answering. The thirst must have been stronger than he'd thought and he was losing the plot. "Uh. Sure. I'm fine." He stepped back to close the door.

"What about the dirty towels?"

"Is it ok if I drop them outside the door later?"

"I guess." Rebecca gave him a concerned stare then turned around and walked back down the hallway to the stairs. Something was definitely off with him.

Zach closed the door, dropped the bundle of towels into the chair beside it, and walked over to the mirror. She was right. He didn't look good. He needed more blood... and soon.

Once night had set in, Zach stepped out of his room, dropped the towels on the floor, closed the door behind him and stalked along the hallway, hands pushed into his jacket pockets. He'd received a text telling him to go up to the church to collect another bottle of fresh blood. Why that location? Couldn't they have delivered it to him like they had the previous time? As he reached the bottom of the stairs, he pulled his hoodie up over his head, crossed the entry hall and headed out the door.

Rebecca spotted him just as she finished setting the tables in the dining room for breakfast the next morning and decided to follow him. *What's he up to?* She whipped her light-weight jacket off the coat rack next to the front door, pulled it on and slipped outside. When she reached the sidewalk Zach had crossed the street heading in the direction of the church on the hill. *Why is he going up there?*

She waited a beat before stepping off the curb and continuing her pursuit. Keeping to the shadows, she tugged her cell phone from the pocket of her deep purple coat and pressed speed dial for Eli. "Hey, it's me. I'm following Zachary Ridgeway. He's heading up to the church."

"Why would he be going up there and why are you following him?" Eli got up from the kitchen table, crossed the living room and stepped out onto the front porch. Both Paige and Linda were already asleep and he didn't want to disturb them.

"I sensed something was wrong with him earlier."

"In what way?"

"He didn't seem like himself and that's why I'm keeping an eye on him."

"So what are you thinking?"

"I don't know. I just knew I needed to see where he was going."

Eli opened the front door, reached in and snatched the car keys off the table. "I'm on my way. Where are you?

"I'm almost at the bank."

"Wait there till I get to town."

"If I wait for you he might disappear."

"Then stay in touch and let me know where he ends up."

"He's still heading in that direction." She stopped at the Moon Grove Bank & Trust and peered around the corner of the red brick building. Zach had crossed the road and was on his way up the steep incline on Harper Street that led to the white church on the hill. Their church.

"Ok. Keep with him but be careful. I'll be there as soon as I can." Eli climbed into the four wheel drive, started the engine, spun the wheels in a gravel spray U-turn, and sped down the dirt drive and onto the main road that connected to the highway. He should be in Moon Grove in twenty minutes.

Eli swung the Jeep around the corner heading to Harper Street. He hadn't heard back from Rebecca and his gut told him something was wrong. He revved the four wheel drive up the steep incline, sped into the parking lot and pulled up about twenty feet from the double doors to the church, which were sitting wide open.

His eyes roamed the entire area before he stepped out of the vehicle. Where were Zach and Rebecca? He pulled his pistol, checked the clip, and eased his tall frame closer. The church was in darkness and his wolf hearing detected no sounds. He wanted to call out but knew if anyone was still in the building they would know he was there. They probably did already.

A shadow appeared in the doorway and Eli stopped short, raising his weapon. "Show yourself," he called out.

The figure was female. "I have your pet inside. Are you really intending to shoot a defenseless woman, Sheriff?" Yana stepped out into the moonlight, a smug smirk on her pale face.

"You're far from defenseless. Now show me."

"I believe we can make a trade."

"What are you talking about?" Eli kept his gun aimed at Yana's forehead and wouldn't hesitate to fire on her if he had to.

"You have Gregor. Do you not?" She took a step closer.

"Stop!"

"Very well."

"I don't have Gregor. Why would you think I do?"

"Because he went into town this morning to visit your girlfriend and has not returned to us."

Eight vampires emerged from the surrounding trees. Eli's eyes moved around the circle of immortals. He was outnumbered with no way of escape.

"Where's Zachary Ridgeway?"

Yana snapped her fingers and Zach appeared in the doorway holding Rebecca, who was bound and gagged, in front of him, his pale eyes glowing. "He is here, as you can see." Her glossy, deep red smile widened, exposing her canines. "I will release your bitch when you return Gregor to us."

Eli's gaze roamed the others around him. All male. "How do I know you'll keep your word."

Yana sauntered up to him. "Because I want my lover back. You give me what I want and I will give you what you want." She glanced over her shoulder at Rebecca.

"I don't have him but I might be able to find out where he is."

"Good. Make sure you do." She turned around and strutted back to the pair in the open doorway. "You have twenty four hours to fulfill my request." She walked up to Rebecca, brushed a pointed, black polished fingernail across her captive's cheek, drawing blood. "Or she dies."

FORTY FIVE

*S*o Zachary Ridgeway had been part of the council's plan all along. How could I have been so ignorant to the fact? Why hadn't I seen it or sensed it? Eli stalked into the police station, his wolf pack, minus one, waiting for him inside. "Thanks for coming on such short notice." He ran his gaze around the curious faces in the room. "We have a situation."

Bobby folded his arms, his butt planted on the corner of his desk. "What kind of situation?"

"The vampires have Rebecca."

"What?!" All voices chorused.

"She was doing some surveillance work and followed Zach up to the church only to be ambushed by Gregor's team."

"Why would they want her?" Paul asked, a concerned frown crossing his handsome face.

Eli sighed. "Because we have Gregor Petrov."

"When did this happen?" Ryan stepped up with hands on hips.

"This morning. He was in a session with Paige and mesmerized her and drank her blood then went into convulsions."

"I don't understand," Rosemarie said from behind her desk. "I thought Paige's blood would enhance a vampire's abilities."

"Yes, that would normally be true, Rosy... but... I initiated Paige so her Lycan genes are activated. Gregor thought she was still human and when he drank from her it poisoned him."

"Good." Bobby rounded his desk and plonked down in his chair. "One less bloodsucker to worry about." His gaze moved to his boss and he smiled. "Glad you finally stepped up as Alpha. Wasn't that difficult, was it?"

"Thanks, Bob, but you have no idea. Anyway, Gregor's not dead. Doc Hoskins has him over at his surgery. I asked him to do what he can to keep him alive."

"Why would you do that?" Cooper asked. "He's the enemy."

"For the very reason we're here. They have Rebecca and plan to kill her if I don't deliver him to them in the next twenty four..." Eli glanced at his watch. "Twenty two hours and twenty five minutes." He paced, stopped and turned around. "And there's one more thing... Zachary Ridgeway is working with the council. His wanting to find out the truth about Charlene's death was a ruse to keep me busy, I think, so that my headspace was elsewhere and not in the upcoming battle."

All voices bombarded him at once – Bobby saying I knew it. Rosemarie saying I never trusted him from the beginning. Paul saying we need to end him? Ryan asking how didn't any of us pick up on that? Cooper saying I want to be part of the pack.

Eli raised his hands. "I know. I know. Let's just focus on getting Bec back. Ok?" His eyes moved to his young deputy. "Do you, Cooper? Do you really want to be part of our pack?"

The young man nodded. "You bet. I want to help you, Sheriff Blackwood."

"Maybe you should give it some more thought."

"Nope. Don't need to. It's all I've been thinking about."

Everyone's eyes moved to him.

"What?" He shrugged. "Don't ya'll think it's a natural progression? I'm already on your team."

"Cooper, you're a lovely young man. Wouldn't you prefer to stay human, get married one day, have kids?" Rosemarie asked.

"Why? I don't have any family... except all of you. I can be of use. I'm strong and healthy and I really want to do this. Besides, I can still marry and have kids. Bobby has." He turned to look at Eli. "What do ya say, boss?"

"If I do what you ask, Cooper, there's no turning back. You're sure about your decision?" Eli walked over to him.

"I'm sure, Sheriff."

Eli's eyes roamed the faces of his pack. "What do you think?"

"We could use another pack member," Bobby said. "We're down one with Craig being killed."

"Bobby's right, Eli." Ryan told him. "We could use a couple more."

"Agreed," Paul said.

Eli's gaze moved to Rosemarie. "What about you, Rosy? How do you feel about it? You seemed to have reservations."

"Oh, well, I guess if it's what he wants then he has to do it."

Eli turned to his deputy. "You'll need to remain in a holding cell until the change is complete."

Cooper stepped up to him. "That's fair. I wouldn't want to go all animal on anyone. When can we do it?"

"Right now, if you want."

The deputy swallowed hard. "Oh. Sure. Ok. Let's do it."

Eli looked at Bobby. "Can you prep the cell for Cooper?"

"Sure thing, boss." Bobby crossed the office and stepped through the door to the back of the station.

"Paul, I want you to pay Doc Hoskins a visit. Take Ryan with you just to be safe. See if there has been any improvement with Gregor and find out if there's anything we can do to speed up the process. He needs to be on his feet when I take him out to the cabin."

"On it." Paul headed to the front door, but before leaving he turned around and said, "Good luck, Cooper. Welcome to the pack."

"Yeah," Ryan said. "Welcome to our pack." He and Paul headed out the door.

"Cooper? Why don't you go out back to Bobby? I'll be there in a minute."

"Sure. Ok." Cooper made his way out to the cell block.

Eli glanced across at Rosemarie. "Why don't you go on home, Rosy? There's nothing more you can do here for now."

Rosemarie picked up her purse and came around the partition. "Look after Cooper, Eli."

He rubbed her arm. "I will. You have my word."

"Goodnight then." She crossed the station to the office door but before leaving turned around. "He's young and impressionable. I hope he knows what he's getting himself into."

"He'll be fine, Rosy. I promise."

Rosemarie nodded, opened the door and stepped out onto the porch.

Eli gave a heavy sigh and headed out back.

Bobby was outside the second cell when Eli came in. Cooper was already naked beneath a dark blue robe because once the change occurred and he shifted into wolf form his clothes would be decimated.

The sheriff stepped up to the bars. "You're one hundred percent sure about this, Cooper?"

His young deputy nodded. "Yes, sir, I am."

"Ok. Come over here and pull up your sleeve."

"What are you gonna do?"

"All it takes is a scratch or a bite." Eli's eyes glowed yellow and his right hand elongated, along with his nails.

"Wow! Will I be able to do that? Go part wolf, I mean."

"Not at first, but with time and practice, yes, you will." He reached for Cooper's arm and nicked the flesh with one, sharp black claw. "You'll feel weak and dizzy at first. Then your body will begin to change. Your bones will extend, joints will shift, and your muscles will be stretched to their limit. I won't lie to you, Cooper, it's a painful process. But like Bobby said that day in the woods it does get easier to handle over time."

"I understand. So we can change at will?"

"Our particular pack can. Some can't. Some are governed by the full moon."

"Wow!"

"Bobby will stay with you while you go through the change. Once the shift is complete and you're in wolf form, he'll bring you some raw meat. It's essential that you eat it for strength."

Cooper nodded again. "Ok."

"How're you feeling?" Eli folded his arms.

"So far so good."

Eli turned to his deputy. "Bobby, keep a close eye on him and keep me up to date, ok?"

"Yep, will do."

The sheriff left the cell block and headed to his car still berating himself for not picking up on Zach's deception. It had cost them time they didn't have.

When Eli stepped through the front door Paige was sitting on the sofa waiting for him. He closed the door, dropped the keys onto the small table, walked over and sat down beside her. "What are you doing up?"

"I heard you drive out of here like the devil was on your tail and I couldn't get back to sleep knowing something was wrong." She stared into his eyes. "Something is wrong, isn't it?"

Eli gave a heavy sigh. "Yeah. The vampires have Rebecca."

"What?!" She reached for his hand and gave it a firm squeeze of support. "How did that happen?"

"Zach."

Paige frowned. "I don't understand. What has he got to do with it?"

"He's been playing with us… well, with me at least. He's working with Remus and the other vampires. It appears he lured Bec up to the church and they captured her."

"Oh, Eli."

"Yeah. Yana gave me an ultimatum – return Gregor or Rebecca dies."

"What are you going to do?"

"The only thing I can do. Give her what she wants otherwise she'll kill Bec."

"Is he doing any better?"

"The last time I spoke to the Doc, Gregor was semi stable but still unconscious."

"If Yana and the others find out he's been poisoned they'd think it was deliberate."

"Yes, they would. But they won't find out."

"How can you be so sure?"

"Who's going to tell them? Not anyone in our pack or Doc Hoskins." Eli stood up and headed to the kitchen. "Want some coffee?"

"No, thanks." Paige followed him over. "I can't sleep as it is."

"Could be the Lycan genes kicking in. We don't need as much sleep as humans do."

"Oh? I didn't know that." She folded her arms over her pink robe. "That explains a lot then."

"It'll take some time for your body to adjust. Just try to go with it. Makes it easier." Eli's gaze moved to the hallway. "Linda asleep?"

"I think so. I didn't check but there's been no movement."

Eli set down his mug and walked over to her. Brushing stray strands of hair from her face he smiled and said, "Want to fool around?"

"I'd..."

At that moment, his cell phone chimed. "Dammit."

When Paul and Ryan reached Doc Hoskins' medical practice the place was in total darkness. Both men gave each other an uneasy frown and climbed out of the car, leaving the doors open. If the doctor was inside monitoring the vampire then why weren't the lights on? Paul stood in silence and used his super sensitive hearing to see if he could pick up any sounds within the building. Nothing. "That's odd." His dubious gaze moved to his companion and he whispered, "Something's not right here."

"Yeah, I'm with you on that one," Ryan said, his eyes also roaming the dark building.

Paul tugged his cell from the pocket of his dark blue work pants, keyed in the surgery number and pressed the phone to his ear. The line rang out and no message bank kicked in.

"Anything?"

"No. Not even a voice message." He took his police issue revolver from the glove compartment, checked the clip, and he and Ryan made their way to the front entrance along the narrow side street. As the pair got closer to the glass door they could see the receptionist's body lying on the floor in a pool of blood just inside. "Here." Paul shoved his weapon into Ryan's hands, raised his pants leg and unclipped a small pistol from a holster at his ankle. "Can never be too careful these days."

Ryan's stomach flipped over as his eyes met the scene before him. The receptionist's throat had been ripped out. There was no point in checking for a pulse. Her staring eyes told him she was dead. If he didn't know better, he'd have thought another wolf did this. "Where's the Doc?"

"Good question. Let's move in as quietly as possible. Gregor could still be somewhere inside. Not having a heartbeat makes it difficult to pinpoint him."

Ryan nodded, his serious gaze meeting Paul's, the weapon gripped tight in his hand. "Silver?" he asked, raising the pistol.

"You bet. Never leave home without it anymore." Paul went in ahead of him. "Stay close to me and if anything moves shoot first ask questions later."

"What if it's the Doc?"

"By the look of things he's either dead or turned. So, like I said, shoot first. Got it?"

"Yeah. Got it."

Another body lay beside the reception desk. Male. Possibly a patient or another doctor who worked at the clinic. Paul leaned down and pressed two fingers into the guy's bloody carotid artery. No pulse. He ran his bloodstained fingers down his pants leg and the pair continued moving through the dark, their nocturnal vision scanning every inch of the corridor and open doorways. So far no sign of the vampire or the doctor.

"Let's try the emergency room down the back," Paul whispered, motioning with his head.

Ryan nodded and remained close.

When the pair reached the double doors, Paul eased one back and peered into the unlit space. Still no sign of life. He stepped into the room, Ryan at his back, and ran his wolf eyes around the chaos. Doc Hoskins was on his back, arms spread wide, eyes staring upward, his pale face in an agonized grimace.

Paul crossed the room while Ryan stood at the open doorway, gun raised, peering over his shoulder along the corridor. If anything moved he *would* shoot.

Squatting down, Paul checked for a pulse, although he knew it was pointless. Doc Hoskins was dead and Gregor was gone.

Eli listened to everything Paul told him before speaking. Doc Hoskins' medical practice had been turned upside down and his staff killed. The Doc was dead and Gregor had disappeared. "Call the crime scene cleanup crew and get them over there ASAP. We can't have regular patients turning up there in the morning to witness what happened. I think I have a good idea where Gregor has gone. I'm going to get Archer Hamilton to go out there with me. Get everyone together at the station and I'll be there as soon as I can."

Paige frowned up into his honey colored eyes. "Please don't go out there without backup, Eli. There are too many of them now."

He touched her cheek with gentle fingers. "I won't do anything stupid. I promise. I just want Archer to tell me if Gregor made it back there. If not, we need to find him fast.

Maybe your blood changed him into a rampaging monster. By the description Paul gave me it's more than likely."

Paige gasped. "Could that happen?"

"If it didn't kill him, which it hasn't, then it's changed him. He's a threat to our town and has to be stopped."

"What can I do to help?"

Eli drew her close and held her. "Wake Linda up and wait for my call."

Paige nodded. "Ok." She stepped out of his embrace. "Please be careful."

FORTY SIX

Archer Hamilton was on the street when Eli screeched into the curb and threw the door open from inside. "Get in, we have no time."

The editor climbed into the four wheel drive and closed the door. "You think he's gone out to the cabin?"

"I'm hoping he has, otherwise I have no idea where he is. We can't have him roaming Moon Grove attacking the residents." Eli stepped on the gas and hurtled along the road.

"So you think Paige's blood had caused some kind of reaction?"

"Yes, I do. From what Paul told me about the scene at Doc Hoskins', Gregor has gone rogue. Or worse."

"I thought Paige's blood was meant to enhance our abilities, make us stronger." A nervous quiver trembled through his gut. Would he become a monster like Gregor?

"That was before."

"Before what?"

"I initiated her into our pack." Eli thought it would feel good telling his rival that he'd lost her but it didn't. They had come to respect each other.

"Oh, I see." Paige had made her choice then. "It's no secret that Lycan blood is poisonous to us just the same as vampire venom is poisonous to you."

"Except Gregor had no idea Paige had turned."

Archer sat bolt upright in his seat. "What if he goes out there and attacks his team?"

Eli frowned at the editor. "Why would he?"

"If he's as crazed as you believe he is then he could. Rogue vampires don't care whose blood they drink."

"That would be the answer to our prayers. There would be no war." Eli pressed the accelerator to the floor.

"We might need some help out there." Archer folded his arms.

"Let's see if my instincts are correct first. Once we know for sure we can call the others. I say let nature take its course, if Gregor does attack his team, then we'll deal with him afterward."

When Eli reached the location of the cabin he turned off the headlights, pulled his Jeep into the scrub so it was out of sight, and pocketed the keys. He wasn't giving the vampire any chance to escape. He checked his weapon and re-holstered it before heading to the house hidden in the trees, Archer beside him.

"When we get closer, you wait in the trees like last time while I take a look around," the editor told him. "I can circle the house in seconds without him knowing I'm there."

"That might've been before he changed. What if he senses you're outside?"

"Let's hope he's too preoccupied with massacring his team."

"Be careful, Archer."

"Hey, that's the first time you've called me by my actual name. We're progressing."

"I'm serious."

"I'll only be a few seconds." He evaporated into the night like a shadow.

Eli's cell vibrated in his pocket and he snatched it out. "What is it, Paige?" he whispered.

"I brought the cavalry. We're at your Jeep."

"How did you know where to find me?"

"Yana told me about this place while she had me captive. Because she planned to kill me I guess she didn't think it would matter."

"Who's with you?"

"Bobby, Linda, Cooper, Ryan, Paul and Nathan the local vet."

"Why did you bring Nathan with you?"

"He has a tranquilizer gun. I thought it could be useful. And he can administer first aid if necessary."

"Ok. You're right. He could come in handy. Just stay put until we know if Gregor's here."

"We will."

Archer rocketed toward him like a dark blur. "He's been here but he's long gone."

"What about his team?"

"They're all dead. Torn limb from limb." He passed the Lycan tome to Eli. "This belongs to you, I believe."

Eli took the book and ran his eyes over the worn leather cover. "Thanks. I wonder where he could be."

Archer's serious gaze met his. "I don't know. There's something else I need to tell you, Eli."

The sheriff frowned. "What is it?"

"Zach's body's in there."

Eli's eyes widened. "And Rebecca?"

He nodded. "I'm sorry."

Tears stung the back of Eli's eyes and rage burned inside him. "We need to find him… *now*." He turned on his heel and stalked back to his car and the others. "Listen up. Gregor's killed his team along with Zach… and Bec."

"What?!" everyone said.

"He's a serious threat to our town. We need to split up and comb every inch of Moon Grove until we find him."

"I have four tranquilizer pistols in my car. If we break up into four groups of two we can each take one and if we do find him we can knock him out, take him to the police station, and lock him in a cell," the vet suggested.

"Thanks for offering to help, Nathan. I appreciate it." Eli's eyes moved around his team. "Let's get organized. We need to find Gregor before he kills someone else. And remember to keep your distance. Radio in if you locate him."

Gregor climbed the curved, ornate concrete steps up to the front landing and stopped outside the double black doors. He pressed his ear to the glossy wood and listened. Nothing. The council members wouldn't be in repose as it was early morning and still dark out. Where were they? He had a score to settle with Remus for what he'd done. He had lied to him about the O'Connell woman's blood and now he was transforming into a monster not a super warrior.

He reached for the handle, gave it a sharp twist, tossed it to one side and eased the door back, taking in the dark interior before stepping across the threshold. Gregor stood in silence and used his immortal hearing and senses to find the members. They had to be here. They never ventured out often. He stalked across the entry hall and slid open the double doors to the library. Empty. A sound somewhere in the mansion caught his attention and he swung around. *Where was that? Upstairs?*

He listened for the sound again. *There!*

Gregor flew up the carpeted staircase and dropped onto the landing. His eyes roamed the shadows. There were three doors on either side of the hallway on this level. Were they hiding somewhere on this floor? He moved along the passage without a sound, stopping at each door and leaning in to listen for sounds from inside before swinging the door open. No one. He retraced his steps and took the second staircase up to the next level. The mansion also had an extensive attic and cellar which he would explore if he found no one up here.

A creaking floorboard caused his ears to prick up and he eased his tall frame along the hallway to where the sound had emanated from. A satisfied smile spread across his bloodied face and his clawed hand moved to the ornate, white knob. The door was locked. A guttural growl rumbled from his chest and he raised his size fourteen boot and kicked it in, splintered wood flying everywhere, and stormed into the room.

Eli cruised the street, his nocturnal vision searching for any sign of movement on the deserted streets, Paige in the passenger seat beside him. It was after three in the morning and none of his team had spotted Gregor. Had he left Moon Grove? Eli didn't think so. So where was he? Bobby radioed in to say he and Linda had done a thorough sweep of the south side of the town with no results. Paul and Ryan had also radioed in to say they had seen nothing to the north. Archer and Nathan hadn't yet checked in, but Eli had given the directive to everyone to keep looking. Gregor couldn't be allowed to murder anyone else in their town or to escape.

"He has to be somewhere," Paige rationalized. "Where would he be likely to go?"

"That's a good question. Maybe we should think like a deranged vampire on the loose." He gave her a thin, unamused grin.

"Hey, that's not a bad idea. Who did he associate with here?" Her psychiatrist rationalizing technique kicked in.

Eli thought about the question for a moment. "No one, as far as I know." A sudden look of awareness crossed the sheriff's face. "Unless he went up to the mansion."

Paige frowned. "You mean the council's home?"

"I can't think of anywhere else, can you?" Eli got onto his radio. "Meet me at the council manor ASAP." He swung the Jeep around.

"Do you really think he'd be there? Wouldn't Remus and the others finish him off?"

"It would depend on how strong he's become. Despite not wanting him to gain strength from your blood it appears that he has, since he turned rogue, so anything is possible."

The sheriff and his team converged on the mansion at the same time, cars skidding to a halt on the front lawn of the extensive grounds. Eli threw open the door of his four wheel drive and climbed out, his team joining him in front of his car. "Gregor could be inside. We need to be prepared for a fight because he won't give up easily and there'll be no way to reason with him. I don't think the tranquilizer guns are the answer here so this is a shoot to kill situation. Understood?"

Everyone nodded.

"How do you wanna do this, boss?" Cooper asked.

"I think we need to go in front and rear and try to take him by surprise. Watch your backs, and remember shoot to kill."

Eli's team dispersed. Bobby, Linda and Nathan heading around back, Paul, Ryan and Archer following Eli and Paige up to the front entrance.

The doors stood wide open and when the sheriff and his group reached them Eli knew Gregor was still inside. He turned around. "All senses on high alert. Ok, let's go."

Gregor gripped the shirt collar of the man cowering in the closet and yanked him out into the room. "Where is Remus and the others?"

The old man's body shivered in the vampire's grasp and his voice quivered. "I – I don't know."

"Do not lie to me." Gregor raised him into the air.

"Why would they tell me? I – I'm just a servant."

"You are more than that, Roger, so tell me the truth and I will let you live."

"I swear I don't know where they are."

"I do not believe you." Gregor shook the manservant with such force his neck snapped with a sickening crack. "Ugh." He tossed the body onto the carpet, turned and stalked out of the room and headed for the stairs to the storage area in the ceiling. *Remus must be up there.* He thrust open the attic door, his menacing gaze roaming the narrow, wooden staircase before taking that first step. Gregor climbed the treads with caution his ears listening for any movement above him. All was quiet.

"Remus, show yourself." An amused smirk crossed his distorted features. "I know you are up here." He reached the top of the staircase and stepped onto the dusty wooden floor, his eyes searching the shadows in the ceiling. "You will not escape my wrath for what you have done to me." He could feel the monster inside him clawing its way out. "Remus!" He whipped around the moonlit space, knocking over furniture and other items covered with gray, dust ridden sheets. They were not there.

Gregor flew down the stairs and through the open doorway into the hall; Eli shot him with a silver bullet in the shoulder. The Russian's knees folded beneath him, black blood spreading across the chest of his white T-shirt, and he went down. Eli fired off another shot. It hit the vampire in the other shoulder. "That's for Rebecca."

A smile spread across Gregor's face and he coughed out a laugh. "You think silver can kill me now?"

"Probably not. But taking off your head will." Eli turned to his pack members. "Shackle him and load him into the wagon. We'll take him into the woods and do what needs to be done." He returned his gaze to the Russian. "Where's Remus?"

"I do not know. If I did he would be *dead*."

"Get him out of here." Eli watched Paul and Ryan haul Gregor down the staircase, Bobby and Cooper behind them.

"Archer, can you sense anyone in the house?"

"I've already tried. Remus and the others are not here."

The sheriff frowned. "I wonder where they are."

"Someone must've warned them," the editor said.

"Yeah, it seems that way. But no one knew?"

"Someone must have."

Paige came up the stairs and walked over to the pair. "I thought it was a shoot to kill situation. Why is he being taken into custody?"

"I felt the need to hurt him for what he did to Bec. Besides, silver won't kill him it appears."

"He's cunning, Eli. What if he escapes?"

"He won't. We're taking him out into the woods and beheading him. Then we'll burn the remains."

"When?"

"Now. This is finished." He headed toward the stairs then turned around. "Coming?"

Archer motioned for Paige to go ahead of him and followed her and Eli down the staircase. Linda and Nathan were standing at the bottom of the stairs. Just as the trio reached the lower level, Cooper staggered into the entry hall covered in blood and collapsed on the floor.

The group raced over to him and Eli knelt down and lifted his deputy's head onto his lap. "What happened?"

Cooper gasped and blood spilled from the corner of his mouth. "He – he got away."

"Where are the others?"

A single tear slid down the young man's cheek. "They're…"

Eli's head snapped up and his eyes moved to the open doors. NO!

FORTY SEVEN

A couple of days after Gregor's escape, Archer entered the station with three men and asked to speak to the sheriff. Rosemarie walked across to the closed door and knocked. "Eli? Mr. Hamilton's here to see you." Her eyes returned to the four standing on the other side of her desk then back to the door. "Eli?" She reached for the handle but the door opened.

"I heard you, Rosy."

"Oh?" She gave him an unsure smile. "Ok. Did you want them to come through?"

"Sheriff. I need to speak with you."

"All right, come on in."

Archer opened the partition gate and motioned for the three to step in ahead of him then followed them over to Eli's office. Once inside, the sheriff closed the door leaving Rosemarie in reception alone. Cooper was in the hospital over in Bellehurst and the other members of the pack were in the County Coroner's office. Tears slipped down the receptionist's face and she swiped at them with her handkerchief. *Bobby, Paul, Ryan and Rebecca. Gone.*

How could this happen? Her sad eyes moved around the empty space.

The door opened and Paige stepped into the station. "Hi, Rosemarie. How are you doing?"

"Not so good. We've lost some good people because of that vampire, a vampire the council brought to our town." She sniffled, and another tear slipped down her cheek. "I don't know what to do with myself, Paige. My heart aches so bad right now."

Paige came around the desk and wrapped her arms around her. "I know. I feel the same. It all seems like a horrible dream."

Rosemarie nodded and wiped her face. "Yes, it does."

"Eli in his office?"

"He's got Mr. Hamilton and some other men in there with him, hon."

"Oh? Do you know who they are?" Paige's gaze moved to the glass office, the vertical blinds drawn so no one could see in. New vampires in town?

"I don't. He didn't say who they were."

"That's ok. Eli will probably tell us later." She gave the woman a thin smile. "Are you free right now?"

The receptionist's puffy eyes moved to the wall clock. It was 10.30 AM. "Well, it's morning tea time so I guess so. Why?"

"I thought we could go grab a coffee and get you out of here for a while. What do you say?"

Rosemarie blinked back more tears threatening to spill. "I'd like that."

"Good. Grab whatever you need and let's go. We'll pop the closed sign on the door for a bit."

As she and Rosemarie stepped out onto the porch, Paige glanced back through the glass door. What was Archer up to?

Archer pointed to the vampires beside him. "This is my brother, Max. And these guys are Blake and Christopher."

"Good to meet you. We need to find Gregor Petrov and rip him apart." The bitterness in the sheriff's voice didn't go unnoticed by his visitors.

"Do you think he's still nearby?" Max asked, a look of skepticism crossing his face.

"Yes, I do. I think he'll want to finish what he started with the council."

"Have you located Remus?" Archer folded his arms.

"Not yet. But it's only a matter of time. They can't have gone far."

"So you don't think they'd abandon Moon Grove to save their own skins?"

"They've been here too long. They believe they own this town, so, no, I don't."

"Ok. Could someone be hiding them?"

Eli nodded. "Yeah. But who and where... I have no idea right now."

"Can we help?"

"Do you think you could pick up their scent or vibration or whatever it is that you do?"

Archer thought about the question for a moment. "They're ancients. Might be more difficult to trace, but I'm happy to give it a try."

The sheriff's gaze moved to the three vampires beside the editor. "Are you prepared to hunt Gregor down and send me intel when you've found him?"

The trio nodded. "Hell, yeah," Max said. "After everything that's happened you should be the one to end him."

"Yeah, I should." He looked at Archer. "If you want to do a sweep of the town and see what you can pick up that would be appreciated." He returned his gaze to Max. "When do you want to get started?"

"How does right now sound?" Max's eyes moved to his companions and they nodded.

"Now sounds perfect." Eli stood up and shook Max's and the other two vampire's hands. "Thank you."

"Don't mention it. No one's safe with a feral vampire on the loose." Max, Blake and Christopher headed for the door. "We'll be in touch."

"Ok. Be safe."

Archer hung back. "I'll let you know if I get something."

"Thanks." Eli walked him to the door and noticed the office was empty. "Looks like Rosy's gone out for a bit." He understood why.

"Yes." The editor crossed reception and opened the door. "I'll keep you posted."

"Archer."

"Yeah?"

"Thank you."

"I haven't done anything yet."

"You know what I mean."

He nodded, gave Eli a smile, and stepped through the door.

Eli's office phone rang and he rushed back in and snatched the handset off its base. "Moon Grove County Sheriff's Office, Sheriff Blackwood speaking."

"Sheriff, it's Remus. Have you found Gregor Petrov yet?"

"Where are you?"

"You didn't answer my question."

"No. We haven't found him yet. Where are you?"

"That is privileged information, Sheriff, and you don't need to know."

"How do you expect me to keep you safe if I don't know where you are?"

"We are in good hands and are perfectly fine. The fewer people that know our whereabouts the better."

He had a point.

"Someone warned you to get out of the mansion. Who was it?"

"Eli, you should know by now we have many resources."

"Come on, Remus, tell me who it was. Do I have a mole?"

The vampire coughed out a laugh. "Always." The line went quiet for several seconds. "I am sorry for your loss, Sheriff. Despite our differences, they were good men."

"Men you wanted dead, don't forget. And don't change the subject. Craig was working for you... so who else?"

"It was Zachary Ridgeway."

"Couldn't have been. He was already dead out at the cabin." Archer Hamilton popped into Eli's head. "Is it the new editor?"

"We have nothing to do with that Hamilton fellow."

"Stop playing games with me, Remus. Just tell me who it is."

"Don't worry yourself over matters that do not concern you. I am not going to divulge my source, so let it rest."

The sheriff wanted to know who on his team is or was the mole. "I want to know and I want to know now, otherwise I'll send Gregor right to your door."

Remus made a sound similar to a chuckle, but Eli knew he didn't find anything amusing. "And how do you plan to do that when you have no idea where we are?"

"You could be mistaken about that." Eli ended the call leaving Remus to ponder what he'd just said. He'd set up a trace on his laptop as soon as he knew it was the council leader on the phone and had kept him talking long enough to find out where he and the others were.

FORTY EIGHT

Paige and Rosemarie walked along the tree-lined street heading back to the police station. They had had a nice time drinking coffee and eating blueberry scones at the local diner and it had taken their minds off their current situation, at least for a short while. When they stepped into reception, Eli was just coming out of the door to the small kitchen out back with a mug of coffee in his hand. "Enjoy your break?"

Rosemarie rushed through the partition gate and up to him. "Eli, I'm sorry I went out without telling you, but you were busy."

Eli wrapped an arm around his plump receptionist and gave her a tight squeeze. "You don't have to square it with me before going on a break, Rosy. It's all good."

"That's a relief. I mean, I did leave the station unmanned and all."

"Not an issue. Hope you had a good time. Lord knows we all deserve it after everything that's happened." Eli headed to his office door then turned around. "Oh, Paige, can I see you for a minute?"

"Of course." She smiled at Rosemarie and followed him into his office.

Eli sat down behind his desk. "Close the door, would you?"

Paige's right eyebrow arched and she did what he asked. "What's going on?" She crossed the office and perched herself on the edge of the chair in front of his desk.

"We have a mole."

"We do? How do you know?"

"Remus called…"

"Where are they?"

"I'll get to that. He told me someone tipped him off and that's how they were able to get out before Gregor arrived at the mansion."

"Did he tell you who it was?"

"He wouldn't. He lied and said it was Zach but he was already dead."

"Do you have any suspicions?"

"None. I'd hate to think it was Bobby or Paul or Ryan or even Rebecca. It wouldn't be Cooper, that I know."

"Oh, Eli, surely it wouldn't have been any of them. They loved you too much."

"Yeah, I know. But money speaks louder than words sometimes. And Remus would pay well for information."

Paige eased her rigid spine against the backrest. "I can't believe it would've been one of them."

"I thought it might have been Archer Hamilton, but Remus said he doesn't know him."

"How can we know who to trust then?"

Eli sighed. "I don't know. Remus said there are always spies in the camp."

"Meaning?"

"He has eyes and ears everywhere."

"I still won't believe it was Bobby or Rebecca or…"

"If it wasn't one of them then we still have a mole in our midst."

She hated to say it, she even hated to think it, but if Eli was sure it wasn't Cooper then Linda was the only one left. "What about Linda?"

Eli's serious gaze met hers. "I was just wondering the same thing."

"Well, she did work for Mayor Redmond and he was involved with the council. Maybe she was leaking information back to them from Ross's office too."

"It's possible. Although I'd like to think it wasn't her."

"She told me she was Wendy Eli's informant."

Eli frowned. "She did? When?"

"When she first started working for me."

Eli was silent for some time, allowing the information to sink in.

"You said you knew where Remus was?"

"Yeah, but I'll keep that under wraps for now."

Paige frowned into his eyes. "You're not thinking I could be the mole, are you?"

"Of course not, sweetheart, but if I'm the only one who knows then it can't cause any problems, can it?" All of a sudden, he wasn't sure who he could trust. Paige had been abducted and who knew what the vampires did to her while they had her. Linda seemed the likely candidate, but he wasn't going to share information with anyone until he knew for sure.

Archer circled back and did another sweep of the town. He hadn't picked up any residual vibrations or scent so where had the council members disappeared to without a trace? He pressed the Bluetooth button on his console and called Eli's cell. "Hi, Eli, it's me. I don't have anything to report. I couldn't find any trace of Remus or the others."

"Thanks for trying. I appreciate it. Have you heard anything from your brother?"

"No, but I don't think they've had enough time yet. And I'm sure he'll call you before he calls me."

"We need to find Gregor as soon as possible. Now that he's murdered his team he might be considering creating a new one and we all know what that would mean."

The editor's forehead wrinkled into a deep frown. "You're right. I'll give Max a call and see if he's found anything. Let me call you back."

"Sure."

Archer pressed speed dial for his brother's number. "Hey, it's me. Any luck?"

"We're heading out on the highway to that abandoned medical center. Gregor was injured, right?"

"Yes, he was. Eli shot him twice with silver."

"Ouch!"

"Yeah, but it had no effect on him. He was injured of course."

"Then it could be the perfect place for him to hide. It's well out of the way of anywhere from what I saw on the map and there's bound to be old medical supplies out there. He'd need to keep the wounds clean until they healed."

"Yeah, depending on how fast he does heal now. Be careful. Don't get too close. And call the sheriff as soon as you find anything."

"Will do."

Archer ended the call and pressed redial. "Max is on his way out to that abandoned medical center you went to when Paige was missing. He thinks Gregor might've gone out there to lay low for a while and heal."

Eli jolted out of his seat. "It would be the perfect hiding place for him right now. I'm on my way. Meet me out there."

"Ok. I'll see you soon."

Paige frowned at Eli. "What was that all about?"

"Archer's brother thinks he knows where Gregor's hiding."

"Are you going there?"

"You heard what I told Archer." He rounded his desk. "Are you coming?"

FORTY NINE

Eli rough-roaded the Jeep over the broken concrete drive and pulled up beside the black, Ford e350 parked in front of the double doors of the abandoned medical center. His mind wandered back to when he and Brent had come out here and the thought crossed his mind about where Paige's brother might be right now. He hadn't been in touch for a while and Eli hoped he and his mother were ok. Archer's brother, Max, climbed out through the jagged glass hole to meet him. "Hey, Eli, Archer said you were on your way." He ran his gaze around the deserted, unused street. "Where is he?"

"He said he'd meet me out here so he shouldn't be too far off. Find anything inside?"

"Nothing so far, but we haven't been here long."

Eli spotted Blake and Christopher standing just inside the doors.

Paige stepped out of the four wheel drive, rounded the hood, and stood beside him. Extending her hand she said, "We haven't met. I'm Paige."

"Good to meet you. I'm Max, Archer's brother." He turned to look at the broken doors. "And those two are

Blake on the left and Chris on the right." Both gave her a brief wave.

Paige roamed Max's face. "Yes, I can see the resemblance."

"Hey, don't hold that against me." He winked and grinned.

At that moment, Archer's Mercedes convertible pulled up at the end of the driveway. Not the kind of car you'd force over debris. He walked up to the group. "Ready to go in?"

"Yeah. We were just waiting for you and getting acquainted." Max turned on his heel and stepped back through the broken door.

Eli motioned for Paige to go ahead of him then followed her in, Archer behind them.

Max looked at Eli. "You've been here before, right?"

"Yeah, when Paige was abducted. We thought it'd be a good place to hide someone. Turned out she wasn't here."

"So you'd have a fair idea of the layout of the place." Max ran his eyes around the gloom. "Where do you wanna start?"

"Maybe check the ER first to see if Gregor has been here to tend his wounds. If we find something then I suggest we head underground. I've been doing a bit of research and it appears he'll go through further changes before his metamorphosis is complete."

Paige stepped closer to Eli. "What kind of changes?" she asked, a quiver in her voice. She might be a wolf, but right now she still felt human.

"The only way I can describe it is like Dr. Banner morphing into The Hulk."

"So in other words we're dealing with a monster?" Archer frowned.

"Yes. And a dangerous one. We need to keep our distance because a bite from a creature like him will kill... instantly." Eli wasn't looking forward to the face to face confrontation but had no choice, they needed to end him before he turned or killed anyone else.

"Any idea how to kill him?" Blake asked.

"He laughed at me when I shot him with silver bullets. He said silver wouldn't kill him and he was right."

"I guess the only way to finish him would be decapitation." Max glanced over his shoulder. *Did I just hear something?*

Eli noticed. "What is it?"

Max shook his head. "Just spooking myself, I think."

"Did you hear something?" Eli stood with hands on hips, his eyes moving in the same direction.

"Nah, like I said, just spooking myself."

"Ok. Let's stay together and head to the ER. And keep your wits about you. If Gregor is here we need to find him before he finds us." Eli led the way.

The ER still had some old medical equipment and cabinets filled with ampules, injections, bandages and other surgical items in it, the cubicles were empty of all gurneys except the first one. Eli crossed the room and when he reached the curtained rectangle he found bloodstained gauze, an open bottle of antiseptic and two, bloody silver slugs lying in a kidney bowl along with a pair of tweezers. "He's been here."

"Maybe he kept moving," Paige said, hoping she was right.

"He'd need to stay out of sight for a while until the wounds healed."

"Eli, he was strong enough to... to kill some of our pack. What makes you think he'd need to hide out until he recovered from the gunshots?" Paige had the feeling Eli was underestimating Gregor.

"No supernatural creature heals instantly. He has to be here resting somewhere."

"So where do you wanna start?" Max crossed the room, eyeing the bloodied equipment sitting on the gurney.

"Downstairs. I doubt he'd be up here."

"Is there more than one way out? We really don't want to be trapped down there with a crazed, rogue vampire."

"Unfortunately, no. The other doors at the end of the corridor have been blocked with a mountain of dirt from the outside. The stairs are it. There's an elevator but with no power..."

Max nodded. "Ok. How do you want to play this one out?"

"We stay together. We check each area downstairs including the morgue fridges. He doesn't need to breathe so it would be the best concealment while he's healing, and if he is in one of them we'll have him. He won't be able to get out."

"Which way?"

"This way."

The five followed Eli to the stairs he had taken the last time he'd been here.

Vampires could see perfectly in the dark, werewolves only so much. Eli pulled a small LED flashlight from his jeans pocket, flicked it on and handed it to Paige. The group moved with caution through the gloom, checking every open door and crevice they could find until they reached the morgue. Eli turned around, his voice low. "If he's anywhere it has to be in one of the fridges. We've looked everywhere else."

Archer stepped up to him. "If he is, what do you plan to do?"

The sheriff thought for a moment. "He'll be trapped, so we need to take off his head. Anything else might not work."

"I was thinking setting him on fire in there." Max smirked.

"Vampires have been known to survive being burned, and, besides, he's a different kind of creature now who knows what he can withstand." Archer roamed the dark space with his nocturnal vision.

"My brother is right. If silver couldn't touch him..."

"Ok. Then we need the axe. It's in the trunk of the Jeep." Eli glanced along the shadowed corridor to the stairwell.

"I can go," Paige offered.

"No. It's not safe."

"You said yourself you didn't think he'd be upstairs. I'll be ok. And it won't take that long. I'll be back before you miss me."

"I'll come with you," Archer said.

Eli's gaze darted to him. Was that a bolt of jealousy pulsing through his veins? "No. I'll go."

"I'll be fine." Paige turned and headed back along the corridor. Just as she reached the stairwell Gregor pounced on her his large fingers wrapping around her throat.

"NO!" Eli shouted. "Let her go."

A deep, throaty chuckle escaped the misshapen vampire's lips. "I am no fool, Eli Blackwood." Gregor leaned in and sniffed Paige's throat. "She smells so good. And look what her blood has done for me. Nothing can harm me now." He shoved her forward, maintaining his hold on her. "If you do not do exactly as I say I will snap her neck." He tightened his grip.

Paige opened her mouth trying to suck a small amount of air into her lungs, her face flushed.

"All right!" Eli raised his hand. "Just don't hurt her."

"That depends on you, doesn't it?" Gregor took another step closer, the stairwell now several feet behind them, his large frame blocking their path. "I wonder what would happen if I scratched her." His red eyes met Eli's and he gave a smug grin. "Should I try it? Or maybe I should go ahead and bite her. What do you think?"

"What do you want, Gregor?" Eli's voice echoed along the dark corridor.

"My freedom."

"And where would you go?" Max asked, pointing to the grotesque monster in front of them. "Have you looked in a mirror lately?"

"I would go wherever I choose."

"I don't think that's gonna work for you buddy. People are gonna notice."

"Enough!" He opened his mouth and leaned in to sink his fangs into Paige's throat, but as he did his body started jerking and he released his grip on her.

Paige dashed out of the way and ran into Eli's arms.

Gregor's knees buckled and he hit the floor with a loud thud, face down, his body twitching.

Cooper stood behind him, one arm in a sling and a taser in his other hand turned to full strength. He held his finger on the trigger to make sure the electrical current kept the monster down. "Whatever you're gonna do, do it now!" he yelled.

Blake came out of the morgue with a rusted bone saw in his hand. "This should do the job." He walked over and handed it to Eli. "You want to do the honors, Sheriff?"

Eli eased Paige out of his embrace, snatched the saw from Blake's hand, and stalked over to Gregor. Without hesitation, he sliced through the vampire's thick neck until the blade came out the other side and Gregor's head rolled across the linoleum. "That's for the lives you stole."

Archer walked over to Eli with a bottle of clear alcohol and tugged a cigarette lighter from the pocket of his pants. "We need to burn the remains."

"Go ahead. My job's done." Eli took Paige's hand and headed for the stairs. "Thanks, Cooper. How'd you know we were here?"

"No problem. Rosemarie told me and I thought you might need some back up." He gave the sheriff a goofy grin, turned and followed him and Paige back up the stairs.

"Good old Rosy."

Max and his companions stepped over the headless corpse and stood on the other side while Archer splashed the alcohol over it then stepped in front of his brother, flicked on the lighter and dropped it onto the body. It caught alight in seconds. The four remained in the corridor until Gregor turned to ash, which didn't take long because he was a supernatural creature. Afterward, Archer scooped what he could into a container and sealed it then poured the remaining alcohol onto the residue and set it alight to make sure there were no essences of the vampire left. He would give Eli the container to bury in consecrated ground to be sure no other vampire could resurrect Gregor at a later date.

When the four emerged from the abandoned building, Eli was leaning against the front left fender of his Jeep, arms folded, waiting for them. He'd sent Paige back with Cooper but wanted to offer his appreciation to Archer, his brother, and his companions for their assistance.

"I couldn't leave without thanking you for offering to help and coming out here. You didn't have to."

"It's all good," Max said. "That's why we came to Moon Grove."

"Are you planning to stay for a while?"

Max's gaze moved to his brother then his companions. "Yeah. We were thinking about it."

"Good." Eli realized that the council's original plan had been set in motion and executed despite his efforts to prevent it. Gregor had been sent to the town to annihilate his pack and had successfully completed his mission single-handedly. Eli hadn't even had time to grieve the loss of his wolves and best friend, nor had he had time to find out if Linda was indeed the mole. Something he'd need to pursue. His wolves would receive the sendoff they deserved with the help of his Alpha female, Cooper, Clary and Rosemarie. His thoughts returned to Paige's brother, Brent. Where was he?

FIFTY

The four bodies of his wolves lay covered with white sheets up to their necks on wooden rafts on the edge of the river. Bobby, Paul, Ryan, and Rebecca had been part of Eli's pack since they were in their late teens, before he became Sheriff, and it would be strange not to have them by his side from now on. He swallowed the painful lump in his throat, a dagger in his hand, a tear sliding down his left cheek. He swiped it away and sniffed back the urge to allow his emotions to get the better of him, his jaw clenched to prevent his chin from quivering. He was their Alpha, and he would stand tall and keep it together to honor his brave comrades.

Paige could see the distress on Eli's face and her heart ached for him. She walked over and linked her fingers through his. Cooper, Rosemarie, Clarissa and Archer, his brother and companions, Bobby's wife, Barbara, and their two kids stood behind him in solemn solidarity for their fallen. The editor had made a pledge to offer his support anytime the sheriff needed it. He also promised himself that he would tell Eli about drinking Paige's blood and the real reason he was in Moon Grove once things settled back into a normal routine, if that was possible.

Eli ran the sharp blade along the skin of his left palm, dipped his index finger into the blood and painted the Lycan symbol onto each of his dead wolves' foreheads. When he stepped back, Cooper joined him and Paige and they linked hands and chorused a guttural howl of mourning together, the sound echoing high into the tall pine trees surrounding them. Paige lit the wooden torch and handed it to Eli and he set the first pyre on fire and pushed it into the water, followed by the second, the third, and finally the fourth, Bobby's. "Farewell my wolf family. May the Lycan spirit of Tundra guide you to your rest."

After the ceremony, everyone drove into Moon Grove to Pete's Bar to toast those who had lost their lives fighting Gregor. The place reminded Eli of the night Jake's body had been discovered and he downed his scotch in one shot, the amber liquid burning all the way into his stomach. He hadn't told Paige what had really happened to her uncle and he thought it best not to. She should be allowed to remember him the way he had been, the way she'd known him. She had been through so much since she'd arrived in the town and she had grown so much because of it. He sat in the booth, his eyes on her beautiful face as she talked to Rosemarie and Clarissa, and wondered what the future held for them as Alphas of an almost non-existent pack. There were other wolves living in the area but they had remained solitary for many years. Would they be willing to join him to protect their town from supernatural forces that threatened it? The question would eventually need an answer. He knew he had an ally in Archer Hamilton and realized that his initial reservations about the vampire had been unfounded. He had proved his worth to Moon Grove and Eli was grateful for the allegiance.

The saga with the council would continue until he could find a permanent way to deal with Remus, and the battle over the moonstone ring would also rear its ugly head again some time in the future, if not because of the governing body then someone else craving its power. The word had spread about its existence and it was only a matter of time.

Paige's honey colored wolf eyes met his and he smiled, his sadness hidden beneath the desire to make her happy. He had lost good people and his heart ached right now but life had to go on. Tonight, Paige would be back in her own home with him right alongside her. As far as he was concerned, they would never spend another night apart... ever. The time he'd wasted trying to protect her had been futile and now that he belonged to her and she to him their lives would become one from this moment forth.

Clarissa said her goodnights and Paige and Eli climbed the front steps of the house. The night was clear and warm and he suggested they sit on the swing seat for a while, even though it was almost midnight. Paige had the feeling he wanted to talk to her about something so she went along with his suggestion and sat down, him beside her. It made her heart happy having him here again. She had missed him so much. When their eyes met he leaned in and pressed a gentle kiss to her lips. "Paige, there's something I want to tell you."

"What is it, Eli?"

He let out a sigh. "Now that we're back together I'd like to tell you about Michelle."

"All right." She realized she should have asked who Michelle was.

Eli frowned into her eyes. "Do you know already?"

She nodded. "I found the photograph in the bureau."

"Ah. But you don't know what happened to her?"

Paige nodded again. She couldn't lie to him. "The corner of the coroner's report was poking out of the frame."

"So you decided to read it?"

"I'm sorry, Eli. I know it was an invasion of your personal space…"

"It doesn't matter. I'm not angry about it but I'd like to explain what really happened."

"Ok." She reached for his hand and linked her fingers with his. "I'd like to know."

"There had been some deaths in our town and we found out a renegade wolf had come to Moon Grove. He'd remained one step ahead of us at every turn and this particular night I was out with the pack searching for him. The only thing we didn't know was he'd circled back and was heading for my home. Michelle had been asleep when he'd broken in and by the time we realized and I got there he'd killed her and scrawled a message on the wall in her blood."

"Oh, Eli, I'm so sorry." Tears stung her eyes and she squeezed his hand.

"That was the reason why I avoided new relationships. I didn't want anyone else to be a target just because of what I am."

"And that's why you broke up with me? Because of what happened to Michelle?"

He nodded. "I couldn't let anything like that happen to you. But here we are. A lot has happened and you've been right in the thick of it."

She rubbed his hand. "And I'm fine, Eli. I am."

"I won't doubt that anymore."

"Michelle... she wasn't Lycan, was she?"

"No."

"Did she know about you?"

Eli gave a heavy sigh. "Not at first. I tried my best to keep that part of my life separate from my personal life with her, but she found out."

"How?"

"She must've had her suspicions and one night she followed me. The pack and I were on the outskirts of town, we were hunting a vampire who'd taken a child, and we all shifted before heading into the woods. She'd stopped down the road and walked up to where our cars were parked and she witnessed the change."

Paige gasped.

"Yeah. When I got home she wasn't there. She'd packed a suitcase, left me a note, and had gone to the Inn in town. She wouldn't talk to me or let me explain. She stayed there for a month without any contact and then one day she walked into the station and told everyone there she knew what we were." Eli stood up and walked over to the porch railing. "She told me she still loved me despite what I was and she'd try to make our marriage work."

"I don't know what to say."

"You don't have to say anything. I thought it was time for you to know. I don't want any secrets or lies between us."

Paige walked over to him. "And neither do I."

At that moment, a hooded figure crossed the lawn.

"Hey, stranger, I was wondering when you'd show up." Paige met her brother at the steps and gave him a hug. "It's good to see you."

"It's good to see you, too." His eyes moved to Eli. "I'm sorry about your pack, man."

"Thanks. I appreciate that." He walked over to the front door and opened it. "I'll give you two some space."

Paige swung around. "You don't have to…"

"It's ok. I need some time on my own anyway." Eli stepped into the house and closed the door.

"How are things with you?" Paige asked.

"Ok. I came here tonight because of two reasons."

"Oh? What are they?" The pair walked along to the swing seat and sat down.

"First of all, do you think Eli would have me as a pack member?"

"Are you kidding? Of course he would. But what about the council?"

"I figure if I stay out of their way it shouldn't be a problem. They don't leave the mansion very often anyway."

She hugged him again. "Thank you. We need all the help we can get right now."

"So I can talk to him about it?"

"Absolutely. What's the second thing?"

"Mom wants to see you."

Paige's eyes widened. "When?"

"Soon. But you'll have to come to her. She won't set foot in this town."

"That's understandable after everything that's happened." Her heart thumped against her ribs. She was going to see her mother after all these years. "Will you tell her that I'm looking forward to it?"

"Yeah, I will."

Paige's gaze rested on the front door. "Just give Eli a couple of days and then talk to him."

"Sure." Brent stood up. "I'd better get going. I'll come back and let you know when."

"Ok. I'll wait to hear from you." She smiled and watched her brother cross the lawn and disappear into the night.

A few minutes later, Eli opened the door and stepped out onto the porch. "Where's your brother?"

"He's gone."

"Everything all right?" He sat down beside her.

"Yes. My mom wants to see me."

Eli reached for her hand. "That's good news."

"I know it is… and I'm excited about it but… it will be like meeting a stranger. I don't know her." She frowned into his eyes. "I'm scared, too."

"And that's understandable, Paige. You were only five when your parents disappeared." He wrapped his arm around her shoulders. "But it will be fine. You'll see."

She sighed. "You're right. I know it will."

"I made hot chocolate. Want to come in and have some?"

"Sounds wonderful. It's been one hell of a day." That was an understatement.

"Yeah, it has."

321

Paige leaned in and pressed her lips to his. "I love you, Eli Blackwood."

"I love you, too, Paige O'Connell." He stood up and held out his hand to her. "Let's go inside."

She smiled up at him and took his hand. "Why don't we take that hot chocolate up to the bedroom?"

Life would go on despite the loss of the people they cared about and a new phase would begin in Moon Grove. Eli was determined to do whatever he could to relinquish the council's control on the town, however long it took. Now that he had his Alpha female by his side, together they would establish a new werewolf pack that would enforce the laws without fear or threat.

He would look into Linda's involvement with Ross Redmond and the governing body to see if she had been the one who warned Remus about the impending danger. He hoped he was wrong about her. But, then, if he was it would mean one of his pack had been the mole and he didn't want to contemplate that. And what about the hidden key the mayor had given him? Could whatever was inside the safety deposit box lead to the council's undoing? Eli planned to find out.

For now, though, life would return to some kind of normality. Eli knew it wouldn't last for long. He knew he would need to recruit new wolves into his pack as soon as he could to protect the town against future threats. He would also have to request new deputies to assist with law enforcement because Bobby and Paul had died in the line of duty, at least that's what the official report would say.

Until then, he would make love to his beautiful Alpha female tonight to ease the sorrow in both their hearts and strengthen the bond between them because tomorrow would arrive with its own set of supernatural issues to deal with and they would need to be ready.

Did you love the book?

Let other readers know by posting a
review on Amazon
Visit the author's Amazon page below
Author.to/MaggieAnderson

READ AN EXCERPT FROM
BOOK THREE
WOLF LOVER

ONE

Paige flicked off the overhead light and crossed the shadowed office to the glass door. Eli would arrive at any minute to pick her up. It was after nine and she was tired and hungry and just wanted to go home, kick off her heels, and relax on the sofa in his arms for a while. Her business had picked up over the past few weeks and she had several new clients, for which she was grateful. Were they human? Not one. She realized her patients were more likely to be of the supernatural kind, now that she was a wolf. As she reached to open the door a figure appeared in the alcove outside, startling her. Paige gasped, jerked her hand away and stepped backwards. Her breathing quickened, along with her heart rate, and she took another tentative step back. Who could it be?

Life had been quiet for a short while and it had felt good not to have to look over her shoulder all the time. But she knew it wouldn't be long before a new threat of some kind ventured into their town. The dark shape stepped closer to the glass and Paige dashed out of the way so she wouldn't be seen. She snatched her cell phone from her purse and pressed Eli's number as she sidled around the room to the door leading to the kitchen and back exit. Eli's voicemail kicked in. "Eli," she whispered, "someone's at the door of my office and I'm heading out the back. Please hurry."

Paige made her way along the short hallway and into the kitchen. When she reached the back door her cell vibrated in her hand and she jumped. It was Eli. "Where are you?"

"Stay inside until I get there. I'll deal with whoever it is."

"I thought I should get out the back door and meet you in the next street."

"Paige, please just do as I ask."

"But…"

"I'm only about a minute away."

A noise echoed along the hallway. "I think they're trying to break in."

"I'm almost there. Please stay inside. It's the safest place for you."

Paige didn't think it was the safest place. "Eli, I need to get out of here."

"Paige…"

She rang off, dropped her phone into her purse, snapped open the locks on the rear door, and whipped it open.

The hooded figure was right in front of her. "Hello, Paige.

Paige's anxious eyes widened and she sucked in a shocked gasp.

www.ingramcontent.com/pod-product-compliance
Lightning Source LLC
Chambersburg PA
CBHW022134170626
46807CB00005B/1934